TERMS OF SURRENDER

BOOK ONE

HARLOW

KARYN RAE

Published by Karyn Rae Publishing

Visit Karyn Rae's official website at www.karyn-rae.com for the latest news, book details, and other information.

Copyright © Karyn Rae, 2018
ISBN: 978-0-9960922-4-1
Library of Congress Control Number: 2018943938

Edited by: Lindsey Alexander
Cover Design by: Humble Nations
Formatting by: Guido Henkel

For the women:

My mother, Sandra Hillier
My mentor, Christi Nies
My friend, Alli Ritchey Wideman
My coach, Kelley Wolf

PART ONE
NOW

12:00 a.m.

THE REMAINING HOURS OF HER LIFE DRIPPED AWAY IN synchronization with the fluid in the finger-smudged IV pouch. The bag was already half-drained. A background orchestral of machinery worked in melodic rhythm, rising and falling in pitchy tones. No one piece was more important than another. Each shift in my back-wrenching metal chair added another instrument to the orchestra, augmenting the monotonous cadence of minutes ticking away in Mother's life.

The hospital's stark yet ordinary Sheetrock walls matched Mother's milky-gray irises and translucent, paper-thin skin. For a woman who prized youthful beauty, Mother looked old in that bed. The years had stripped her hair of color, and the illness had drenched her skin in a cadaverous glow.

I thought for sure a line of aristocratic Charlestonians would have stretched down the corridor by now, each with thought-provoking summations of how she had affected their lives. Right behind the nostalgic would be the greedy, eager to witness her final moments—if only for a story to share at the next twenty cocktail parties. But the room was as empty as the heart that beat inside her chest. There was not a pillow fluffed, no vital taken, no mass of concerned seersucking bootlickers.

I expected a flock of nurses to be diligently checking the tubes coiling around her upper body, while fiddling with the continuously beeping machines. Instead, a wilting debutante occupied a remote-controlled bed in an unattractive and generic hospital room, which reeked of diminishing Old South grandeur. If Vivian Ausby had caught a glimpse of herself here—in what she would certainly consider to be humiliating circumstances—she would have pulled the plug on her own.

I sat uncomfortably, waiting for Beth, waiting for the tirelessly spinning hamster wheel in my mind to slow down, waiting for the machines to stop, waiting for something to happen. If there were an award for wasting your life on someone, I would have won the blue-ribbon prize. "Most in Denial" is another award I would have won. As I took in the spectacle of how ordinary Mother's death would be, I couldn't force back the thought: *I told you so. You brought this isolation on yourself.* But the motherly side of me—which after forty years with this woman was thankfully still intact—only pitied her. The juxtaposition of these thoughts was a familiar war I waged upon myself, one that dated as far back as I could remember. Unfortunately for Vivian, after decades of tirelessly manufacturing her grandiose prestige, her only actual legacy happened to be the person who irritated her the most: me.

I didn't make a move toward her.

A family takes years, decades, even a lifetime to become dysfunctional, and our particular brand of dysfunction was by now as impenetrable as the downtown Queen Anne mansion where it had begun. As I stared at her bony and for once unmanicured fingers, my conscience implored me to take her hand in mine. *She's my mother; she only has me and Beth.* Even my daughter, Evie, wanted nothing to do with her—mostly on my behalf. She'd seen firsthand the frigid cold Mother was able to create right there in the heat of the Lowcountry. The guilt of ignoring the sympathetic and womanly voice of reason immediately began shaming the obedient child who, after all these years, still hid inside me.

As far as Mother was concerned, I had shamed my family on several occasions. In my younger days, it seemed as though the harder I reached to be the person she wanted me to be, the less likely I was to actually become that person. From the friends I chose to the man I fell in love with—not to mention, most blaringly, the red birthmark that swallowed my left leg—I had, over the years, diminished the opulent Ausby name. The truth was that I had spent my life trying for a perfection that was never obtainable. The pain of that kind of knowing had sharp teeth and grit, and a lingering that never faded.

Those childhood memories flooded my thoughts.

Through no fault of my own, I had been a wisp of a girl, one made seemingly of strawberry mist. My blazing-red hair matched the birthmark on my leg, both of which were noticeable across a crowded room. Those were my only noticeable characteristics, though. For the daughter of a Charleston neighborhood as exclusive as South of Broad, I lacked those qualities that kept up the charade of grandeur that was tended to like a rare orchid in our part of the city. I was as out of place there as a midday moon. Unlike Mother, I had never commanded a room by stature or beauty alone. The art of small talk was lost within my shyness, and the animation of my flirtation was one-dimensional. I was the awkward kind of girl who wrung her hands together or shoved them deep into her pockets. I'd had two arms my entire life, but once surrounded by a crowd, I had no idea what to do with them. When asked a question, I always hoped that a *yes, ma'am* or *no, sir* would suffice. These unfortunate traits only grazed the surface of why Mother considered me a genetic disappointment.

I felt tears working their way to my eyes. I only wished they stemmed from the sadness of our current situation, instead of anger about our past.

Splintered rays of yellow light from the lamppost outside Mother's room slipped in through the institutional blinds, freckling the tightly tucked hospital-grade blanket. I got up to twist the clear plastic rod, letting in more light.

It won't be long now.

A quarter moon cast deep shadows, only broken by the Spanish moss that clung to the massive branches beyond the window. As I stared through the window and into the parking lot below, a lone man paced in front of the entrance doors. He made exaggerated gestures, as if his hands were giving a lecture to his heart, only pausing to sweep them through his hair. It was apparent that he was trying to talk himself into some kind of decision. Four floors up, and through the muddled fog of a Carolina night, I couldn't quite make out his features. The pacing man seemed to abruptly make a decision and, finally, walk through the front doors. I admired this stranger's decisiveness. I wished I had the same moxie.

Like Mother's room, the hospital grounds were sparse in the darkness, and like Mother's machinery, the security lights hummed their own song. Beyond the window, the serpentine branches of an aged oak tree dipped and bowed in the wind. Life was happening everywhere. Everywhere but this room.

Each heartbeat less surefooted than the one before, and each moment bringing us closer to the final one: Mother's heart was giving out. Over the years, I had given mine to unrequited relationships, so that pieces of my heart had scattered all the way from the Ashley River to Folly Beach and back. A loveless marriage, a broken friendship, and the dull ache of lost love had left my heart still functioning, but irreparably damaged. As a child, I used to believe that life would somehow magically repair all its undoings. As an adult, I'd grown to know better. I had spent my entire adult life trying not to be like Mother, but we had both ended up with a broken heart. I shuddered to think of the coincidence. Even though I didn't want to be the type of middle-aged woman who was consumed by the regret of irrevocable choices, here I was, the poster child for remorse.

This was not how I'd pictured my fortieth birthday.

Where's Beth? What's taking her so long?

Just when I thought I couldn't spend another minute alone—well, with Mother, but alone nonetheless—a van pulled into the roundabout. Beth Chaney's fading ginger curls pranced around her head as she hopped out the rear passenger door. I couldn't help but smile at the sight. Instinctively, I smoothed back my own hair, the strawberry coils wrapping around my thumb. Beth's hair was the first thing I had noticed about her, and it was the first reason I trusted her on the day we met. The draw I felt toward her was immediate. Twenty years of her bottomless loyalty had proven my inclination right.

As Beth opened the rear double doors of the van, a hospital attendant rolled out a luggage cart from the lobby. Beth directed her obedient valet as to which paintings to load onto the trolley.

You've got to be kidding me. What does she need those for?

Tried and true, Mother could always count on Beth to do her bidding. Twenty-plus years ago, Mother had brought in Beth to work for our family. When she first arrived, her job was to take care of my ailing father, but through the years, Beth had completed every task asked of her with a vivaciousness that I sometimes loathed but always admired.

Spinning the fully loaded cart toward the hospital doors, Beth nearly ran over a man walking out—the same perplexed man from earlier. The two seemed to know each other. They paused for a brief hug before parting ways, and then Beth's figure disappeared inside.

When he was beyond the brightness of the hospital lights, the man stopped and looked up at me—directly at me. Startled, I stepped back into the darkness, snapping the blinds shut. Curiosity got the better of me, but when I took another look out the window, the man was gone.

Beth announced her arrival at the door with muttered cursing and heavy panting, along with a lobby cart stacked with more possessions than a dying woman should care to have.

"It's stuck on the doorknob. Help me," Beth pleaded.

Grabbing the brass poles, I tried to come to her aid, but instead I tipped the jammed dolly too far to one side.

"Grab the top! It's going over!" I whisper-shouted, panicking at the noise we were making.

Before we could stop it, the loaded cart toppled, and the paintings clattered to the floor. One on top of another, they piled up and spread out across the doorway, making a racket. Beth steadied the cart upright, while I quickly gathered as many canvases as I could hold. As I hurried to line the frames along the wall, a shadow appeared in the doorway.

We had poked the bear.

The hallway lights shone into the darkness of the room, backlighting a ferocious-looking woman dressed entirely in white. Her wide stance supported her heavyset frame, two meaty arms crossed sternly over her chest. The woman wore the tightest bun I'd ever seen. It seemed to pull the skin on her face back an entire inch.

We'd heard whispers about the nighttime manager and the little patience she had for troublemakers on her floor. A seen-and-not-heard behavior was not only required but enforced by this night-shift dictator in white. We had been warned that Nurse Boone ran a tight ship, and any resemblance of a mutiny resulted in visitors walking the plank—right out the front doors.

"Ladies," she began in an unexpectedly soft voice. "Is this the manner in which you usually conduct yourselves?"

"No, ma'am," we whispered in childlike unison.

"Do I need to go over the rules?" she asked, cocking her head farther to the side.

"No, ma'am," we repeated, both of us still frozen in the same position she had found us in.

"Am I going to have to come back in here again tonight?"

"No, ma'am."

"Uh-huh," she breathed, harshly pursing her full lips together into a thin tight line, before silently disappearing out the doorway.

"Whoa, she's scary," Beth finally whispered. We both began to snicker like schoolgirls, which quickly turned into a slumber-party cackle. "Hey, hon," Beth said, jabbing me in the side with her elbow, "happy birthday."

"Thanks for remembering."

"I'd never forget your birthday."

"It doesn't feel that happy, yet."

"Then I don't suppose this is going to help."

She pulled out a folded-over page from her jacket pocket. The article had been torn from the interior section of *Papier and Pen*, a notoriously crude Charleston tabloid. The magazine was trash, at best. The headline in today's edition: Divorced. I didn't need to read the article to know that it was about me.

"Quite a gift to get on your birthday," Beth remarked.

I agreed. "It's bad enough that it had to be final on this day, of all days—at Patrick's request, of course—but why do they have to make it front-page news?"

"Don't think of it as a bad thing." She paused in thought before finishing. "Think of it as free advertisement. You're single, and now all those eligible bachelors won't be confused about your marital status." She was teasing, but her voice quickly became serious. "This is a gift, Harlow. You need to trust me on that. You've always been better than him, and he's never deserved your loyalty."

I couldn't disagree with her there.

Come on," she added, picking up one of the paintings. "Let's figure out where to put these."

12:30 a.m.

STANDING IN THE CENTER OF MOTHER'S HOSPITAL ROOM, BETH turned several circles, continuing to glance back at the framed artworks while mentally calculating the perfect position for each piece. She pulled out a sheet of paper from her back pocket and began consulting her diagram, checking off numbers as she found them on the back of each canvas.

Ausby Fine Art was our family-owned-and-operated business in the heart of the Charleston arts district, which teetered along the east side of Broad Street, four blocks from our family home. I don't have too many childhood memories that don't include the smell of freshly baked pastries, the sound of horse hooves on cobblestone, and the shade of a Spanish moss canopy; all were senses of comfort I could count on as I accompanied my daddy on our walks to his work. That time in my life was something I longed for still, yet I would never go back to it if given the choice. I couldn't bear to bury my father again. I had only this one heart of mine, and to survive his death again would surely break it for good. The pain of the thought was a sharp slap that put me back into the moment, back into the hospital room.

"Why are we doing this?" The bitterness in my voice was undisguised.

"Doing what?" Beth echoed without looking up. Her body was hunched over a large framed portrait.

"This," I said, jutting my hand out in the direction of several canvases leaning up against the wall. "You know as well as I do that they should be in proper storage. Patrick would have a fit if he knew we were moving the art. Why does she need these here, anyway? Are they for visitors to envy, or is she really planning on taking them with her to the afterlife?"

Beth let out a long sigh before straightening up. "Harlow, I couldn't care less what your ex-husband Patrick thinks, an attitude I wish you'd mimic. Can we just put the pieces where Vivian wants them without an argument?"

For the life of me, I couldn't understand why, for years, Beth had worked tirelessly to please an unpleasable woman. Mother had always expected us to do what she said, often before she said to do it. I tried to fathom why Beth bent over backwards to follow every social-climbing request. I wondered how she could be so emotionally devoted to a tyrant who did nothing but push her around, when I was emotionally detached from the same woman, who had barely laid a hand on me in twenty years. My crime, in her eyes, was getting pregnant.

"Fine. Whatever you say," I conceded, lightening the tone of my voice. "Tell me where they go."

I could never stay mad at Beth. She had a way about her. Beth was the kind of woman who made you feel welcomed and loved the moment she met you—the opposite of Mother. Kindness exuded from every smile, every look Beth gave me, and I'd come to love her like my own kin. Even though I hadn't met her until the cusp of adulthood, my knees were practically calloused from thanking God for bringing her into my life.

A smile appeared at the corner of her lips, satisfied by my acquiescence. "You always were a good girl. Maybe too good," she teased with a wink. "Although it's hard to choose just one, it is one of the things I love most about you."

She was right about being a good girl. Despite what Mother thought, I *had* been a good girl. On the other hand, being an exemplary grownup, well that just wasn't the case. I had certainly fallen short of becoming an admirable adult.

As we worked together, Beth would call out the number on the back of a canvas and then direct me on where to place it. Mother had given specific instructions to Beth that each painting should line the wall in an exact spot. Since I had decided to swallow my opinion of the stupidity of this task, we actually made quick work of the job.

"Hold up," Beth said as I placed the last canvas against the bland wall. "We're missing one. A small one."

"How can that be? The entire room is lined with paintings. There isn't space for any more. You must be mistaken."

As her head tilted down, her eyes shifted up, and she stared hard at me through the nearsighted portion of her bifocals. "I'm not mistaken, because I've already made all of my mistakes. See," she said, holding out her hand-drawn picture-map, "a three-by-three canvas is supposed to go in this spot here." She pointed to a sliver of empty wall space. "Right between the Thiebaud and the Kinkade. It probably got left behind in the van. Could you be a dear and run out to the parking lot to get it?"

"Now? But it's dark out there."

"Of course it's dark. It's nighttime."

"What if that man is still out there?"

"What man?" she scoffed with a chuckle.

"There was a man in the parking lot."

"Don't be silly, Harlow. This is South of Broad. You'd have a better chance of spotting sequins at a funeral than a murderer on the street."

"I'm not kidding! He looked right up at the window before he disappeared. You saw him. You were hugging him, for God's sake."

"You saw him, saw us out there?" Her voice had changed from disbelief to mild panic, startling me. "Did you get a good look at him? What did you see?"

She fired off questions faster than I could answer. This was completely unlike Beth. Something was up with her.

"No, I mean yes, I saw him, but just barely. Geez, what's with the twenty questions? Who was he anyway?"

"I'm sorry. I didn't mean to raise my voice. It's just that…" Her voice trailed off as she turned toward the window. "Ohhh," she sighed, drawing out the sound as long as her breath allowed. "It's probably time. You'll know soon enough anyway."

Turning her around by her slumped shoulders, I asked, "Time for what? What on earth are you talking about? Who was that man, Beth?"

"If you'll please go get the last canvas out of the van downstairs, we'll have us a little chat when you get back. Sound good?" she asked.

Suspicious and all-around weirded out, I left Beth standing at the window and patiently waited for the door to click shut behind me as I stepped from Mother's room into the hall.

Downstairs, like a turtle from a shell, I poked my head out from between the front-entrance automatic doors. I didn't care if Beth did know him. I didn't want to be alone in an empty parking lot with any man at midnight. *Coast clear.* I hurried along and spotted the large *Ausby Fine Art* decal in the distance. This Mercedes was the newest vehicle to join the fleet.

I despised it.

The luxury van gave the opposite impression from the one my father had tried to make when he'd opened the art gallery forty years ago. It was also a glaring reminder of what an egotistical prick my husband—ex-husband—had turned out to be. To be fair, we never imagined ourselves getting married at twenty years old, but when you come from old Southern money—by that, I mean the kind that goes back to Fort Sumter and the first shots of the Civil War—and you find yourself unmarried with child, you shut your mouth and do exactly as you are told, even if it concerns something as important as the rest of your life. Vivian Ausby wouldn't stand for people saying she was anything less than perfect.

Even though they would, in the most glad-happy, your-ship-is-sinking type of way.

The light flickered on as I opened the rear door of the van, one of four Patrick had purchased for the gallery. His wastefulness enraged me.

One. One van is all we have use for. We only have one driver on the payroll. How is he supposed to drive more than one vehicle at a time?

The lengths Patrick went to stroke that Peter Pan ego would embarrass even Tinkerbell. *I'd like to take a handful of her fairy dust and shove it straight down his throat, until his rear end burns from diarrhea glitter.*

Grabbing the small boxed canvas that had slid under the passenger seat, I said all the things in my head that would make me feel better, knowing full well that I would never actually say them aloud to Patrick. Southern ladies were discouraged from speaking unkindly to their husbands—current or otherwise. It would completely throw off the balance of perceived power. We were taught to bottle our real emotions, put on some lipstick, and hang in there until cocktail hour. Drinking your feelings was never discouraged South of Broad.

The apron of air-conditioning instantly cooled my fuming thoughts as I walked back through the doors of the hospital's main entrance, canvas in hand.

"Hold the elevator, please!" I called out as the doors slid together.

A manicured hand sliced through at the last second, forcing the doors back open.

"Fourth floor please?" I politely requested, stepping inside.

She wasn't dressed to the nines, but she had put much more effort into her appearance than I had, especially for a hospital visit in the middle of the night. With a little help from Manolo Blahnik, her long tanned legs traveled almost up to her neck, while her effortlessly beachy brown waves stretched down her back, coming to rest atop her yoga-firm rear. Ever since I had known Lexi, she had always managed to look as though she had just walked through brisk air-conditioning. Lexi Pratt was the envy of every forty-something first wife in Charleston. She had looks to kill, money to last her a lifetime, and a long line of men who were dying for her to break their hearts. Currently at the top of that list was my ex-husband.

I wouldn't allow myself to look down at my oversized sweatshirt, ballooning out over faded, baggy leggings. I wouldn't give her the satisfaction of watching me cower from her glamazon height. I also didn't have enough guts to continue to look her in the eyes. Unfortunately for my self-esteem, my sight settled on my sandal-clad feet.

My port-wine-stained foot stuck out from my cheap flip-flop; my big toe was cranberry-colored, like the udder of a pregnant cow. This left foot of mine was a constant reminder that I was different, and somehow inadequate. The sight of my toes recalled the voices of numerous plastic surgeons, who shook their heads in regret that I was "unfixable." Until I had first heard that word, I hadn't realized that I was broken. They had been right, though. Normal wasn't something I would ever be—not by society standards, anyway.

I hated the sight of my feet, especially when they were alongside flawlessly manicured and appropriately colored toes.

"How dare you come here," I whispered. "You have some nerve, Lexi Pratt."

She didn't speak. Only a quiet but audible breath escaped her perfectly coral lips. Maybe the sound she made was one of haughty disgust, because she was just as repulsed by my foot as I was. Maybe it was annoyance that she was confined in a small space with the newly ex-wife of her longtime lover. Maybe it was because I had made a point to use her last name, which I knew she *and* her mama hated. Maybe her fat, over-injected collagen lips couldn't completely close, and by default, she made that sound when she breathed.

19

"Mother is struggling for her last breaths," I hissed. "You have no right to be anywhere near this hospital. I don't care if you *are* sleeping with Patrick; you *aren't* part of his family." I had to concentrate on my words to keep my inflection stern. Confrontation wasn't a specialty of mine. Still, I needed her to know that despite the doormat I had allowed myself to become, I wasn't going to let her wipe her feet on me. At least, not that night.

"Harlow, if you'll let me explain," she began in a defeated voice.

"You've had years to explain yourself, and also to stop crawling into bed with married men. Your word is as trashy as that god-awful orange lipstick you've smeared across those ridiculously fake lips. I'm not interested in anything you have to say."

The elevator made a loud commotion announcing its arrival on the fourth floor, and the doors took their sweet time to open, delaying my ability to dramatically storm off. I held my ground and didn't look away, even though I was out of clever things to say. I couldn't believe those words had come from my mouth. I had spoken to only one other person so harshly in my life, and coincidentally, it was to Lexi's older sister, and my ex–best friend, Savannah Pratt.

Turning toward the panel, I repeatedly tapped the open-door button, praying that I would escape this elevator unscathed. That's when I felt her hand gently rest on my shoulder.

"My condolences to your family, Harlow. I'm sorry about Vivian. Really, I am."

Without turning back around, but meeting her eyes in the mirrored walls of the elevator, I cautioned, "Stay away from me, and stay away from this hospital. You can have Patrick, because he's more trouble than he's worth. I guess you haven't figured that out yet."

Finally, with a *ding*, the lit-up number four faded, and the doors opened. Focused on a confident exit, I turned and looked back. In the elevator's mirrored panels, I saw Lexi's finger lighting up the number nine.

1:00 a.m.

I WALKED BACK TO THE ROOM IN A DEFEATED SHUFFLE, THE miniature canvas feeling heavier in my hand than it should have. Newly polished floors chirped beneath my sandals with each step, the whirl of a floor buffer still audible in a not-so-distant hallway. I tried to soothe my anger with the knowledge that I shouldn't care about Lexi, because I didn't care, but then again, I did care, and then I didn't. It was the typically indecisive behavior of a woman who felt deeply and scared easily. It was the story of my life.

Patrick and I were officially divorced, going on an hour now. I shouldn't have cared what tawdry affair he had humiliated himself with. That was a solid *don't care*. But Mother had made him executor of her will. She had left him the house, the business my father had started—everything. Not me, her only daughter, but him. She had gone to painstaking lengths to cut me out of any inheritance. What unabashed nerve. So, of course, I cared about that. I had dropped out of college the winter semester of my junior year, and I'd spent the last twenty as a homemaker raising a child. I had no real skills that translated to the working world. No one to go back to, and nothing moving me forward. Only a clear and violent separation from Patrick and Mother. In that, there was something that felt good, fated, what I had always wanted, just not the way I had wanted it. I should have been more careful about the things I wished for.

"Did you get it? What's wrong?" Beth whispered, immediately noticing the slack in my posture as I entered the room.

My voice soft and false, I replied, "I'm fine. This was the only one left in the van." I laid the canvas down on an unapproved corner of the dresser. "I saw her. In the elevator, I saw Lexi Pratt." The tears came, but I honestly didn't know for what—or whom—I was crying; my face had just become inadvertently wet.

"Oh, honey, please. Please don't do that," Beth urged me, while standing from her chair and gently guiding me into her seat. She knelt in front of me, taking my hand as she spoke. "It's a shame you had to see her tonight. I know that wasn't easy for you."

"She said she was sorry for me. Can you believe that? *She's* sorry for *me*. What right does she have to be here, feeling sorry for me?"

Beth took a deep and purposeful breath before she spoke. "She's here to see her sister."

I was so stunned by her words that I couldn't speak. It must have shown on my face; Beth quickly jumped in to explain.

"I was going to tell you that Savannah was back in town, but then Vivian fell ill, and I thought I'd wait until she got better. Vivian's health declined so rapidly that I didn't have time to tell you, and then once we got here, I didn't want to tell you."

"When were you going to get around to telling me?"

"I am telling you."

"This doesn't count as telling me! I saw Lexi in the elevator. You had to tell me."

"Fair enough, but now you know. And let the record show that, technically speaking, I did tell you."

"Cut it out. When did she get back? Why is she in the hospital? What's wrong with her?"

Beth put her arms out to me in an attempt to distract from more questions. "All I know is that Savannah showed up on her sister's doorstep a couple of days ago. The state of her appearance scared Lexi into calling for an ambulance. Savannah has been here since. It's cancer, Harlow."

I had to swirl the emotions in my mouth before double-swallowing the information, unsure if it—if anything—would stay down. I had known Savannah for twenty-five years. For fifteen of those years, she had been my best friend. I hadn't spoken to her for the rest. The thought of her, and of what she had done to our friendship that night, plagued my heart with enduring hurt. The betrayal was compulsive, irreversible, and unforgivable—just like Savannah.

Beth, as usual, seemed to hear my thoughts. "Come on, Harlow, she's really sick. Go up there. I know you want to."

"It's been too long, and too much has happened. I wouldn't even know what to say to her now."

"I love you, and I forgive you. That's what you say. But, yes, you're right: it has been too long, especially for anything that has to do with that mouth-breathing idiot ex-husband of yours. Go make it right, even if you weren't the one who made it wrong."

"I don't know, maybe I'll wait until the morning. It's late."

"Death and forgiveness are usually intertwined, but it's best to do one before the other." She stood over me, one hand on her hip and one finger pointing toward the door. "Harlow, march!"

1:30 a.m.

Even though I knocked softly, the echo still reverberated down the empty hallway. I wondered if the night-shift dictator was restricted to the fourth floor, or if Nurse Boone had free range of the hospital. I cracked the door open and slid through the narrow slot, unwilling to find myself in trouble with her again.

A wheelchair with a duct-taped rip in the seat sat catty-corner to the bed. Soft glow from a nightlight illuminated the outline of a tiny body. She turned and looked at me as I stood in her cramped foyer. The sight was shocking. The illness had stolen so much of her thick auburn hair that a grayish scalp showed through in spots. When I saw how ravaged her body was, how she had managed to age twice as fast as I, any resentment I had carried into that room vanished, forgotten. The forgiveness was that simple, that pure, right there in a bleach-soaked hospital room.

"Savannah," I whispered, not from fear of disturbing her, but from the size of the lump in my throat. I moved toward her, gingerly placing her hand in mine and kneeling beside her bed. Gone was the rebellious girl from my memories; only a shell of her was left.

"Hey, you," she whispered.

"What's happened to you? What's wrong?" The words choked me with regret.

She smoothed the hair back away from my face and smiled. I couldn't tell if her teeth were unnaturally yellow, or if their hue was from the glow of the unfortunate desktop lighting.

Her voice came out unsteady and soft, like a torn piece of silk. "You always were a bleeding heart and a sucker for the sick. I just figured this was the best way to get you to talk to me again, so I got cancer—more like cancer got me. I was diagnosed a few years after we stopped talking. Or rather, *you* stopped talking," she said, now smiling through her eyes instead of her yellow teeth.

My first instinct was an apology, but for what I wasn't sure. It was what my upbringing had always commanded me to do. So, like a good Southern woman, it's what I did. "I'm sorry," I whispered. "I'm so sorry I shut you out. If I could take it back, I would."

She scooched herself up on a pillow and hit the remote button on her bed, raising her head. "Would you stop? You have nothing to be sorry about, except that hideous outfit you're wearing, and the fact that you didn't divorce Patrick years ago. Other than that, you've done nothing wrong, so don't apologize. I'm the one who slept with him while you were married, remember?"

The night it happened flashed through my mind. Bits and pieces, sounds and smells bloomed. Images of Savannah's hair swinging across her naked back, the roar of Patrick's voice cheering for more. Them having sex in our bed, not even bothering to turn off the lights. The residue of that cruelty found me, and it pushed against a door I thought I had closed.

She saw me picturing the image, and in an uppity voice that was clearly mocking Mother's, she teased, "Now, Harlow, don't be ugly." Her voice returned to its new normal as she continued. "Sorry, I went straight for the joke. It's kind of what I do. How'd you know I was here?"

"I was wandering the halls and saw a pineapple outside your door. It was a logical guess."

Her eyes got wide, her stare perplexed. "There's really a pineapple?"

"No, but I can joke too. Beth told me where to find you."

Her stare turned into a wide grin as she said, "Well done, Low. I see you've turned yourself into a true smartass."

25

That couldn't have been further from the truth. "I wish, but no. I'm still as square as the day you met me."

She reached out her hand and clasped her bony fingers around my wrist. "I like you square. I always have." I didn't know how to respond to that. Over the years, Savannah had used my trustworthy etiquette to her advantage, leaving me as carnage on several occasions. I think she knew that I was now picturing that. "Well, this is awkward. Listen, I'm sorry, Low. I don't know what else to say. Me, speechless. Can you imagine? Vivian would love that. Speaking of, how is Vivian? Still emotionally constipated?"

An unladylike snort-laugh escaped before I could cover my mouth. Savannah had the ability to do that to me. I wasn't sure how, but I had forgotten about that. "No, not constipated, just emotionally illiterate. She certainly isn't swinging from the rafters, and her porch hasn't seen a pineapple in years. Not since you stopped leaving them there. Actually, she's dying."

"I've heard that, and for what it's worth, I'm sorry about that too." Savannah pursed her lips, seemingly recalling the memories. "God, she hated me. Remember how mad she'd get, never missing an opportunity to point out that I was from *off*. She always thought I was up to no good—which I usually was, so kudos to her for that. With her tight jaw and that permanent resting bitch face, just the way she looked at me—I never had to wonder where I stood with her. Her face said it all. All the pineapple punch at the ball wouldn't warm her up to me."

I couldn't help but giggle at what Savannah had said. "She did have a resting bitch face. She might have even invented it. And she was afraid of you. You were different, and different can scare people. If it makes you feel better, it wasn't just you. She thought anyone from *off* was suspicious."

Even though it had been a long ten years of separation, the ease of our childhood conversation was quickly coming back.

"Seriously, Low, I have no excuse, and for the last decade I've regretted how much I hurt you." Her grasp tightened on my wrist as her eyes focused on mine. "Forgive me, okay?"

"Okay," I agreed. "It was a long time ago, and Patrick was never worth fighting over—still isn't."

"Hmm," she muttered. "Are you talking about Lexi?"

"That's his current one. The back of a long line, though."

"Damn, he's working his way through the family. You just missed my sister. She mentioned that y'all had words. I'm assuming it's the reason she didn't stay. You'd think an S.O.B. snob like Patrick wouldn't come within ten feet of a last name like Pratt. He must really be lowering his standards. That man gets more ass than a toilet seat, always has. How can you live with knowing your husband is through with you and off with another woman?"

"You'd be surprised by what we can live with. In his defense—his only defense—he isn't through with me, because he never really got started. The only thing Patrick ever loved about me was my weakness. One night was all it took. But I don't want to talk about him. Van," I whispered, stroking her arm, "you were my best friend. I'm sorry it took until now for me to talk to you again."

Her breath shallow from all the talking, she answered, "I know, Low. I love you too."

We sat in the muted darkness recalling a thousand different memories that spanned more than twenty-five years, all buried too deep to fully dig up. She smiled as a thought seemed to come to her. "By the way, happy fortieth birthday today."

"I can't believe you remembered that. Thank you."

"Of course I remembered. Forty is a milestone that should not be forgotten. I've been waiting a long time to tell you that. We both have."

Confused, I asked, "What do you mean? Who's 'we'?"

"Have you talked to him yet?"

"Patrick? I doubt he'll be wishing me a happy birthday. We still talk, though. Not so much since Evie went to college, but we still live in the same house. He's too prideful to leave, and truth be told, I don't know where to go. We're roommates more than anything else, both of us trying to avoid each other. I'll have to rent a place for me and Beth until I can figure out what to do. The divorce is final today."

Savannah scrunched her face in thought before she spoke. "I'd like to say that I'm sorry about that, though I'm not. You're better than him and always have been. But don't act like you don't know what I mean. You know damn well that I'm not talking about Patrick."

Despite my answer, I did know exactly whom she meant. Even though I had only a fraction of the memories with Jade Ryan, they'd been enough to carry me for the last twenty years. Having his name on the tip of my tongue lifted me, crushed me, and roiled my insides in nautical waves, but ultimately, it saturated me in a light that the years with Patrick hadn't been able to completely snuff out. Jade was my first love, my only love, and the kind of love that I knew only came around once.

I no longer searched for his face among passing strangers or prayed for him to be on the other side of every opening door; the delusions had eventually vanished, but the longing never ceased. For years, he was the last image that swept across my mind at night—sometimes finding his way to my dreams—and the first thought that opened my eyes. I never dared to mention him aloud; I only whispered his name in my heart. Because with that one word, anyone would see through me, see right through to my core, and know that after all these years, I was still in love with him.

"I don't want to talk about him either."

Van just shook her head, disappointment oozing from her expression. "You can't even say his name. Christ, Harlow, you haven't grown up at all. Still a mouse, scurrying around your life."

"That's not true!" I whisper-shouted. "I've seen him from time to time, but it's been a while. In fact, the last time I talked to him was only two years ago." My sight found the ceiling as my confession hit my lips. "I might visit his woodshop on occasion."

Savannah smiled. "You do have some slut in you."

"It's not like that. I go on demonstration days, and I stand in the back. I suspect he never even knows I'm there. The day we actually spoke was a disaster. I was a complete bumbling idiot. It's just—"

"How was it, seeing him again?" she interrupted with a sly smirk.

I couldn't have stopped the smile even if I had wanted to. "Like falling back into a beautiful dream."

Savannah was suddenly quiet. She was staring at me, but it was a strange and uncomfortable look. Quickly, I changed the subject. "What about you? Any torrid affairs?"

"Humph," she breathed, although the sound came out as more of a chuckle. "I haven't had sex in years. Is it possible for a vagina to atrophy, or hermetically seal? I could tell you if I could manage to get a closer look at my own, but I don't think Nurse Boone approves of that behavior."

I giggled. "You're sick." As soon as the words came out of my mouth, I realized the gravity of what I had said. "I'm sorry, Van. I didn't mean…"

She locked her eyes on mine. The thinness of her skin showed every ridge and valley of her jawline in a cadaverous contour. "Two years is a long time, Low. Twenty is ridiculous. You need to talk to Jade."

Her skin was thin, but she was still tough. I was grateful to skate over my faux pas.

Twenty years already? Some days it seemed like only yesterday that Jade and I were together, and other days it felt like a hundred years ago. Sometimes I told myself that I was just going for a drive, but when I crossed the Ashley toward James Island, I realized I had known where I was going all along. The closer I got to Folly Beach, the harder my heart pounded in my ears.

"Something about the way he sands the wood leaves me full—until the next time I need to take a drive again." For the first time in two decades, I admitted aloud, "Even after all these years, I can't seem to let that time go, let him go. And truthfully, I haven't tried."

"That's a lot to say about someone you don't want to talk about." A pitying look washed over her face, and her brows furrowed together as she pursed her lips, suddenly quiet again.

"What's wrong? Should I call someone?" I asked, starting to panic.

"No, no, I'm fine. I was just thinking," she answered, patting my hand. "Do you remember the store we were going to open?"

"Of course I do." I recalled the memory with warmth. "The art gallery: Van-Low Studios. You would run the front of the house, and I was going to put my business degree—the one I never got—to good use on the books. I haven't thought of that dream in years. What made you remember that?"

"I don't know, just you and me talking like old times, I guess. We put a lot of miles on the joggling board that sat on your front porch. It feels good to remember. Hey," she said with a sly smirk, "remember Caroline Coker?"

Every high school has a mean girl, and Caroline Coker was ours. With her year-round tan and that Barbie convertible she drove, she made my teenaged years unbearable.

"Ugh," I mumbled, rolling my eyes. "How could you think I would ever forget her? I hated her and her ridiculously perfect feet."

Savannah measured her words, so as not to go into a coughing fit. "Only you would hate someone for their feet. There were way worse things about her than her toes—like her mouth, for instance.

God, she was awful. You'll be happy to know that all that mean came back to her, and it's now situated directly on her ass."

"Nooo!" I gasped, dragging out the word to match the depth of my shock.

"Yep. Fatter than a hog at Founder's Day."

I doubled over, laughing as quietly as possible. "I had forgotten you talk like that."

"Like what? I'm just saying that she spent a lot of time being cruel to you—on account of your birthmark, and also being so skinny—and now, time is repaying the favor. A fat ass is the best punishment, and hers busts out like a can of warm biscuits. Lord, you were thin, though. Pale, too. Like a Charleston vampire."

I got up to use the bathroom but kept talking through the crack I left in the door. "Don't say that. I wasn't *that* pale, just conscientious."

"Harlow, you were almost see-through."

I waved her words away like a gnat, steering the conversation away from myself. I was sick of thinking about myself. "Caroline seemed to settle down toward the end of college."

"Only because she blew most of the Calvary Prep lacrosse team in a closet one Friday night. Apparently, she wasn't so good at it. By Sunday morning they had come up with a nickname: Choker Coker. Remember that? That was the best."

The satisfaction in her voice made it clear that she relished the memory.

Going solely on looks and family money, Caroline Coker embodied everything an S.O.B. mother wanted in a rising debutante daughter. Golden rays of sunlit hair, a svelte figure with a perky chest, and skin that tanned. The list of necessities wasn't long, but her beauty was nothing short of perfection. Being born with such beauty must have left no room for kindness, because she was just as feared as she was admired. I distanced myself from her back then whenever possible.

I made sure to double-wash my hands, paranoid about spreading germs. "That name was not nice. I felt bad for her when people started making fun of her. I know what that feels like, and it can ruin you. Remember how many doctors Mother took me to? Every time I walked out of another office *unfixable*, I saw a part of her die. I did see Caroline a while back, down at Ryan and Son's workshop. She didn't look heavy to me. It must have been two years ago, because it was the same day…"

And just as his name formed on my lips, like a ghost from my past, he materialized on the other side of the door.

2:30 a.m.

Being in the immediate presence of Jade Ryan again—something I had wished for countless times—left me terrified and delighted. It was strange how I could feel two opposite emotions at once, fully immersed in both, yet unable to unbraid myself from the fringe they tangled me in. I stood in confused silence, like the opaque haze of a dream, and I couldn't trust reality over my recollection of the past. Our eyes met across the room for a long and motionless moment.

His hair was darker than the last time I'd seen him. What had once been a shade of worn leather was now the color of wet dirt. Even from across the room, his signature scent of lemon oil furniture polish was noticeable. I loved it, and I hated it. More so, I hated myself for remembering that detail about him.

His stature was solid and broad, and the room melted away when he spoke. "Hello, Harlow."

To hear my name come from that voice again. It was surreal and uncomfortable and beautiful—everything that had kept our memories alive inside of me. He didn't clear his throat, shift his feet, move his hands, or even blink. He held my gaze as if we were the only two people in the room, in the world even. It was exactly like our very first meeting, only twenty years before. I let out the breath I hadn't realized I was holding.

"Hello," was all I had in reply, too numb to feel the words come from my throat.

I looked at Savannah, ready to explode at her for asking him to come meet me here. This must have been what she meant by saying that people had been waiting to wish me a happy birthday. Another typical pain-in-the-butt stunt, which Savannah was known for pulling, bullying you until you were exactly how she saw you fit to be. As her eyes drew away from me, I noticed what her sight had settled on: a pair of small feet behind the beautiful man.

With petite shoulders that curved toward Jade's lower ribs, she had wrapped her arms tightly around his waist. She was still and quiet, shy and buried, and she was the spitting image of Savannah.

Savannah finally spoke. "Harlow, this is my daughter, Penny."

Well, forty is starting out super. Am I hallucinating, or am I having just about the best birthday ever?

Penny came around from behind Jade to lean her head into his stomach. With one fluid motion, his arms crossed around her like a shield, the tattooed sleeve of his right arm running up alongside her ear. Without looking up at him, and continuing to stare at the stranger who'd used her sick mama's bathroom in the middle of the night, she asked, "Daddy, who is that woman?"

So, no on hallucinations, and yes on this top-notch birthday.

With only one word, that little girl had managed to squeeze my stomach into a nauseating twist. She had called him daddy. I couldn't believe I had missed it before, because now, looking for answers from Savannah's uncomfortable expression, it was all I could see. That and a diamond band on her left ring finger.

Jade answered his daughter, "This is Harlow. She's a friend of Mommy and me."

A sickening wave of realization came over me. That sentence felt like a throat punch.

"Why is she here?" Penny asked.

"Just to say hello, darling."

"Oh," the little girl exclaimed, now seeming pleased. "Hello, then."

She greeted me so merrily, so innocently, and her spirit softened me right there in that moment. I got down on one knee, coming to eye level with her. My selfish desires were no match for the image of a clinging child in her dying mother's hospital room. No child should have to endure this scene and watch her mama waste away. Even if she didn't know it at the time, these days would haunt her and steal a piece of an already-short childhood. I had learned plenty about that when I lost my father. The reality of the entire situation was devastating.

"Hello to you as well," I crooned. "My, you're a pretty thing. I bet you're smart, too."

Her eyes bulged as if I had cracked a secret code, and she let out a sharp gasp.

"That's exactly what my daddy says: that I'm smart, especially for a seven-year-old, and my mama says that I'm her pretty Penny."

"I think that suits you very well, Penny."

Her words were like daggers, but the way she said them actually made me grateful to be engaged in this conversation, instead of the one I knew was waiting for me when this darling little girl walked out the door. She unclenched Jade's hands and unexpectedly walked over to me, her arms engulfing my neck in a tight squeeze.

Her breath smelled of sleep and hard candy, her ruddy cheeks still sticky from the remnant of a treat. Her voice came out in a steady whisper, but not like a child who hadn't mastered the art of speaking yet. She sounded more like a patient and assured older version of herself. Kneeling, Penny ran her finger along my purple splotched foot. The colors were highlighted against the sterile white of the tile floor.

I was used to questions about my birthmark, and I never minded a child's inquiry. They usually came from a nonjudgmental place of genuine curiosity, excitement even: Did you drop something on your foot? Can it change colors? Does it make you feel hot? Will it go away? Does it hurt?

To my surprise, she had no questions. Penny seemed to already know the answers.

When she rolled up her three-quarter sleeve to mid-arm, I smiled despite myself. Different in color and texture from mine, but all the same in the eyes of the clear-skinned general population, Penny had a birthmark too. Blush and carmine splattered the crook in her right arm, where her skin was creased like the deflated rubber of a popped balloon. Her enthusiasm for comparing our abnormal similarities managed to fill me—even temporarily—with an exponential amount of goodness. It was the kind of grace, I supposed, that could only be found in the heart of a child.

She leaned in toward my ear, her whisper strong. "You're even prettier than my daddy said. They're going to make me go back to bed now, but come back and see me, okay?"

"Okay," I agreed. The word came out of my mouth as an afterthought, as if I had no control over what I was saying.

"Promise?" she asked in a way that was surely her mother's, as though she were closing a deal.

"I pinky promise."

I suddenly longed for the days of Evie's childhood. A time when I could revel in our closeness, distancing myself from the rest of my life—a glass partition that enabled me to never fully engage in the future, as well as an excuse to live in the past. I missed being part of a child's life.

Jade turned to Savannah. "I'm sorry she's awake, but she had a nightmare. I promised that a kiss from you would send her back into good dreams. You know," Jade said, picking Penny up and kissing her cheek, "it's very late, so I'm going to tuck you back into bed next door. These ladies have a lot to talk about. Give Mommy a kiss, okay?"

He leaned her over to hover above Savannah, and I heard Savannah whisper, "Good night, my pretty Penny. I love you."

"I love you more," Penny said with a yawn.

"I love you most," Savannah replied.

As Jade wrapped the little girl around himself, she nuzzled her tired eyes into his neck, getting lost in the darkness of her curls. He paused before turning toward the door. Jade was very much a fixture of strength in the hospital room, but at the same time, he emanated a sense of loss. His eyes said something I couldn't fully understand; there was a palpable tension that tore me in two. He stood quietly, again holding my gaze as if a glance could render memories. I was uncertain if he was going to go back twenty years and dredge up the awful night of our breakup, or if cutting me into a thousand pieces with only a look would do the trick. I felt small and unsteady, degraded somehow. Yet he completely surprised me by saying, "It was really good to see you, Harlow." With that, he walked out.

Upon the soft click of the closing door, Savannah tried to seek comfort in the blank wall, clearly unexcited about discussing this turn of events. Her silence was so thorough that I wondered if she had managed to fully retreat from the reality of the moment.

"She's beautiful," I offered, still won over by four feet of sweetness.

"Thank you. I'd hoped you two would hit it off. Jade takes very good care of her. He's a wonderful father."

"How long have you two been married?" I whispered, less from shock and more from anger that she hadn't been upfront with the truth the moment I walked into her room. Savannah had done some twisted things in her past, but this one was a punch in the face. I didn't think I could have been more surprised; there wasn't anything that would have prepared me.

"Four years, but Low, let me explain."

Even though I had no right to be, I was livid, and she knew it. "Funny, that's the same thing your sister said to me tonight. A little advice for the Pratt girls: if you didn't go behind people's backs, you wouldn't need to do so much explaining." The tears were threatening, and I had to get out of there before they broke through. "Why did you let me go on about him? What was the point of encouraging me to talk about him, or even bringing Jade up in the first place? Was it for enjoyment, humiliation, or to get back at me for shutting you out for so long? You sure haven't changed much either."

"Hey!" she said, her eyes wide and hurt filled. "That's not fair."

"No? Since when do you care about fair? Maybe I should have seduced Jade on one of my trips to his workshop. I should have laid him down and thrown myself at him, just like someone else I know. Then I would have slept with your husband, too. Would that make things fair?"

I bolted for the door without waiting for an answer, unwilling to humiliate myself further. I couldn't believe we were here again, in this hurt that always seemed to find our friendship. I used to think she just wanted what I had, but it seemed clear that Savannah didn't spend time thinking of others. She only had eyes for herself. I'd spent years excusing her behavior, categorizing her mistakes as parental failures or the luck of the nurturing draw. The excuses had run out—like our friendship, my patience, and, as far as I could tell, the time she had left.

3:00 a.m.

As I hurried down the hall, the squeak of his shoes against the freshly waxed floors sounded behind me before his voice did.

Jabbing the down button outside the elevator door, I pleaded, *Please, God, please open this door. I'm begging you. I can't face him.*

"Harlow, wait!" he called, running up toward me.

The industrial lights illuminated the colorful ink embedded in his skin, as the sensation of longing for him burst against the belly of my heart. That's when I noticed it: a magazine jutted from his hand.

Jesus, I thought. *Does everyone read* Papier and Pen *before dawn?*

He knew I was divorced, knew I couldn't and shouldn't have tried to make it work with Patrick, knew that everything he told me twenty years ago had been right. That night seemed to surround our silence. Surely he also knew that I was picturing it, picturing him, and I had my suspicions that the memory he recalled was quite the same.

There was an entirety to the silence that surrounded us. The joy and the pain mingled, too coiled for words to untangle.

His fingers nervously intertwined before he spoke, the only betrayal of his emotions. "How are you?" he asked.

I took a long moment before answering. "I'm fine, thank you. And you?"

"Good," he replied. "The shop has been really busy, so that's nice. How's your daughter, Evie? How's Beth?"

The ridiculous small talk was beginning to make me uncomfortable. "Um, she's fine. I'm fine. We're all fine. Look, we don't have to do this, you know."

"Do what? Talk?"

My mood was seeping into my tone. "Act like we care about each other's lives." Drained of emotion, yet still full of hurt, I said to the floor, "I need to get back downstairs."

"Don't do this," he said. I heard an inkling of desperation in his voice, which I chose to ignore. "Don't run off this way, not again. I know what you must be thinking, but let me explain."

"Again, I'm fine. There's nothing more to talk about, and you don't owe me any explanation. You're entitled to live your life." The dishonesty in my voice was only partially disguised.

There was so much that I wanted to ask him, wanted to say, but our memories felt fragile, and I didn't want to risk the chance of breaking them. Memories of him were all I had. I watched his hand massage the flowers that were tattooed from the wrist to the shoulder of his right arm. There must have been a hundred flower petals in just as many colors, waving back and forth to the rhythm of his fingers. Twenty years ago, only a fraction of those flowers had hung around my shoulders and held me tight. He'd had a lot of work done since then, clearly on some sort of mission to leave no skin on his right arm uncolored. As his hand raised his shirtsleeve, I noticed the one tattoo that stood out from the rest. It was an exact replica of Penny's birthmark.

He is a good father, and Penny is lucky to have him. I wish Evie had been that lucky, too. I was wishing for something for the thousandth time: that Jade had been her father, Beth her real grandmother. It was another prayer, another wish that would remain scattered to the wind.

Snapping out of my self-pity, I suddenly panicked. *What's taking this elevator so long?* I poked the button so hard that I should have knocked the thing clear off the wall.

"Look up!" he scolded me, a demand I had heard from him before. Frustration had infused his voice, and he was having a hard time keeping the volume down. Softer then, he said, "Look at me, or you're going to miss this and let it pass you by."

An unfair viciousness rose within me, seemingly lifting my gaze with the force of venom alone. I let the meanness come over me as I pictured him with Savannah. Strangely, it wasn't the thought of them having sex that hurt me—hell, she had slept with half the town—but the trivial and ordinary exchanges of a marriage. The laughter of an awkward moment, the inside joke of a shared memory, all the inconsequential moments that you think aren't important at the time, but that you later find were the most extraordinary ones. I couldn't believe he had married her.

With a tinge of cruelty, I suggested, "You should get back to your wife."

The wickedness wasn't lost on him, and he dove right in. "Oh, so I'm the bad guy here. I'm the asshole in this situation? Have you forgotten what got us here, forgotten that night? Or are we now rewriting history in an attempt to make you less responsible for the past? I made promises to you that YOU wouldn't let me keep. All that stupid Southern guilt you have—stop apologizing, and start living your life. That's sure as hell better than any bullshit apology."

"Don't you dare curse at me, Jade Ryan. I'm not rewriting anything, you smug bastard. I'm only stating a fact. She is your wife, and I'm not the one who should be apologizing for it."

Summoning all his reserve, he replied, "Okay, so I *am* the bad guy. Thanks for clearing that up." In the fractious but eerie silence that followed, he turned to walk away, but in the same instant, something compelled him to turn back. Taking in a breath that seemed too deep for him to hold, he reared up and shook his fists as he blurted out, "YOU BROKE MY HEART!"

All I could do was swallow the pain of that statement, because he was right. I had broken his heart. I had broken both of our hearts.

He said in a much softer voice, "I'm sorry. I didn't know all of that was going to come out of me. It's just that you don't know the half of what you're taking about, and if you would just listen—"

I didn't listen. "You should have told me you were married to Savannah when we spoke at your store."

His voice came out a whisper, but his words were clear. "Why? I've seen you there plenty of times, Harlow. I notice you every single time. Are you going to try and convince me—and yourself— that you're just interested in the rocking chairs I make? I've seen the way you look at me. I know that look, because it's the same way I'm looking back at you. Just let me explain."

The elevator doors finally opened, and I backed inside. Unable to trust my morals alone with Jade in an elevator, I raised my hand to stop him from following me. It didn't stop him from blocking the doors. Irritated in the most grateful way, I tried not to notice how handsome he still was. And his beard…My God, his full beard intensified every rustic and masculine feature I had fallen in love with so long ago, enhancing every bit of him as a man. My body ached from the sight of him, and I tried not to choke as I drank him in.

"I just see you in an entirely different way now." *Lie.* "We were over a long time ago." *Another lie.* "You're free to live your life with whomever you please." *Now*, that *was the truth.*

I removed his hands from the door, but not before taking a moment to remember what they felt like on me, around me, inside me. To see him was hardly bearable, but willpower is a mighty shield, a trick of the mind and heart. When our hands connected, his touch bypassed my brain, traveling straight down to my muscle memory, and even after all those years, my hands still remembered every bit of him. The mind may go gray with age, but the heart never forgets.

The doors slowly erased his face as they closed before him, but the sound of the elevator descending couldn't drown out the rapid beat of my heart. I was alone in a box of sadness and regret and the lingering scent of lemon oil. Suddenly feeling the heat of the encounter, along with the blood rushing to my already purple toes, I slid against the wall and down to the floor.

I must have ridden up and down that elevator ten times before I came to my senses. Although he had been for a time, he wasn't mine now. I had known that for twenty years; there was nothing different about that tonight. I might never be over Jade Ryan, and that was something I was just going to have to continue to live with, surrendering to loving someone I could never have.

Even though the conversation I was having with myself was very adult, there was still the college girl inside of me who wasn't ready to listen to reason.

I loved her for it.

3:30 a.m.

As I entered Mother's room, a breeze from the opening door found its way inside, threatening to lift a stack of loose-leaf papers and scatter them across the tile floor. Foggy-eyed and clearly exhausted, Beth hovered over the documents as though she were harvesting organs. I had grown accustomed to seeing her hunched over, sitting cross-legged on the floor, and working on yet another project. She was beautiful to me. Even in the early morning hours, she was as sturdy as the Carolina pines whose massive girth threatened to block the stars at home. Often, and in numerous ways, I was reminded of how much I loved her. Not for the things she did, but for the way she loved to do them. I hadn't asked her for much in my life, but I hadn't needed to, either. She gave wholly, in a way that lightened your step, softened your voice, and padded your heart.

Beth worked entirely too hard. Through the heat of breezeless summers and the yellow of pollen-covered springs, Beth had stayed with us. She had been an agent of compassion for our family, and an ocean of mercy for me. My soap opera was the last thing I wanted to drag her into tonight. She deserved better than that, better than this family.

"What the heck are you doing up?" I asked. "I thought you'd be dead to the world by now."

"I wanted to see how it went."

"It wasn't entirely smooth, but nothing with Savannah ever is. It's nice to see her again."

"How'd she look? Is she okay?"

"She didn't look so good. I don't think she has a lot of time left. I did meet her daughter, though, and she seemed lovely."

"Yes," Beth said in a faraway voice, a smile breaking on the corner of her lip. "Anything else?"

My suspicion arose. "Why? Should there be anything else?"

"I guess not. Just curious is all. I'm proud of you for going up there. Maybe you should plan on going back up after some sleep."

Penny's sorrel doe eyes filled my mind. "I kind of have to. I made a promise."

"That's great. Van-Low back at it again." Beth chuckled through a yawn, while stretching her arms up over her head. She raked her fingers through a mass of graying red hair, instantly giving herself a fiery fro. "You know," she continued, "no one came to see Vivian today. I realize that not many of her old crew is still around, and the ones that are left are somewhat incapacitated, but no one's child brought flowers. Not a single store that Vivian has frequented for the last seven decades even sent a card. That bothers me. I thought Southerners were raised better than that."

"I guess you get what you give. It's late. Why don't you crawl into the rollaway bed, and I'll sleep on the chaise? Besides, it's too late to be working, or contemplating the psychology of manners. What could possibly be important enough to deserve attention right now?"

"I'm finishing the seating chart for the gala tomorrow night. Well," she said, checking her watch, "technically speaking, it's after midnight, so I guess I mean the gala tonight."

Completely thrown for a loop, I exclaimed, "Wait, we're going through with that?"

"We certainly are. Why would you think anything different?"

"Oh, I don't know, logic? We haven't talked about the gala in a week. I guess I assumed that when Vivian was admitted into the hospital, we would call it off."

"Vivian sent the invitations out weeks ago. It's a big deal for the gallery, and for the clients—the biggest night of our year. This tradition goes back forty years; there's no way it's going to end on my watch. Plus, she made me promise not to cancel."

"She's in a coma! I promise, she'll never find out we canceled. It's insane to go through with this. We've been up all night, we're both exhausted, and I've had quite the trot down memory lane right here in these hospital halls. Besides," I said, sliding to the floor in a defeated huff, "I really don't want to put on something fancy."

"Are you worried about your speech?" Beth asked, completely ignoring all the reasons I had just given her.

"Are you trying to be difficult? No, I'm not worried about my speech, because I won't be giving a speech, because there won't be an audience, because we are canceling."

"It's her last wish, Harlow. Anyway, you don't even have to write a speech. Vivian already wrote it for you."

"Of course she did. The master puppeteer pulling the strings on all her indentured servants."

"Stop being so dramatic. No one is forcing you to be there."

"Okay, then, I'm not going tonight."

"Oh, yes you are."

"You just said I wasn't being forced."

"You knew that was crap the moment I said it. Of course you're being forced. Plain as day, I'm forcing you; we both know that. I just needed something to pull you down off your cross." She flippantly waved the words away from her, to keep them from fluttering back to us.

"At least you're being honest. Thanks, I guess."

"Today is all about honesty, Low. We have to right things—to make everything right and try to send Vivian out in a peaceful body. It's the only way, and it has to get done today. Believe me, you won't want to miss this one, or let it pass you by."

Taken aback by her statement, I couldn't help but stare blankly at her. She matched my gaze, head cocked, brow raised.

"What's that supposed to mean?" I asked as she got up and came to sit next to me, lovingly draping her arm around my shoulder.

It seemed as though she was going to say something, but her voice started, only to immediately pause, coming out as just a breath. She began again. "It just means to pay attention to your life, darling. For twenty years, you've let it pass you by. Sometimes you need to close your eyes to truly see, because what you'll find is the image of your heart."

I could feel her words. They were vast and dark and gaping, and I was drowning in them, drowning in myself. I wasn't the woman I was supposed to be, and I was terrified that I would never become her. With the reality of my fourth decade closing in upon me, the passage of time was inescapable, and I felt as though my life were being held together by a thin strand of hope.

"I'm forty," I whispered. I didn't know if I was just making the statement or begging for it not to be true, but I certainly wasn't celebrating it. Resting my head in the bend of Beth's arm, I whined, "I don't want to be forty."

With light strokes of her soft fingers, she smoothed out the wisps of hair gone rogue against my forehead. "Milestone birthdays can often feel heavy at first, but they have a way of lessening the weight of the previous years, leaving you lighter than you ever imagined. Trust me on this, because I've had a few of my own—birthdays and regrets. Embrace this day."

"It's easier said than done."

"Most things worth doing usually are." She paused, seemingly careful to choose her next words. "You've served your time, Harlow. You've done your penance. You've pummeled yourself for two long decades over one single night. A minuscule fraction of a moment has held you prisoner for half your life. What if you gave yourself a birthday present, a real gift? What if after all these years, you forgave yourself? Not for failing to live up to Vivian's expectations, or for getting pregnant at the wrong time, or even for falling in love, but for staying in love. Because the love is what's gotten you to forty."

Her tone wasn't accusatory, just measured and mindful. Confused, I lifted my gaze to hers.

"Uh-huh, don't think that after all these years with you, I can't see it—the way you still feel about Jade, about all of us, really. You don't have to read between the lines. Just turn the page, honey. The best part of your love story is yet to come."

I let the silence swallow me up. Her words chewed on me in the darkness.

Beth chuckled. "Obviously I'm going to have to get some sleep, because apparently I'm going to spend the rest of the day either kicking your butt or dragging it around town, and I haven't worked out in years. I'm already exhausted."

Her smile sliced through the thickness of the moment. Her happiness was infectious. It was always something you wanted to catch.

She got up and rummaged through her makeup bag. I watched her slather Vaseline all over her face, her reflection shiny in the bathroom mirror. When she caught my gaze, she teased, "Now that you're forty, you better start adding this to your nighttime regimen. Maybe I'll buy you a case of it for your birthday." She held up the economy-sized jar like a commercial spokesperson.

Over the years, Beth had sworn that her perfect skin was strictly the result of the moisturizing effects of Vaseline. Each night, she coated herself from head to toe with practically a second skin, wiping off any excess on squeaky door hinges or stuck drawers, lubricating herself first, and then half the house on her way to bed.

I had never believed her claims of the majestic powers of petroleum jelly, but the youthfulness of her skin had on several occasions caused her to be mistaken for my young mother. I didn't just love that; I reveled in it. Mother and Daddy were always much older than my peers' parents. Already in her mid-eighties on her last birthday, Vivian was well into her forties when I came into the world. After Beth took up residence with us, Mother had been mistaken for my grandmother on several occasions, a correction she never dignified, much too content with her ego to give chase to comments that were clearly beneath her.

Beth and I went to our respective sleeping surfaces—her on the rollout, me on the chaise, face to face in the cramped hospital room. Like a bear about to hibernate, she made a racket getting herself snug underneath the covers. As her breathing began to regulate, I had to find another way to occupy my mind. Or, more truthfully, I had to find a way back to him.

The fastest route back to him that I knew lay in my overnight bag.

I fished around the inside of my tote for the comfort I could always rely on. The frayed cloth of the worn-out binding feathered across my fingers, and the sensation felt warmer than a wood-burning fire. I placed the familiar book in my lap, the sheets serenading me with every stretch and bend. Even though I had read it a million times over, *The Call of the Wild* remained my favorite book, one I could always return to. The craft-paper backing continued to erode underneath the thin hunter-green fabric, and the once magnificent gold-embossed title was all but gone. Only a few random letters still showed.

Through the years, I had spent countless hours engrossed in Jack London's words—which I assumed were life advice—about a man who had disobeyed his parents and set out on life-threatening adventures, all for the sake of creating a life on his own terms. Although I couldn't relate to John Thornton's fortitude—my life had been one obeyed order after another—I certainly idolized his defiance of those who stood in his way. For me, it wasn't just a book, but a map to a different life.

I ran my thumb back and forth over the inscription on the title page. The words were now only a reminder of a time gone by.

Don't forget to look up.

Forever yours,

Jade

"I remember the day I met you, Harlow," Beth said, her words clear in the darkness. "Do you remember the day you met me?"

As I closed my eyes to the life-keeping sounds of Mother's machinery, I opened my memory to the light, something I had done frequently. One memory poured after another, until I was overcome by a stream of them. The way he closed in on me when he wanted me to listen, the back and forth of decades of friendship, and the love for a woman who, for going on twenty years, had saved me from myself. Just as if a window had opened, the past came rushing in, and I could remember everything.

Before rolling over to the weight of sleep, I answered Beth simply, "Of course I do. It was the summer that changed everything."

PART TWO
THEN

Chapter 1

The mild frost of winter had long melted, and the bounty of spring began to thrive in the private gardens and along the tree-lined streets of the narrow peninsula known as South of Broad. Although similar in composition to any other street in America, Broad Street and its residents were far from common. Bordered on the east by the Cooper River and on the west by the Ashley River, Broad Street was the imaginary cutoff of the most exclusive borough in downtown Charleston. Rows of palatial Georgian, Greek Revival, and Charleston Single House mansions lined the cobblestone squares; three-tiered piazzas seemed to triple the grandeur of any given home. Strategically planted screens of trees boxed in lush courtyards, growing high enough to let the offshore breeze in and keep the tourists out, while also providing just enough of a glimpse for an onlooker to gawk in curiosity.

As a daughter of the region and a born-and-bred Charlestonian, I had grown fond of the mystery the city provided. Alleyways and shortcuts, hidden courtyards and breezeways, all anchored by palmetto trees: these Southern staples guided the way through a variety of open-air markets. Like old friends, they didn't change, never faltered, and always showed me the way home. This was my Holy City, laid out in squares and blocks, where any desire could be found around the next corner.

I emerged from a less-than-hidden alleyway and spotted the third-floor piazza of our sunlit coral-colored home. I took my time in reaching it on the walk back from the family gallery. The flowering cherries and heavy-budded crepe myrtles offered a continuous rain of flower petals, carpeting the sidewalks as if I were a bride. The delicate wind-swept blooms twirled between my steps, swirling a potent fragrance that no perfumer could ever duplicate. Bathed in vivid beauty, springtime in Charleston was surely made by the hand of God: a living, breathing work of art.

Despite the delectable afternoon balm, nausea reared as I approached the gate. I didn't know what—or who—would await me. A few weeks before, my father had suffered a massive stroke. To deal with the necessary medical interventions, Mother had hired a continuous stream of nurses, who flowed through our house. Some lasted only hours; none lasted more than a couple of days. Of course, their departure had nothing to do with my father and everything to do with Mother.

As I reached the house, the latest victim stormed out of the garden's cast-iron front gate and onto the street. The climbing vine–covered iron egress slammed behind her, in solidification of her termination. Dressed in blue scrubs and swirls of sweat, she stomped down the sidewalk right past me, her shoulder bag swinging as violently as her arms. Some had quietly skulked off, while others had pretended not to cry, but this woman made no bones about her anger. Stopping short, as if compelled by the Lord, she turned on a dime and huffed back to where I was standing. Her chest heaving, her breathing ragged, she shook her head and her fist, seemingly unable to speak. I thought she might have a stroke of her own.

Finally, she exclaimed, "That woman in there is a pin in the seat of society!" She waved her pointed finger in the air around me. "She's incredibly rude, and her expectations of home health care are unrealistic and, suffice it to say, completely beyond the scope of nursing. I have never been treated so badly in my entire life. Your mother doesn't need a nurse, she needs Jesus! Good luck with Mommy Dearest. I need a drink."

My only retort was silence, because *yes*—yes to all of that. She'd hear no disagreement on my end of things. As she huffed off, I could picture the carnage-filled scene inside. Hospice care roadkill was Mother's latest specialty. Reluctantly, I forced myself through the gate and into the direct line of fire.

Upon the slam of the front door, Mother called out, "Why are you home?"

I followed her voice to the garden and found her lounging with a book on the second-floor piazza attached to her room. A Tuesday afternoon at home or a Friday night social held no variance in Mother's wardrobe. Per usual, she was in full dress and makeup. Even into her sixties, her taut skin created the illusion of eternal youth—science fiction youth. From her flowing dresses, which kissed the backs of her calves when she walked, to her marcelled, pin-tucked waves of brunette hair, lustrous lips stained a fire-engine red, and cloud of Chanel Nº5, Vivian Ausby was a Southern delicacy meant to be seen at a distance rather than enjoyed up close. Any Charleston social climber who knew what was good for them made a point to praise her old-Hollywood attractiveness, her full-bodied hair, and her fashionable wardrobe, purchased from only the most upscale boutiques on King Street. The reason for their infatuation was obvious; she *was* beautiful. But in my experience with Mother, her beauty was only skin deep. From where I stood, the attraction that people had to her was easy to understand, and even easier to despise.

The heat of the recent termination had floated away with the breeze, another worry to unburden herself from. The Botox had either frozen her face or melted her brain, because she didn't seem panicked in the least about the lack of medical care for my father. I suspected that the bourbon and ginger sweating on the table had played a hefty hand in her unusually pleasant mood. Her bridge group must have just dispersed, although I wasn't sure if they actually played cards. I imagined that some of the ladies didn't even know the rules of the game. Who was to say? Children weren't invited, so I could only speculate. The one constant I was sure of in their weekly games was alcohol. The spirits ran high; the ice stayed cold. The cocktail-drinking, tartlet-eating, gossiping group of red-lipped debutantes kept the corner stores stocked with booze, and the city full of lies.

She looked out toward Fort Sumter. "I used to know everyone who lived in these homes," she said, seeming to be speaking more to herself than me. "Now, on any given night, half of the windows along these streets have strangers in them. Outsiders from *off* buy second homes here, throwing their new money into modern renovations, giving no thought to the rules of historical preservation. To live South of Broad is to live in the apex of goodness. Entrepreneurs try to suck up all that's unique here, and then they leave their gaudy hotels and failed restaurants when they've had their fill. What they have yet to understand is that they do not exist without us. We are the foundation of this fine town. It's a travesty, that's what it is." She looked up at me as though she hadn't noticed I was standing there. With her history lesson on pause, she asked again, "Why did you say you're home?"

I respectfully answered her, "Patrick said he could handle closing the gallery on his own tonight. He suggested that I take the rest of the day off."

"That was very sweet of him to suggest. In fact, *I* would suggest that he's a little sweet on you. Wouldn't you agree?" she asked, her painted eyebrows moving up and down suggestively.

"Mother, I've known him since we were both in diapers. If he wanted to date me, he would have already said so. Besides," I added, glimpsing at the birthmark that peeked out from under my floor-length skirt, "I'm not his type of date."

"Oh, says who?" she asked in her poo-poo voice, flicking her wrist dismissively. "Your family is rich and attractive, your bloodline runs red with patriotism, and your home is immaculate. So you have the leg flaw. You'll just keep it covered. Any society gentleman could easily overlook that one teensy blemish. The rest of you seems fine. Who wouldn't want to come to this beautiful home to pick you up and take you out?"

I think she had forgotten that she was talking about me—or to me—because as the bourbon sloshed inside the cut-glass tumbler, her pep talk became self-consoling. Mother would have loved the opportunity to date herself. She would have made herself very happy. I could sense her disappointment every time my leg accidentally became unrobed. My obvious flaw seemed to reflect on Mother herself, a reminder of her failure to achieve perfection. Despite her grandiose dreams of my future marriage to a worthy aristocrat with a similarly sterling bloodline, even if I had been the type for Patrick, Patrick was not the type for me.

Truth be told, he had made some vague passes at me over the last few weeks, but they were more offhanded than anything else. I had known Patrick for a long time, and I think he was just bored. Monotony was the one thing we truly had in common. He didn't want me; he just wanted to be entertained. A glass of bourbon and a theater ticket would have held the same amount of enjoyment for him.

Patrick came from a solid WASP family, with status, money, and clout to boot. The McDade family owned a chain of local pharmacies, where the S.O.B. families purchased most of their WASP pills. I had grown up all but attached to the leg of my daddy, tagging along on every errand I could talk him into, and the original McDade pharmacy, just past Rainbow Row, was a favorite stop of mine. This was before they had franchised, back when the McDades owned only the one store. I think it was probably the last time in my life I saw them happy. Life and money, and either too little or too much of both, had a way of hardening people. Mr. McDade would wave to me from behind the glass partition, and his wife always had a sucker and a kind word for me from behind the register. Probably out of some human grace, but mostly social necessity, back then the McDades were always very friendly to my family and me.

It's well known that Charleston WASPs go to college at The Citadel, the esteemed landmark military college. The McDades were no different in their expectations: their perfect Patrick would go there too. His path paved of cobblestone gold, there was a time when Patrick was well on his way to ripening into a handsome and powerful young man.

One night changed all that.

After a damning sexual assault scandal during his senior year of high school, the board at The Citadel thought it best for Patrick McDade to refrain from applying. The details of that night were legally sealed, though even a vault lock isn't stronger than a Southern rumor mill. Despite the whispered speculations, only Patrick and that tourist from Texas would ever really know the truth of that night.

The only absolute about the scandal was that McDade family money had kept Patrick out of jail. And his actions had kept him out of The Citadel.

With The Citadel off the table, Patrick enrolled at the College of Charleston, and not long after, he called on my father for an internship. Although it was strange and almost unheard of to jump ship, he decided not to pursue the family pharmacy business. Instead, he set his sights on the arts. My daddy, a kind and forgiving man, agreed to mentor Patrick and save his family from another embarrassment. I think he thought that at the very least, he could help shape an egotistical boy into an honorable man. My daddy liked to dream big.

In an attempt to focus on something that mattered, I tried to change course from Mother's topic of choice. "I don't want to talk about Patrick. What are we going to do about Daddy? Should I call another agency? I ran into the nurse on my way in. I don't think she's coming back."

"She's not invited back," Mother exclaimed, as if it weren't a job but a party invitation. "Someone is coming this evening. I need you present to greet her."

"I won't be here tonight. Savannah is coming by, and we're going to her house. I'm staying with her tonight."

"You'll just have to change your plans. Must you continue to see that dreadful girl? She's pedestrian in the most unflattering way. I mean really, what kind of a name is Pratt anyway?"

The Pratt family had long been a thorn in Mother's side—five years, to be exact. In a city like Charleston, where your last name is a first question, Ms. Pratt, Savannah's mother, couldn't come up with the right answer. And the fact was, she never would. As far as Mother was concerned, new-money outsiders from *off* had no business buying property in downtown Charleston, and especially South of Broad. When rumors of a potential heritage-house listing had hit the garden-party circuit, everyone was abuzz about the prospect. Surely the new homeowners would be of Southern descent, adding value to the most esteemed borough south of the Mason-Dixon. Once Mother got wind of the buyer's information—the realtor was a longtime client of the gallery, as well as a desperate clinger—she caused all kinds of trouble.

Ms. Pratt *was* from the South, just not the right kind of Southern. Ms. Pratt (no Mister) hailed from a tiny Southern community. A recent lottery winner, she had been awarded millions by her state, and she finally had the money to give her girls a better life. According to her—and the years of *Southern Living* back issues displayed proudly on her built-in bookcases—there was no better life than in Charleston, South Carolina. Little did she know that even with all her millions of dollars, status was the only thing in Charleston that money couldn't buy. Her naïvety wasn't completely her fault. As an outsider, she never could have understood the reality of native Charleston requirements, the codes of social behavior, or the masks of Southern niceties. Though it didn't take her long to figure those out.

During Mother's first inspection of Ms. Pratt's background, "Pinehurst" said everything Mother wanted to hear. Affluent, exclusive, and the cradle of American golf: the North Carolina enclave was only the best of the first world. However, Pinehurst, *West Virginia*, just didn't say the same thing. Mother's first order of business was to completely stop the sale of the home, but since that was ridiculous—and illegal—she next tried to buy the property out from under Ms. Pratt. She started a "historical preservation" fund. Knowing the right people who were skilled in the right things, she almost got it done. Money from anonymous donors poured in upon Mother's stern suggestion (and a little blackmail—she had dirt on almost everyone). Vivian seemed to function around the officiousness of Charleston bureaucracy. For Mother and her cocktail ladies alike, the city's rules were pliable, to say the least. They intended to keep it that way.

Ms. Pratt continued to throw an increasingly unreasonable amount of money into the till, and she made the owner an irresistible offer he couldn't refuse. Coincidentally, the seller was quickly relieved of any and every S.O.B. membership and figuratively blackballed from their self-important society. Once the sale hit the market, Mother hit the fan.

The majority of S.O.B.s are lovely people with a strong sense of community and a common adoration of historical architecture. The Holy City has always been distinguished, with neither a palmetto nor a pearl out of place. Charleston women consider themselves the finest in the land, and many of them are. I truly loved most of the families I had grown up with. However, in any orchard, a rotten apple can disguise itself among the ripe. Vivian happened to be the most creative and offensive in the bunch.

Like a rational adult from *off*, Ms. Pratt assumed she had won the battle, and that was that. What she hadn't realized was that she had started a war—a quiet war of looks and whispers, lost invitations, and hushed laughter, all disguised by the pretty mask of Southern politeness. Politeness is manners and upbringing, nothing more. Often, it can (yet shouldn't) be confused with acceptance, but the two couldn't be further apart. Of course, these secrets to Southern charm aren't handed out in tourists' brochures or openly discussed behind iron fences. In fact, these built-in rules are spoken so softly that no words are needed at all. If you need to be told, you're on the wrong side of the gate.

I was the first to admit that Savannah Pratt certainly had her flaws, but she was different from the silver spoon–fed girls, including me. Much to Mother's horror, I liked different. Just like her mother, from the get-go, Savannah didn't fit into Southern society. The difference, though, was that she didn't care to. Savannah didn't appreciate the way Vivian had spearheaded the initiative to shun and embarrass her mother. In fact, Savannah didn't care for anyone who went out of her way to ridicule others. In backhanded retaliation, Savannah had started her own silent war with Vivian—by leaving pineapples on our front porch.

To an outsider, the pineapple is a lovely, colorful symbol of kindness and Southern hospitality, but for those in on the secret, they're a symbol of swinging. As in, multiple sexual partners, whether you're single or married. Since Vivian Ausby was the epitome of unfailing decorum, anyone could clearly see that she was the victim of a continuous prank. Lord have mercy, those pineapples drove Mother to the edge of madness. Which is why Savannah kept leaving them on our porch. I privately reveled in Savannah's improper behavior. There was something unhinged and feverish and explicitly unapologetic about her.

"Savannah and her last name are fine, Mother. She's been a good friend to me. Do we have to keep having this same conversation?"

"Just because she's friendly doesn't mean you have to follow her around. You're not a stray dog, you know. And tell her to stop leaving pineapples on my porch. I know it's her that's doing it. Only someone as trashy as Savannah would find that funny. What people must think," she speculated, shaking her head with disgust.

Mother had always cared about appearances. Most days, she cared for little else. I closed my eyes to keep from rolling them. "Yes, ma'am, I know I'm not a stray dog."

"Perfect, then you'll be here."

Mother had a way of getting what she wanted, when she wanted it. Before you realized what was happening, she had already gotten her way.

"Yes, ma'am, I'll be here. I'm going upstairs now."

After closing the door behind me, I dropped my purse and flung myself onto the pastel floral print of my monogrammed comforter. My bedroom was hardly a refuge, but it was my only escape from Mother's watchful eyes. I lay amid the chaos of the grossly matching sheets, curtains, wallpaper, and even lampshades of my third-floor suite. In Mother's house, floral reigned, so naturally, the sickly-sweet blossoms of Lilly Pulitzer were the foundation of my bedroom décor.

I was still perpetually seen as a child; even my closet walls were painted with childish pictures. Fairytale princesses climbed tangled vines along the closet ceiling, while storybook characters gathered along the wainscoting, reading children's classics on toadstools and clouds. It was no use asking for anything different, or even for a fresh coat of paint to cover the juvenile art. Having a conversation with Mother was like walking through a swarm of bees. On a slim chance, and by the grace of God, you might walk away unscathed, but more often than not, she would sting you.

Chapter 2

I MUST HAVE HEARD THE PHONE RINGING, BUT I COULDN'T PULL myself out of the haze in time to answer it. When I finally picked up the receiver, someone else in the house had already answered. Patrick's voice was the one I recognized; I had no idea who the woman was.

I didn't remember falling asleep. The slanted rays of light now broke through the lace-bordered curtains, casting an evening distortion across the carpet. I grabbed a T-shirt and freshly laundered skirt out of the closet and jumped in the shower.

The stranger's voice drifted up from the kitchen through the air ducts in the floor. The home's archaic boiler system funneled sound up and down the walls more efficiently than a megaphone. My parents still thought I couldn't hear them fighting when they were two floors down. The sounds of our old house gave the impression of a perpetual guest, or another person who lived with us, but one we never saw. Despite the cacophony, the house still held some secrets.

The woman was saying something about my daddy—something about me. I turned off the water to get a better listen, but I only gathered particles of information, none of which made any sense.

"When are you going to tell her?"

"You know when. We made a deal, and I expect you to stick to it."

I couldn't imagine what that meant, but it was assuredly none of my business.

With my hair air-drying, I quickly slathered foundation over my fair-skinned freckles and topped my lashes with two coats of mascara. Teeth brushed, and then red lips. Leaving my room "undressed" was not allowed in Mother's home. Debutantes were always ready for a social caller. I was sure *they* were. I'd heard about Mother's glory days since I was old enough to listen, but *I* was not—neither a debutante, nor frequently called upon.

A wide staircase covered in hundred-year-old heart pine floors wound up the side of the foyer—a real showpiece. I tiptoed down the spiral staircase in my kitten heels, dispersing my weight onto the intricately hand-carved railing as best I could. No shoes were to be worn on the stairs, in an attempt to keep the scratch marks to a minimum. But the house was over two hundred years old, and the only things that stood out on the stairs were its scratch marks. The staircase was covered in them. I didn't disobey the house rules often, but I chalked up my defiance of this one to safety. My pantyhose were so slippery on the constantly waxed wood that twice I had taken a tumble—once going up, once down. If I wanted to wear an above-the-knee skirt that didn't hide my birthmark, Mother insisted on my legs being covered with pantyhose. Break a rule or break my neck: these were my choices.

I found them in the kitchen, Mother perched on the woven sea-grass stool, cradling a teacup. I doubted it was filled with anything herbal. Medicinal, yes. Herbal, no. The guest was coming out from the pantry, her arms filled with the appropriate ingredients for baking cookies. A smile graced her lips when she noticed me, but my reaction to her was altogether different. Looking at her was like being offered a glimpse into the future. We weren't exactly twins, but we could definitely pass as family— maybe distant cousins. A petite nose and almond eyes, skinny chicken legs and a flat chest: these were noticeable similarities. But the hair. Her hair took my breath away. A different style and cut— she had to be twenty years older than me—but the color was almost identical. I was immediately drawn to her.

A redhead living in the land of bleach-blonde Barbie dolls tends to stick out. Add body freckles and a purple leg, and you're a flashing neon sign. In my twenty years on Earth, I had never met another redhead. My mother was a brunette, and my daddy had never been anything but gray. It took some time for me to say so, but I was immediately intrigued.

She dropped the ingredients on the counter and walked toward me. "Harlow," she said—a statement, not a question.

As her arms encircled me, I looked to Mother for guidance, but she was flipping magazine pages while drinking her "tea," paying no mind to the scene playing out before her.

I didn't want to embarrass the woman; politeness was an essential character trait of mine. Acting natural, I pulled away. "Yes, hello. I'm Harlow. You must be the replacement nurse. I'm sorry, but I missed your name."

"Yes!" she exclaimed, slapping her thighs and startling Mother so that her drink sloshed out of her cup. "Yes, I am. I'm Beth Chaney. I'm so happy to meet you. Would you like a cookie?"

I looked over at the stacks of raw ingredients sitting on the kitchen island.

Her outburst of laughter shocked Mother again. "I mean, when they're finished," she explained, palming her forehead.

"No, Ms. Chaney, I'm fine. Thank you for asking, though. Maybe I'll have one later, when I get back." I turned to go.

"Wait!" she called out. "A boy named Patrick called, and he's having trouble with"—she turned to a note on the counter —"reconciling the receipts. I don't know what that means, but it sounds important. He didn't leave any other pertinent information." Grabbing my hand, she added, "Please, call me Beth."

As sweet as Beth appeared to be, my emotions leaned toward a saltier taste. Heat rose within me and seemed to work as a bonding agent for my clenched teeth. I had told Patrick that he hadn't worked there long enough to close the gallery on his own, even though he'd assured me he had. The gallery was too important to my family. Savannah would have to wait until I was finished there.

I gathered my things and caught the tail end of their conversation in my rush out the door. Mother's distinct bourbon voice said, "Don't get fresh with me, young lady. I was just thinking—"

"Thinking, or drinking?" Beth interrupted her. "Because by the looks of you, I know which one you're rooting for."

I had never heard anyone take that tone with Mother before. Certainly not the help. It was unprecedented and delicious—it made me feel all bourbon*ish* inside. But her comment also confirmed that Beth would be gone by morning.

I FOUND PATRICK IN THE OFFICE ALCOVE WITH A GLASS OF MY daddy's oldest scotch. The room was lit only by a pair of seashell-encrusted desk lamps, leaving the rest of the gallery in the dark. I should have been mad that he was drinking at work, but there was something about the scene that struck me as funny.

Patrick was the type of boy who—only in his father's absence— put on the airs of a grown man. Much like the other boys from South of Broad, he still referred to his father as Daddy, as if that were his first name. True to his Southern roots, he was always dressed like a spectator at a fraternity-sponsored regatta: swooped hair and Sperry slip-ons, popped-collar silk shirts, and gingham-checked or appliqué chinos, all worn together in the boldest mix. Patrick's wardrobe rivaled even the homes on Rainbow Row.

Tonight, though, he looked different. Dressed in standard-issue prep-school chic, he looked somewhat plain, and maybe somewhat less entitled. Gone was the party boy of yesterday. Patrick looked like a kid playing dress up in a successful man's clothes. I supposed that wasn't an entirely foreign concept for him. Maybe it was an altogether natural behavior for him—for both of us, really. We were both doing our best to fit into roles that we hadn't auditioned for, yet were cast in nonetheless.

Sympathy replaced the annoyance I had felt on the walk over.

"What?" he asked, removing his feet from the desk. "You're looking at me funny. Don't I look okay?"

"You look fine. It's just that I've never seen you dressed so...I don't know, grown up before. It's nice."

A look came over him, as a smile slowly spread across his cheeks. It was a look I hadn't seen before. I hadn't had enough experience with boys to know what that look meant.

He broke the silence. "How about you and I grab something to eat?"

"Thanks, but I've already eaten."

"How about a movie then?"

"I can't. I'm headed over to Savannah's house."

"It's dark out. I should walk you."

"It's only a few blocks from here. I've done it a thousand times."

I continued to shoot down his attempts, even though I didn't realize what he was attempting.

A half chuckle escaped his lips as he patted them in frustration. "You're a hard girl to get through to."

Offended by his accusation, I countered, "That's not true. You needed help, and I came over right away. I don't understand why you're accusing me of being difficult."

His eyes narrowed ever so slightly as he moved toward me. "I didn't say you were difficult. I said you were hard to get through to."

I took a step back. "I don't understand the difference."

"That's exactly what I mean, Harlow. I've tried every subtle way I know how—other than just telling you, which apparently I'll have to do—to show you that I like you. Every time we work together, I compliment your outfit, your hair, your smile—something about you. I bring you coffee and pastries from the bakery, and I make myself available to the gallery because I respect your father." He took another step forward. "But it seems like no matter what I do, you don't even notice me."

For the sheer ridiculousness of this insane confession, I almost couldn't stifle my laugh. I couldn't imagine what he was talking about. He didn't like me. Boys like Patrick didn't like me. They liked girls whose fingers demurely concealed a giggle, girls who had perfected the art of flirtation. Not the purple-legged introvert skating by on her parents' affluence.

I just stared at him like an empty-headed cartoon character, dumbfounded.

He continued, "I know what you probably think of me, and rightly so—in the past, I haven't been the best version of myself. But I want you to know that I've changed. Just give me a chance to show you. Let me take you out, if not tonight, then sometime soon. I'll come to your door and everything." His hand found my hip, and he gently pulled me to him. "Let me show you a better version of myself."

His lips came upon mine with skill; his hands held my waist with a firm grip. The initial shock of it stiffened my body, but the lingering touch of our kiss made me unconsciously soften my guard. A part of me expected him to maul me when I didn't stop him, but his intentions seemed to be genuine. He smiled as he pulled away, so I let him kiss me again.

"I had no idea that someone like you would have any interest in me," I confessed.

"To be honest, I didn't used to, but I don't want to be that guy anymore."

In that moment, I believed him. I think he believed himself, too.

THE SMELL OF FRESHLY BAKED COOKIES GREETED ME AS I opened the front door. When I made my way into the kitchen, I was pleasantly surprised by what I saw on the counter. Displayed on the kitchen island, and stacked in a perfect pyramid under a bell-shaped glass dome, were twelve chocolate chip cookies, along with a note.

Harlow,

I enjoyed talking with you today. I hope there are many more conversations in our future.

Much love,

Beth

I lifted the dome and pulled out the top cookie, smiling as I took a bite. In the past, Mother had fired women for big things, little things, even nothing at all. This Beth must have been one hell of a nurse—a cook, too—to have survived the earlier conversation that was just getting started as I was walking out the door. I had never loved being this wrong so much before. I also had never known victory could taste so much like chocolate.

Chapter 3

WITH SUMMER BREAK APPROACHING, FINALS WEEK LEFT NO time for foolishness. Textbooks and study guides littered the dining room table. I was embarking upon the final semester of my sophomore year at the College of Charleston, and I wanted to finish strong. When my daddy passed that spring, I changed my major from elementary education to business, with an emphasis on finance. Though Mother owned the gallery, she had no desire to run the daily operations or stand on the sales floor all day. As I understood it, with a little knowledge and a lot of gumption, I could step into Daddy's shoes and help the gallery at least survive—if not thrive. Still, changing direction felt drastic, and I mourned the path I was suddenly turning away from. I had loved children my entire life; I had begged for a sibling back in my younger days. I hadn't really ever dreamed of being a teacher. I hadn't needed to; it was just always going to be so. Yet the day we put my daddy in the ground, I stopped thinking about what career I wanted and started doing what I needed to do.

Patrick and I had made it through the spring, and he had become somewhat of a fixture at the house. He was always on time for every dinner party, always with a gift in hand. Mother couldn't help herself with talk of a big, prestigious wedding. I found bridal magazines of all kinds strategically scattered around the house. In the nightstand, under the coffee table, and always in the bathroom—her hints were less than subtle. Yet on several occasions, I found Beth throwing them out. Beth had made it through the spring too.

My relationship with Beth had flourished in only a matter of months. She was everything to me that Mother wasn't. She was always ready with a soft word, a hug around the neck, and fluid conversation around the dinner table. Beth quickly became involved in our lives, and that's where she stayed. She was my confidante and cheerleader in all things—all things except Patrick. Cordial but never affectionate, Beth had hardly warmed up to him. I couldn't say that I blamed her. Unlike Mother, I didn't hear wedding bells when I thought of Patrick. But no one was asking my opinion.

Along the way, there were inklings of incompatibility within our courtship. Some were blatant, while others were hidden beneath the surface of polite, gentlemanly gestures. He opened the door but walked through first; he'd offer me iced coffee from my favorite bistro, but then the drink wasn't what I ordered. After we had been dating for a time, it seemed as though coming to my house was more of a highlight for him than our actual date. Beth particularly hated that. More times than I could count, he openly leered at other girls. That was something he either couldn't control or didn't want to. I wasn't entirely sure.

Underneath it all, there was a salesmanship to Patrick, as well as an underlying trace of entitlement. These tinges were all tiny infractions compared to the harsh ways of the world. I understood that. I also knew that for my family's sake, I should work harder to fall in love with him, but there was a part of me that wondered why I had to try so hard. Shouldn't Patrick and I fit together easily? Couldn't we be complementary? Like the sun and moon, when one person sets, the other rises, and this alliance keeps the relationship going. Wasn't that what love was?

On one ordinary but sweltering afternoon, some college kids from the neighborhood lounged around my pool. Rambunctious boys did tricks off the diving board, desperate for attention from the bikini-clad girls lined up in lounge chairs, like delicate elixirs at an apothecary. Beth had driven Mother to a specialty market in Beaufort, so we had the house to ourselves for a few hours.

Savannah's younger sister, Lexi, was there too. Moving out of her awkward stage, yet still in high school, Lexi tried so hard to fit in with the college girls. Just as it was for her mama, social status was a top priority for her.

I had my suspicions that all those kids were only there because Patrick had offered up my house as his own, inviting them as if he had any authority to do so. But since my spine was somewhat collapsible, I didn't have the nerve to run anyone off. Plus, I had been brought up to be a gracious host.

I was slathered in seventy-grade sunscreen, being the red-headed type of fair-skinned that burned in the shade. While I was brave enough to wear a bikini top, my legs were certainly covered. I even wore footie socks, hoping that the others might think I had just forgotten to take them off. There was no way that I was going to pull out my bare feet with someone like Caroline Coker looking on. She and her friends could be cruel. They reveled in jokes about my birthmark, asking me if I needed to borrow a maxi-pad, as if my period were continuously running down my leg. For some reason, they never tired of this game.

They were the type of girls who thought their beauty and social status gave them free rein to say and do as they liked. The unapproachable type of girls, who slipped into their expected upper-class roles with ease. Some looked the part naturally; others had to try a little harder, though all were successful in their quest for beauty and status. Their bodies were proportionate, their hair sun-streaked blonde, their skin smooth and unblemished. They were the epitome of Southern stature. Other than some minor cosmetic differences, they were all basically identical, as if they had all been manufactured in a specialty warehouse. Like some Lowcountry version of Botticelli's Venus, they looked as if they had all emerged from a shucked oyster. Sitting at the pool with them, it was difficult not to feel like a dried-out sea urchin. To be born with such a flaw in a city that glorified beauty was unfortunate, to say the least.

Since their conversations never went deeper than the surface level, the discussion eventually turned to the cotillion's debutante circuit; they had debuted two years ago. Their talk gradually turned to marital prospects. I loathed these conversations.

True to her protective nature, Savannah stood guard over me from a lounge chair. She had a knack for swooping in when their mockery turned in my direction. Never the one to start a fight, but usually the champion at the end, Savannah was a master at deflection.

They were discussing a "rather unfortunate" charity case who obviously didn't belong in the circuit, but because of a societal sponsor, she was allowed to participate. Though the girl's situation had nothing to do with Caroline, she raised her pitchfork first.

"I'll literally die if they let that homely girl from the swamp debut. She barely speaks English."

Savannah chimed in. "No, Caroline, you'll *figuratively* die. You *literally* don't know what you're talking about. See the difference?"

Caroline glared at her.

"It's quite possible that someone was sleeping on the job when you debuted, considering that your grasp of English isn't exactly comprehensive either."

"Why don't you head back to your trailer, mountain girl, and take whatever diseases you have with you?"

Savannah didn't miss a beat. "You're always obsessing over all these debutantes, and I'm starting to think that you aren't just a wretched piece of shit, but maybe a sexual predator too. I kind of feel like I should warn the town about your lust for innocent teenage girls. Maybe they should add you to a list, or put a sign in your front yard."

"Oh!" Caroline screamed, infuriated. "Why don't you just go back to whatever toothless holler you came from?"

Savannah leaned in toward her and made sure to whisper loudly enough for all of us to hear. She tapped her front teeth as she spoke. "Being toothless certainly helps with the blowjobs, Choker Coker. According to the Cavalry Prep lacrosse team, it's a lesson you might be in need of learning."

I thought Caroline's head was going to explode right there by the pool. Despite the venom of the accusation, it was true, and much like the lacrosse team, it was hard for Caroline Coker to swallow.

Savannah grabbed my hand. "Screw these bitches. Let's go inside."

I would rather have played hostess anyway. It kept me from having to endure small talk with these girls who were using me for my pool, a place where they could easily flaunt their perfect feet.

The boys in Patrick's incestuous group of guy friends could be just as callous as the girls. They were skilled at fakery and four-letter words; they were boys who did not doubt their lot in life, even if their sense of purpose escaped them.

"Take off your cover-up and get in, Harlow!" Patrick yelled at me from the deep end of the pool, hollering to keep attention focused on him.

I saw the way those boys barely tried to disguise their snickering, as if my pale and scrawny body in a swimsuit was a joke they could all enjoy.

"I'm going inside to make some drinks instead. Y'all keep swimming."

Savannah headed upstairs and, as usual, left the work to me. After pulling some lemons out of the fridge, I closed the door and turned around, to find Patrick standing almost on top of me. The water from his swim trunks pooled on the hardwood floor beneath his bare toes. He gave me a look that felt like a wave crashing inside my stomach. On several occasions, I had warded off Patrick's advances, but they were becoming more frequent. Each time, they were more assured. He pulled me into the guest bathroom.

His hands quickly found the bare skin of my stomach, and his lips found my chest. He moved with ardent speed. I was sure he was drunk.

"Patrick, stop," I said, trying to remain casual.

His hands moved faster, frustrated by my prudishness.

"Stop!" I repeated, a little too loudly for his liking. His face reflected his annoyance. "We have company," I added.

A sigh came long through his gritted teeth. The muscles in his jawline were taut with control, holding back the anger I knew he felt. His eyes darkened as his finger slid down my cheek.

"Do you know how many girls would like to be standing in your shoes right now?" he asked. "I went out on a limb and made you my girlfriend, Harlow. Your lack of eagerness is growing old. Do you understand what our being together could do for our families? Bringing the Ausby and McDade bloodlines together is everything our parents could want. How selfish are you to take that away from them?"

Pleasured moaning interrupted his speech and trickled down through the walls, amplified by the squeaky box springs of my Jenny Lind bed.

"See," he finally said, raising his eyebrows toward the ceiling, "Savannah gets it. She understands the value of a fuck, especially when your family name isn't worth one." Squeezing my cheeks together so my lips puckered like a fish, he cautioned, "There are just some things that you have to surrender to in this life if you want to be worth anything at the end of it."

The nameless image of the Texan tourist filled my mind. I didn't know if she had heard those same words from Patrick, but I would have bet my life that she'd seen that same face.

"Ouch, you're hurting me," I said, wincing.

Digging his fingers farther into the sides of my mouth, he growled, "Get with the program, Harlow. I'm not going to wait forever."

The knocks came swiftly and suddenly. "Hello in there. I'm sorry to intrude, but the other bathrooms are occupied, and I really have to go!"

Beth's voice filled me with relief and Patrick with panic. The moment he unlocked the door, it flew open from the other side, and Beth, back from Beaufort earlier than I had expected, waddled in.

"Unless you'd like to be a part of my business, I'd suggest you clear out," she said, lifting her skirt in the most unladylike manner.

Patrick put on his best made-for-television smile while we exited the bathroom. I went back into the kitchen and steadied my hips against the kitchen island, my fingers massaging the sore spots around my jawline. He bumped me from behind as he made his way back out to the pool. As the screen door slammed behind him, his arms went up above his head in a touchdown gesture. Hoots and hollers from the other boys accompanied his lie.

I heard a sigh from behind me, and I turned to find Savannah watching us. Amid the pure white of shiplap walls and the precious auctioned antiquities, Savannah stuck out in my home like a rusty nail. With her disheveled hair, low-cut blouse on inside out, and mascara smudged under her eyes, she looked every bit the whore that Patrick had described her to be. And she knew it.

"Come on," she offered, "let's go sit in the front."

Daylight began to fall behind the trees, spinning beams of light onto the warm porch floor under my feet. We swung on the joggling board in silence, and during the slow descent of the afternoon, a realization washed over me. I'd been seconds away from losing my virginity—from losing *myself*—right there amid the indigo swirls of the bathroom's wallpaper. A heated anger bubbling deep within me must have evaporated my tears from the inside, because despite wanting to cry, no tears came.

"You can't let him upset you, Harlow. This doesn't have to be that big of a deal," Savannah said. "He's just a dumbass kid with a dumbass smirk on his face. Just fuck him already. It's just sex. If you give him what he wants, he'll feel like something special, and he'll leave you alone for a while. By the looks of his man-boy frame, it'll be over before you know it."

"Excuse me?"

"You're only making it worse by continuing to turn him down."

"Maybe you're okay with being used by a man, but I'm not."

"Wait," she said, genuinely taken aback. "What makes you think that I'm being used?"

"Please, Van, you haven't exactly been selective in your choice of men. You even slept with Davis, and though he hasn't admitted it, I'm pretty sure he likes boys more than girls."

In true Savannah dialect—a dialect rooted in the twang that rolled along the peaks and valleys of the Appalachian Mountains— she exclaimed, "First of all, those boys aren't using me. Women can enjoy sex too, and if those boys think they have the upper hand in our encounters, then let them think that. Y'all may think that I'm some backwoods hillbilly—and maybe in some ways I am—but at least I'm free. Vivian has you brainwashed into thinking that you don't deserve any pleasure in life, that your job is to serve. Sex is fun, and it's a way to escape the monotony of this stifling Stepford community. This house has a thousand rules—unless you're a man. Then, somehow, it's fine to throw caution to the wind. Trying to understand you people is like trying to pile water." The veins in her neck turned red and popped out with each pointed sentence. "Secondly, we aren't exactly sure if Davis is confirmed to play for the other team."

"Really?" I asked.

"No," she sighed, calming down. "I'm pretty sure he's gay. Why do we always lose the good ones?"

Trying to be encouraging, I said, "Maybe he's just well-rounded, artsy."

"Quit being so naïve, Harlow."

I didn't know what she meant.

For me, sex was always in the future tense, a fulfillment of devotion and duty to the man I would marry. The thought that sex could be fun had entirely escaped me. To Savannah, going to bed with someone wasn't so much about belonging, but owning. Whether she preplanned a torrid affair or made a sweeping decision in the spur of the moment, she assured me that any man she slept with, she slept with by choice.

We rested our heads together as the joggling board swung us, two outcasts thrown into an overcrowded pond. One of us a toad kissing the wrong prince, and the other the white-trash daughter of a bootlicking suck-up.

Beth opened the screen door and popped her head out. "You two okay?" She was asking us both, but she looked only at me. "Is everything as it should be?"

"Yes, ma'am, I'm okay," I replied. "Thank you for asking, and thank you for needing to use the restroom so bad."

"It turned out to be a false alarm. Funny how you can be so wrong about some things."

I swallowed the breath that caught in my throat. She had saved me. And she had known she was doing it.

As if it were just a regular day, and not one of a saved virginity, Beth added, "The party is winding down, and Vivian is lecturing the girls on modesty. They're all very attentive, I'm sure. It's a good thing you don't care too much for them, because they probably won't be back for a while. What are y'all up to the rest of the day?"

Before I could answer, a drunken Patrick swung out of the screen door and stumbled onto the porch, Caroline Coker tailing him like a lost puppy, and Mother following both of them closely behind. Savannah's nostrils flared in disgust, a truck tailgate slammed shut, we all turned to look, and Beth smiled.

Chapter 4

AS IF IT WERE THE WEIGHT OF A CHILD'S TOY, HE CARRIED THE rocking chair above his head in a manner so gentle, there was no mistaking that he had done this many times before. When he set it down, the sound it made against the wide-planked porch floor was just as light. A red *Ryan and Son's Woodworking* logo was embroidered on the breast pocket of his work shirt; his shirtsleeves were in a tug-of-war with his muscular arms.

He seemed to be older than a college student, but possibly without the opportunity of one. The sweat-wetted ends of his dark hair brushed across his cheek, his eyes, and the corner of his lips. A five o'clock shadow grew across his jawline. He was a noticeable type of man, just by shoulder width alone. A man like this was not from Charleston. Where he was from, I couldn't say. I hadn't known the earth grew men like this.

From the moment he walked through the gate, his gaze never wavered. When our eyes met for the first time, it was such a deep stare. His irises were a color of green as unmistakable as a forest.

"Hello, Harlow," he said, holding out his hand in greeting, as if we were the only two people on the porch.

Patrick shuddered, and Savannah elbowed my ribs.

His hands were rough and calloused, the beds of his nails black. He smelled faintly of lemon oil furniture polish, which, like him, I found to be unusual. A trellis of colorful flower tattoos encircled the lower part of his forearm, seemingly climbing to somewhere, but they stopped mid-track. Interconnected layers of leather bracelet straps wrapped his wrist in a mysterious style that I had never seen before, yet I still grasped the general language of rebellion. This man with shoulder-length hair, colorful tattoos, and leather bracelets must have had a motorcycle or a gang or something too cool for me to even know about.

How did he know me? I looked to Mother for help. With a backbone unyielding in even the most blusterous of situations, Mother never broke. She didn't even bend. So it came as a great surprise to me when I looked beyond my shoulder to find her white as a sheet, as though she had been half-drained of blood.

I took his hand in belated reply. It was only a brief exchange, but sometimes the smallest moments are the ones that have the greatest impact.

"I'm sorry," I said. "Do I know you?"

A smile that hung from both ears took over his face. "Not yet."

"Ahem," Beth interrupted. "Harlow, Vivian, this is Jade. He's here to replace the rocker that was damaged by the storm, back in the spring."

"It's nice to meet you," I said.

"I can assure you, the pleasure is all mine."

Making a show of the gesture, Patrick slung his arm around my neck. "Nice bracelets," he said in a snotty tone. "Aren't you on the clock? I'm sure your boss would love to know how wasteful an employee is being with his time."

Another big smile emerged as Jade crossed his arms over his chest. "I suppose he might, if he thought customer service and basic manners were a waste of time."

Infuriated, Patrick threatened, "Well, why don't I call him to find out?"

Relaxing his posture, Jade submitted, "I don't think that'll be necessary, but I appreciate your offer." With an upward quirk of his lip, he extended his hand toward the seat of the rocking chair and asked me, "Would you like to try it out?"

When I sat, the chair, so finely constructed, almost rocked on its own. Cradling my underside with firm back support, the dark varnished wood engulfed me. I ran my hands along the smooth surfaces and found not a single blemish. It was an astonishing piece of furniture—a piece of art, really.

"This is quite beautiful."

Showcasing his upper teeth, he smiled. "That's kind of you to say. I'm glad you like it. It's yours to keep—something to remember me by."

"Do you have more?"

"Of course, I have a whole shop full of them. I'd love to show you sometime."

"This is bullshit. It's a stupid chair," Patrick huffed. "Caroline, take me home."

Caroline's face lit up. Whether it happened in her car, her bed, or her bathroom, I was sure that Patrick was going to get what he wanted. I don't think it really mattered who was giving it to him. I was glad to see him go.

Jade dipped his head. "I'd better get going too. Ladies, Harlow, it's been a pleasure. Y'all have a pleasant evening." He stepped off the porch and made his way back through the gate.

With bulbous eyes, Savannah whispered, "You slut! What the hell was that? Either your prudishness is a theatrical charade, or he has the makings of a fantastic stalker. That man is perfectly molestable."

"I swear that I've never met him." More to myself than to her, I asked, "Did you see how confident he was? He walked right up here as if he belonged. And those tattoos, I've never seen so many on one person."

Almost on cue, his dark and wavy head of hair popped over the ivy-covered privacy wall. "Hey, Harlow, if you aren't busy tomorrow, I could show you around my shop."

As if I hadn't been cloaked in cotillion etiquette my entire life, I shouted back, "I'd love that!"

"All right, then. I'll come by tomorrow afternoon and pick you up. Don't forget!"

Savannah's laugh brought me back to the front porch. "As much as I would love to stick around for this—because believe me, this is about to get good—I have to go too."

I never saw Mother go back inside. When I turned to look back at Beth, her shrug seemed to indicate that she didn't know anything about that man, but her smile said otherwise.

Chapter 5

Just as he had the day before, Jade again stood on my porch. I found it strange that no one had answered the door or invited him in. Unlike the day before, he was cleaned up, dressed smartly, and visibly nervous. He kept rubbing his palms together and then wiping them on his pants. His discomfort made my own dissipate, and I was grateful for that.

"Hello again," I said through the screen door.

"Harlow, it's wonderful to see you. When no one answered the bell, I got worried that you had changed your mind."

"I'm sorry about that. I'm not sure where everyone has run off to. Please, come in," I offered, slowly pushing the screen door open between us.

With quick and inconspicuous curiosity, I watched him study the vestibule. I wondered what box he put me in: little rich girl with a silver spoon, or painfully obedient blue blood without a backbone. He would be right about both, I supposed.

Like most visitors who entered through the main door, he pointed to the picture hanging above the credenza. "This is you." He stated it as if he already knew the answer and was only confirming his rightness.

The photograph was completely wrong for the space, not to mention seventeen years old. A little ginger perched on a wooden swing, her hands clinging tightly to the sailor-knotted ropes on both sides, her green eyes turned toward the sky. The sun bled out in orange and red behind her white dress. The portrait was only a simplistic veil of beauty. What it represented was much more complicated. I grieved for that little girl. I wanted to tell her to bear down at that exact moment, because she needed to be resolute, more calloused, delinquent somehow. The little girl in that smocked dress wouldn't have listened, though. She was far too gentle to understand the harshness of time, and already much too conditioned by propriety to pivot.

Mother and I had argued about replacing the photo with something more appropriate for the space—and less embarrassing to me. Like most of our battles, I lost. I had gotten to the point where I didn't notice the picture upon passing, or maybe I'd purposefully blocked it out of my sight. But every first-time guest in our home not only noticed it but commented on it. The image seemed to pull all the light in the room toward it.

"Yes," I finally answered. "I was about three years old there. It's a little embarrassing that that's the picture our guests are greeted with, but I don't have a lot of say in home décor decisions. So year after year, it stays up."

He stood in the vestibule breathing, as though the picture had taken too much of his strength. His eyes stayed trained on the photo. "I think it's a lovely piece of art. You were beautiful then." He looked away from the portrait and caught my stare. "You're beautiful now."

I was embarrassed by his compliment, and I didn't know how to respond. The awkward silence that lay in wait had found us. Thank God he spoke again.

"Shall we?" he asked, sweeping his hand toward the door.

"I thought you'd never ask."

With its sea foam–green cab, business logo professionally painted on the passenger door, whitewall tires, and wooden truck-bed rails, Jade's vintage Chevy truck was in pristine condition, and I immediately loved it. As I had hoped, the hinges squeaked when Jade opened the door for me, and again when he slammed it shut. I loved that sound. It was more than just a sound;

it was also a place, a feeling. It was a time when people walked to where they needed to go, waved for no better reason than to be friendly, asked about your mama and them, and actually wanted to know the answer. The truck had that same lemony scent that I'd smelled on the porch. I wasn't sure if it was Jade who made the truck smell like polished furniture, or if the truck left the lingering scent on him. Either way, I liked it.

Jade's old Chevy sputtered to life after clearing its throat. Riding in it was like getting a glimpse into the past.

"You're smiling," he said, pulling me back into the present.

"I'm sorry, what?"

"I just noticed that you're smiling. I like that."

"Yes," I agreed, "I like it too."

With the windows down, we took Broad to Lockwood and passed the Charleston Yacht Club. Rows and rows of boats were anchored in the marina, like cars in a flooded parking lot. The farther we got out of town, the brighter my light shone. Heading west over the Ashley River, I smelled the unmistakable twang of brackish water, which slips over the muddy river bottom twice a day, like a comforter over silk sheets. If you weren't born here, the smell stinks, but for those of us who were, the pluff-mud stench—a cross between sweet confederate jasmine and salted egg water—is the smell of freedom.

"You're still smiling," Jade repeated.

"I'm sorry?" I answered.

"Are you always this happy?"

"I'm not sure. I don't think so."

"Also, you apologize a lot, and I'm not sure what you're apologizing for."

"No I don't."

"Yes, you do: yesterday on your porch, today at your front door, and twice already in the car. It doesn't bother me. I just want to make sure you know that you don't owe me any apologies. Not yet, anyway."

"Oh…well…I suppose it's Southern guilt."

"It's what?" he asked with a confused laugh.

"I don't even realize I'm doing it. It's nothing. Something stupid, really."

"Tell me. I want to know about it, about you."

"Southern guilt is a specific type of guilt. It's like an extra chromosome passed down to every Southern-born daughter, and there's no remedy or cure. It makes us apologize for any and everything—a clean house, a dirty house, having a bad day or a good one, wearing the wrong thing or the right one. It's like a disease every Southern-born daughter is infected with." I looked at him with a purposeful smirk. "I'm really sorry about that."

As we both laughed, he teased, "It all sounds terrifying."

"Well, it can be, because once you've been around an obsessive apologizer long enough, you'll never be sure what we're actually sorry about." Teasing back, I added, "If I were you, I'd be very sure before getting mixed up with one of us."

"Thanks for the warning. I'll consider it carefully. Can I ask you something else?"

"Sure."

"What's the deal with that guy at your house, the sloppy smart-mouth? Is he your boyfriend?"

"Patrick? We work together at my family's art gallery. He's probably harmless. He recently decided that he liked me, but I think he's just bored. I'm not his type."

"I don't know about that. I'm pretty sure you're every guy's type. Probably harmless is definitely scary. So, he is your boyfriend?"

"Kind of."

"Kind of," he repeated. "Did he do that to your cheeks?"

Without thinking, I immediately pulled down the vanity mirror to check my reflection. The foundation I had put on earlier had spotlighted the thumbprint bruises along the hollow sides of my cheeks, rather than disguising them. The heat of embarrassment rose to my ears.

"It's none of my business, but you shouldn't be with a guy who treats you that way. There are plenty of men who would love to take you out and show you how a real man acts. Like me, for example. I don't mean to embarrass you. I just thought you should know that you're wrong about him being harmless. He's definitely harmful, and those bruises are only a starting point. I've seen men like him before, and I've never seen one change."

I was taken aback by his directness, and a little offended that he had been studying me. I replied, "You don't know me, and I doubt that you're qualified to make some kind of diagnosis about me or the people I spend time with. I'd appreciate you sticking to the things you do know."

"Oh, you mean less complicated things, like rocking chairs?"

"Yes. I mean no, not just rocking chairs. Wait, that came out wrong. I'm sorry if I'm coming off as rude. It's just that while I appreciate your interest, and I don't disagree with you, there are more things at stake than just my feelings."

A confused look washed over him. "What does that mean?"

"Nothing. Can we talk about something else?" I asked, turning my head to feel the breeze from the open window against my face, while simultaneously closing the opportunity for more of the same conversation.

We moved across James Island, low tide below us, the city in the rearview, and the Country Club of Charleston in the distance. With the traces of the Southern winter long gone, the greens on the fourth hole were a beacon of color across the marsh. Only glimpses of the golf course appeared through the gaps in the towering trees, a device used to keep motorists interested in the luxuries beyond the pines.

"Do you golf?" he asked, watching me stare hard at the club in the distance.

"Only a little. My family gave up on my lack of talent years ago. I did spend many great summers on that course with my daddy. He always let me drive the cart or join in on a game of skins, even when I was far too young to know what I was doing. Mother hated the idea of a young lady sweating enough to stink like a man, whacking away at a golf ball with a bunch of boisterous cigar-smoking men. Daddy liked me out there with him, though. He truly was a master of magic, as well as great at golf."

"He doesn't play anymore?"

"Not by choice," I said earnestly. "He passed away this spring."

"He sounds like a fine man. I'm really sorry for your loss."

I smiled. "Now you're the one apologizing."

Chapter 6

As we entered Folly Beach, we turned onto the dirt shoulder of a numbered state road, and then onto an even smaller path, where a long gravel road greeted us. A cathedral of connected branches intertwined like massive hands, creating a canopy of shade above the driveway. Clumps of Spanish moss dripped from the oak fingers, hanging lazily among the branches as though they had all the time in the world, nothing to wait for but a breeze. The narrow drive opened up to a surprisingly spacious homestead, which was situated on a large plot of land that backed up to Kings Flatt Creek, an inlet of the Atlantic Ocean.

As Jade opened the door for me, a breeze blew in, warm with a tinge of salt. A gaggle of skinny-legged dogs suddenly encircled him. One was too little to compete for his attention. They were barking and jumping, carrying on as though they hadn't seen him in weeks. His clothes were an instant mess. He bent over and scooped up the baby.

"See," he laughed, trying to pet each big dog, but not fast enough for their liking, "this is why I can't have nice stuff. This is Chiquita," he added, holding out the saddest-looking animal I'd ever seen.

"Heavens to Betsy, that is one ugly dog," I said in my sorriest voice, leaning in to let the puppy lick my face. "How did you end up with such a tragic animal?"

"Well," he started, as if they'd had a grand story together, "Chiquita had a rough start in life. I fixed him up and let him stay. He's my sidekick now."

"That's him fixed him up? He's a one-eyed, three-legged Chihuahua. How bad off was he when you got him?"

"Let's just say that both of us look a whole lot better now."

I caught his stare and silently agreed. "Do you live here?"

"I have a cottage on the back of the property. It's not much, but I've always preferred quality over quantity, so it does just fine." He pointed to the farmhouse at the edge of the property. "That's the main house. My parents have lived here far longer than I can remember." He casually slid his arm around my waist and cocked me to the side. "That building on the outer right is the staining barn, and this one here"—he turned me around again—"is the woodshop. The cottage in front is the general store."

"You're the son in Ryan and Son's?"

"That's me."

"Why didn't you say something yesterday, or put Patrick in his place when he treated you so poorly?"

"It wouldn't have changed him or mattered in the least. At the end of the day, he'll still be a jackass. Guys like that are insecure and entitled. I'd rather spend my time on more passionate pursuits."

Whatever box he had put me in, I had done the same to him. If he thought I was a precious little aristocrat, I'd thought of him as a simple laborer. I was beginning to see how wrong I was. He wasn't what I had expected, at least not by a precise definition. He was different, and I liked the excitement of different.

Two women emerged from the screen door attached to the farmhouse. One looked like a teenager; the other had a belly the size of a watermelon. They were carrying empty sea-grass baskets toward a raised-bed garden. Jade waved at them as they passed us.

92

A car pulled in behind us, and the sound of the horn made me jump. Jade waved the driver off, shouting, "You know we're closed, Dr. Beck. Come back tomorrow!"

He gave me his hand in a chivalrous gesture and then placed his other against the small of my back, leaning in as he spoke. "Come on, I'll show you the woodshop."

"I don't want to be a bother. It seems like you're busy."

"I am busy. I'm busy showing you around, if you'll get going. Besides, the homestead is closed on Mondays. Mama is on a quick business trip, and my daddy is probably taking a nap on the back porch. We have the place to ourselves, and you aren't being a bother. In fact, I'm really glad you came."

I pointed to the girls plucking cucumbers off a wooden trellis. "What about your sisters?"

A hearty laugh came from deep within him. "Those aren't my sisters. I'm an only child. They help out around here in exchange for a warm bed and a makeshift family. Come on, I'll show you around," he said, again grabbing my hand as if he had done it a thousand times. He led the way to a beautiful old barn.

The space inside was much more elaborate than the faded exterior had let on. The workshop was complicated and alluring, with shelves and racks and numbered cabinets on wheels. The afternoon sun angled down through the loft windows, highlighting a treasure trove of tools, all arranged by height on pegboards. Industrial barn lights hung from the rafters, each positioned above its own large wooden table. Along the wall were rows and stacks of wooden spindles and spires, grouped by size and girth. A few unfinished rockers stood around the room, in various stages of production. There was a measurable madness in the meticulous arrangement of materials, and Jade emanated a sense of pride as he showed me his space.

My nostrils instantly picked up on the smell of fire. "Is something burning?"

"Wood smells the same when it's cut as when it's being burned. My family has been making these chairs since my daddy was a little boy. Every piece is cut, sanded, nailed, and stained by hand. Our quality is guaranteed, has been for three generations. We have a family farm near the Smoky Mountains, in Tennessee. All of the wood used in our furniture is grown and harvested there." He picked up a bristled block and dropped a wood slat in front of me. "Do you want to give it a try?"

"I shouldn't. I don't want to tarnish three generations of quality in less than ten minutes. Besides, it looks like dirty work."

"What, this?" he asked, drawing a heart in the mound of shavings on the massive workbench. "This isn't sawdust, it's man glitter. Since it gets all over everything, it tends to leave a little sparkle wherever it goes."

He put my hand on the sanding block and closed in behind me. Usually frozen by the approach of a man, my body surprised me by relaxing. His hips fit into the small of my back, and his chest encircled my shoulders with a faint but palpable heat.

"May I?" he asked as he gently pulled my hair away from my face, twisting it like soft-serve ice cream and then tucking it under the collar of my dress. "I was just kidding about the man glitter. The sawdust gets everywhere, and it's a total pain to wash out of your hair."

He leaned his face into the slope of my neck, our cheeks almost touching, while the lingering of his instructions left me almost unable to breathe, in the most exhilarating way.

With his fingers upon mine, we gripped the head of the block together, moving it back and forth in long and slow strokes. The impact of the opposite surfaces in friction left a trail of fine particle buildup along the sides of the slat of wood.

"Always go with the grain," he instructed.

His breath seemed to permeate my skin, enticing the hairs on my neck to stand at attention. "How do you know when the wood is finished?" I asked.

"She'll tell you."

"She?"

"Wood is like a fine woman. You aren't sanding to try to change her; you're only helping her uncover who she has always been. If you move too fast, handle her roughly, or lack the patience she requires, you'll ruin what had the potential to be something beautiful. And each time you fail to meet her requirements, she's forced to be whittled down and turned into something else, something that might not have been her intended purpose."

My heart thundered inside my chest. The more we stroked the wood together, the more synchronized our movements became, all the way down to a controlled and kindred breath.

When he stepped back and away from me, there was a soft but palpable separation, like tearing silk. I couldn't find the words to express how beautifully observant his thoughts were. I stared at the ground, desperate to hold on to this moment, a moment that swirled beauty inside me at a dizzying rate. Even if he was too good to be true, I wanted to stay in the lie.

"Look up," he said, tilting my chin with his finger. "I'm sorry I went on like that. It wasn't meant to make you uncomfortable; there's no ulterior motive here. I've just always thought of my job that way, as a reminder of what I am and who I should be. Sometimes I get carried away, and I probably said something wrong. I do that from time to time."

"No," I said, smiling. "You said everything right."

That moment of silence found us again, but the awkwardness was gone. Our fingers intertwined by natural instinct, despite how very different we were. My delicate, pale skin against the vibrant colors of his, my debutante upbringing versus the freedom of life at Folly Beach, but most glaringly, my carefulness with every word, versus the confidence of his honest way of expressing himself.

"Are you ready to see what's next?"

"Yes," I said, but my answer had nothing to do with rocking chairs.

When he took me to the staining barn, my sense of smell was assaulted again, not by burning wood but by a sharp chemical stench. The kaleidoscope of colors was astonishing, to say the least: a black wood stain of the deepest ebony, a washed brown of tidewrack, the almost clear varnish of pickled oak, and every shade in between—all of it stained by hand. The odor, however, was nauseating, and Jade immediately picked up on my discomfort.

Handing me a face mask, he said, "Put this on, and the fumes won't make you feel sick."

I obliged.

With an enormous laugh, Jade doubled over. "It looks good! Very upper-crust zombie apocalypse. I think you'd fare well in the end times."

Thank God I couldn't see myself. I suspected that I looked like an overgrown ant, minus the antennae. I shook my head.

"No?" he asked with a lingering chuckle. "Okay, that's enough for today. Let's go outside and get some air."

The outside breeze had never felt so fresh. "I don't know how you stand it in there. Don't you ever feel like you're going to pass out?"

"When I was a kid maybe, but after all these years, I'm now immune to the fumes. Is making rocking chairs as exciting as you had hoped?" he asked with a touch of sarcasm.

"It's different than what I expected."

"What did you expect, Harlow?"

I sensed that we were talking about more than chairs now. "Whatever expectations I had when this day started, you have surpassed them in immeasurable ways."

Without so much as a hint of warning, he scooped me toward him and kissed me. Softly at first, gentle touches of our lips together, and then just as softly parting, as he pulled back to look in my eyes.

"I'm sorry," he said shyly, "I should have asked first. I've wanted to do that for a while now."

"Is there more?" I asked, with a ridiculous grin that I couldn't control.

He moved slowly, so as not to frighten me; his fingers tenderly caressed the space between my shoulder blades, fingering the strawberry tips of my hair that hung between them. Each time he retreated his lips from mine, he did so with patience. I was the one who rebelled and took his face in my hands, abandoning propriety and insisting on passion instead.

Although our tongues moved together within the warmth of our mouths, I felt that kiss move all through me. Down my arms and around my heart, into my stomach, weakening my knees: he commanded every part of me, without even asking. I had never felt such weakness within that type of strength. A hidden part of me was suddenly at attention, and a light shone where it had previously been dark.

"That was a kiss," he said, the words almost floating on breath alone. With an enduring shyness, he added, "My heart is still pounding."

An unstoppable smile crossed my cheeks. "You surprise me, Jade Ryan."

"Why? Because someone like you could like someone like me?"

I thought for an instant, but quickly replied, "No, for the exact opposite reason. I'm starting to think that you might be too good to be true."

"I'll have to prove you wrong on our next date."

"What makes you think there will be another date?" I playfully asked.

"There will be plenty of dates—enough to last a lifetime."

"You sound sure of yourself."

"How could I not be? I've loved you my whole life, Harlow."

I had to pause, because I hadn't expected that either. "Loved me? We only just met yesterday."

"Well, I've loved the idea of you, anyway."

The crunch of gravel under oncoming tires announced another arrival along the driveway. A woman sat in her car long after she had turned off the ignition. Jade finally motioned for her to come over. She was not an unattractive woman, but one with the distinct physical characteristics of a hard worker. The weathering in her skin added age to her face, likely earned through laborious hours in the raised beds outside, as well as work inside the house. She was clear about her distrust of me before she ever spoke. A hardened gaze pierced me, as did her cold smile. Her expression said everything she wanted me to know. I suspected that her guarded nature was for her son's sake, and her own. I speculated that she had preconceived notions of a society daughter from a generous house off Broad, and of what exactly I was doing with Jade. There were times, like this one, when I was embarrassed to be an S.O.B.

The grapevine of gossip stretched far, and if you got caught up in it, it would hang you every time. It was best to let people show you who they were before you decided to believe them. I hoped that Mrs. Ryan relied on the same philosophy.

She wasn't unkind, only cautious with her words. Uneven wrinkles were already burrowed into her forehead, and they deepened as she spoke. "Hello, young lady. You must be a friend of Jade's."

"Yes, ma'am, I am. My name is Harlow Ausby."

Like a curtain swept up by a breeze, a look fluttered over her. Her face paled upon my mention of my name. Apparently I had been right about preconceived notions—and about the grapevine. I wondered, but only for a moment, what she thought of me and my family name.

"Well, Miss Ausby, what are you doing all the way out here in Folly Beach?"

"Jade was kind enough to give me a tour of your production facilities, which are fascinating. Your family makes lovely rocking chairs."

"That's kind of you to say. And how did you hear of our little company?"

"I'm sorry to say that I hadn't, not until Jade delivered a rocking chair to my home yesterday. That's when he invited me here."

Her skin paled as if it had cooled ten degrees, but this time, her eyes looked as though they were about to leap from her head. I inwardly panicked. I had known that Mother's tentacles stretched farther than I could fathom, but what could Mrs. Ryan possibly have heard about Mother that was vile enough for this kind of reaction?

Truth be told, this type of response wasn't a complete surprise. I knew families that were nice to us strictly because of the power Vivian carried up and down the Carolina coastline. The humiliation was starting to make me sweat.

In the most casual voice, she said, "It was nice to meet you, Harlow. You best be getting along."

My words were so soft, I couldn't have spit them out even if I were choking. "Yes, ma'am. Thank you for your hospitality."

After a quiet ride home, I didn't think Jade Ryan had much else to say to me. His independence was obvious, but he'd also made a choice to work and live on his family homestead. That scenario revealed his character, as well as his intentions, and he didn't seem like the kind of man who would go against the grain. In fact, back in the woodshop, he had specifically said as much. If his mother had already made up her mind about me, then I supposed Jade had too. I couldn't believe that I had almost fallen in and out of love in the same afternoon.

I braced myself for goodbye as he turned off the ignition. "Thank you for a lovely afternoon. I appreciate your taking the time to show me around. I know Beth is replacing our garden furniture in the coming weeks, so I'll make sure she buys from your shop. Well, goodnight then." I pulled up on the handle to let myself out.

"Wait," he exclaimed with a confused look on his face. "That's it? 'Thanks for the afternoon, and I'll never call you.' That's all I get? I thought we had a good time today. I know I did. You don't want to see me again?"

"Of course I do." I closed the door in hopes that this would go somewhere good. "I just thought…your mother, she didn't seem too thrilled to meet me. I assumed she's already crossed paths with my family, and it seemed like she was crossing me off. It wouldn't be the first time. You just don't seem like the type of man who goes against what his family wants."

"What type of man do I seem like, Harlow?"

My face flushed at the question. "Strong." His smile appeared. "Handsome." The smile grew. "Genuine." He put his hand on mine. "Honest." If I hadn't been so desperate for him to kiss me again, I would have noticed him flinch on that one.

"Slide over here and sit by me," he whispered, pulling me across the bench seat toward him. His hand softly tangled into my hair, and he brought our lips close together, without sealing them. His breath was warm against my mouth. "Don't worry about my mama. She'll take some time to warm up to you. On the bright side, it's taken me no time at all."

I don't think I had ever felt something as good as his hands in my hair or his warmth in my mouth. Our breath heated the inside of the truck, while the cool night air surrounded us. We spent the next twenty minutes fogging up the windows, until our heat had created a full-on barrier to the outside world. With each press of his lips against mine, my body internally pivoted and swayed. Our time together was sweet and unhurried, and he couldn't have been more of a gentleman. Not once did his eyes darken or his hands stray. As I lay against him in the cab, trying to etch every feeling, every word as if it were the last, he drew another heart. This one was on the back windshield. How could he have been out in this world, so close to me, and I hadn't met him yet?

"Do you want to go to the beach tomorrow?" he asked.

I answered without hesitation, "Yes, definitely."

When he walked me to the door, he kissed my hand and told me goodnight. I sat in Jade's rocking chair long after the sound of his Chevy evaporated into the night. It was something to remember him by.

Chapter 7

THE NEXT DAY, THE DISTINCT SOUNDS OF AN ARGUMENT funneled up the staircase and echoed all the way to the third floor. Their words bounced like a rubber ball against the plaster of the nineteenth-century hallways. Privacy would have seemed a given in our house, with its walls made of metal mesh and cement. Instead, almost every thought could be heard. On any day of the week, squabbles between Mother and Beth floated through every room, their retorts easily pushed around by a ceiling fan. Those two women fought like an old married couple, and they were at it again. I paused on the stairs to eavesdrop.

"Why would you do that?" Mother demanded, rattling the place settings on the dining room table with a swift and thorough pound of her hand.

"Are you having some sort of menopausal episode? He delivered a rocking chair, Vivian. He didn't graffiti curse words across the front door. Christ on a bicycle, woman, you need to relax."

"Don't you take that tone with me. Did you know she went there yesterday? As if it weren't already, this is going to turn out bad. And yet everyone thinks I'm the bitch, when I'm just trying to protect her."

Beth mocked her, "Always with the self-centered dramatics, Vivian. You should have a trophy case by now."

"She can't see that Ryan boy again, or go anywhere near that homestead. It will be a disaster."

"What will be a disaster?" I asked.

The arguing women were so self-consumed that they hadn't noticed my entrance into the dining room. Beth fumbled the teacup and saucer, flipping them to smash against the heart pine floors. Mother, on the other hand, froze as if she were a window mannequin at Saks, the flower arrangement she was busying unmoved in her hand.

"What are you two bickering about now?"

Mother cleared her throat, glared at Beth, and then tipped her chin. When she was about to give an unpopular statement, it was usually prefaced with a chin tilt. A dignitary's hesitation or an aristocratic pause, I couldn't say, but when her chin pointed north, I knew I wasn't going to like the words that followed.

With a steady and monotone cadence, she laid it out. "I did not raise you to gallivant around the countryside with two men at the same time. You must have learned that from that Savannah. You have given Patrick the idea that you're interested in him, and you should stick by that. Besides, the two of you work together, and if he finds out about this Ryan boy, friction will ensue. There's no reason to be unkind. Simply tell Jade you're better suited elsewhere."

When Mother meant to be dismissive of people, she would say "this boy" or "that girl." It certainly wasn't a term of endearment, but a clear and concise ranking. Now, calling you by your first name didn't mean she liked you; it just meant that she didn't think you were completely worthless.

Usually a daughter of deep silence, on this subject the words effortlessly poured out of me. "You can't be serious. Where have I gallivanted? You don't even know him. *I* don't know him yet, but I'd like the opportunity to."

"Precisely. You don't know him, or where he comes from. We can't always trust people from *off*. It's best if you keep your interests local."

I could usually look to Beth for help in turning the tables on a clearly one-sided and illogical argument such as this, but she just stood there. She didn't say anything, so I didn't say much else either.

"He's picking me up in half an hour. We were supposed to go to the beach today." I offered the statement as a last-ditch request for permission.

Mother knew how to use her words to hurt. They could rock you so unsteady that you almost tripped over them.

"Oh, Harlow, you can't go to the beach. What about your leg? You don't even swim." Now she was off and running again. "See, this is exactly what I'm talking about. He doesn't have your best interests in mind, and God knows what else he's thinking of doing out there. Take a drive with him, tell him you're sorry, and part as friends—who may or may not see each other again. It will be wrapped up nice and tidy, and Patrick will never be the wiser. Don't you love it when a plan comes together?"

As if on cue, Jade's truck rumbled to a stop outside the side-street garden entrance. Mother excused herself when the doorbell's song rang out, and Beth slumped into the chair at the head of the dining room table.

Seeing him fidgeting on the front porch—with a pineapple, of all things—seemed to make everything okay. Despite the storminess of the previous moments, just being near him relaxed me. He was fixing his hair and smoothing his clothes, trying to fit himself into an unreasonably small box—the same one I had repeatedly stuffed myself into over the years. When our eyes met through the plate-glass front-door window, it made everything even better.

"Jade," I crooned, grabbing his hand and pulling him inside. "I'm so glad you came."

"I'm sorry if I'm too early. I was excited to see you again." As if in afterthought, he handed me the pineapple and said, "Here, this was out front. Now that I'm handing you this, I'm also realizing I should have brought you something that I didn't take from your porch."

"Ha," I laughed. "It's not as random as you think. My friend Savannah likes to have a little fun with Mother. Anyway, don't apologize. I'm glad you're here." Turning toward the dining room, I said, "I'd like you to meet Beth. She's part of our family now."

Usually a bubbling personality, Beth only solemnly nodded her head in greeting.

"Yes, we've met," he informed me.

Her jaw tightened and her eyes became bigger, but Beth stayed quiet.

"Remember the other day on the porch? Beth is the one who called to replace the chair."

"Yes," she finally said, snapping out of her weirdness. "I was. Well, you two have fun. It's a perfect day for the beach. I'm taking Vivian back to Beaufort today." She started nodding her head as if forming a plan. "So we won't be here all day, and we won't be back until later—not until much, much later."

I ran over and hugged her. She was going to bat for me; I just needed to wait for the perfect pitch. "Thank you," I whispered.

"Jade," she added. "It's a pleasure to see you again."

"Yes, ma'am," he replied.

———

I GOT INTO THE CHEVY, AND CHIQUITA GREETED ME WITH KISSES as soft as tissue.

"He's coming with us?" I asked.

"Sure, why not?"

"He's so small. Aren't you worried about him getting hurt?"

"Hardly. This dog has more lives than a cat, and Chiquita likes a vacation day as much as the rest of us. It's nice for him to get away from the bigger dogs. Besides, he knows he's my favorite." Jade leaned across the cab of the truck and gently kissed me. "He used to be, anyway."

We headed west with the music up and the windows down. Freedom—if only for a short time—rolled in with the breeze. Conversation with Jade was easy, the lags infrequent. He was a conscientious listener and a man with a vast understanding of people. I could sense his caring nature. His left hand was on the wheel, while his right held mine tightly, only letting go to shift gears. Being with him was unhurried, and he seemed to hang on to every word I said. It was a pointed shift from my past experiences. Time moved so quickly, I didn't realize we had been talking and traveling for almost an hour.

"Are we lost?" I asked, looking out the window in an attempt to identify the area.

"No, I just wanted to take the long way."

"Which beach are we going to?"

"I doubt you've ever heard of it. It's off the beaten path, but it's worth the trouble. I don't think too many people know about it. I've never seen another soul there. Folly, Sullivan's Island, and beaches like those are so crowded that I feel like I'm not getting away from anything. I've never taken anyone else here."

Chiquita started barking and jumping up against the back windshield. A bee was unsuccessfully trying to get out. He lunged at it, causing it to swerve and fly right under my sunglasses. In an embarrassing commotion, I threw my glasses off, swatting and slapping the air, kicking my legs about until the bee made an escape through my open window. An overly dramatic rush of adrenaline coursed through me. In that moment, I absolutely fell short of the Ausby name, and I could almost hear Mother confirming it. Jade pulled over to the side of the road, probably to drop me there, now that he had seen a glimpse of the real me.

"I think it's gone," he said, clearly trying to stifle a laugh.

"Yes, sorry about that." I breathed a sigh of relief, putting my feet on the dashboard without thinking.

"Please, don't apologize. I thought it was very brave of you to take on that bee and save me and Chiquita from certain death."

I held together what was left of my composure. "Thank you. I appreciate that." I wanted to die.

I felt him staring at me again, and when I realized what he was looking at, my embarrassment turned to panic. I pulled my feet off the dash, and in the same swift motion I covered my leg with the hem of my skirt. My birthmark had been showing. I could only imagine his disgust; if it was even half of mine, it was enough. My eyes fell away from his as he turned the car back onto the road.

"So, Harlow," he began.

Here it comes...

"You go to college, you have a kind-of boyfriend—which we'll get to later—you have a soft spot for ugly dogs, and you are a master bee ninja. Is there anything else I should know about you?"

"Um, no. I think that about covers it," I quietly said.

"I doubt that, but it would have to wait anyway, because we're almost there. You'll love this spot. The water is fantastic, and there's just enough of a wave to get up on a board. Have you ever been surfing?"

"Oh, no, I don't swim," I informed him.

"You can't, or you won't swim?" he asked, genuinely shocked by my statement.

"I can, but I choose not to. Don't act so surprised. There are people who don't swim."

"Yes, I'm sure there are, but you literally live steps away from a large body of water. It seems ridiculous that you don't get in it. What are you going to do all afternoon? Don't you want to cool off in the water? What if you get hot, or get sand all over you?"

The questions were all dancing around the one big one he wanted to ask. I didn't care how sweet he was; at some point I was going to have to discuss my leg. I hated that fact, but it was a fact nevertheless.

"Look!" I said with some heat. "I've been to the beach plenty of times. You don't need to entertain or babysit me, if that's what you're worried about. Go surf, and Chiquita and I will be fine on the shore. Don't make this a big deal."

I immediately regretted yelling at him. The hurt was apparent in his eyes.

We pulled into a beat-up landing of scattered weeds, like a makeshift parking lot. He turned the car off, but neither one of us moved. I imagined he was considering taking me right back home. I heard him sigh as his head fell back against the headrest.

"Just so we're clear, I don't care about whatever you're trying to cover under your long skirts." He turned to look at me. "Whatever flaws you think you're hiding, you're not. And this may surprise you, but I like them, because I'm flawed too. Your birthmark—if that's even what that is—makes you real, and I like reality." He picked up my hand and kissed my palm. "Can you just trust me when I tell you that *you are* the one I've been waiting for?"

No one had ever said something like that to me. Even with those I was closest to, the conversation was always about masking, not showcasing, my birthmark. I almost couldn't breathe.

"Yes," I replied. "I trust you."

"Good. Now let's go have some fun."

The sun was the perfect kind of warm on my skin, the kind of warmth that magically relaxed your brain too. We made a little nest for Chiquita under the umbrella, and he did seem pleased to be out in the world with us. I almost died that afternoon when Jade took off his shirt. Patrick was fit, but Jade was strong—the kind of strength that comes from necessity, not vanity. As he pulled his surfboard against his waist, every muscle in his upper body seemed to contract in agreement.

"What are you waiting for? Let's go," he said, confused as to why I was still clothed and sitting in the shade.

"I told you, Jade, I don't swim."

"As much as I love to hear you say my name, I'm surprised that you're not going to reconsider."

"I promise, I'm fine here. Go play."

"You're really not coming in?"

I pulled my shades down over my eyes. "I'm really not."

"Okay, but don't forget to look up," he conceded. He started his walk to the water.

I enjoyed that walk. His half-clothed body seemed to draw all the light from the sun toward him. It made me hot, even in the shade. I watched him paddle out and glide back to shore on his board, his tan physique gleaming against the water. He had no trouble standing up, even waving at me a few times. Silliness wasn't a characteristic encouraged in the Ausby household, and I admired Jade's natural ability to have fun.

Around the fifth or sixth time out, he caught the largest wave I'd yet to see. White foam compressed into a curl, and Jade moved along the break of the wave, handling it fine—until he wasn't. He wiped out. As his body shot backward into the girth of the wave, his feet sent his board rolling upward, like a piece of Styrofoam in the wind.

I straightened, waiting for his head to pop up through the wave.

Nothing.

The white belly of the board gleamed in the sunlight, still catching the waves without its rider.

I stood up.

Still nothing. He wasn't coming back up.

Chiquita stared at me when I started to pace. "No, no, please come back up." I took off my sunglasses. "Jesus, please, I'm not qualified to save you." As I ran down to the water, a trail of clothes in my wake, I pointlessly yelled for help. The beach's privacy had become a double-edged sword; no one else was out there.

"Jade!" I screamed. My ankles were wet. "Jade!"

I kept moving out. The seconds he stayed underwater began to feel unnaturally long. I was wasting time with panic, taking too long to decide what to do. Uncharacteristically, I dove in and began a furious paddle, planning my descent once I got to the board. The brackish water burned my eyes, while handfuls of it slipped into my mouth as I swam. The coating of salt water inside my throat made it hard to breathe. I stopped to listen for his voice, but I couldn't hear anything over the gurgling in my ears. When I reached the abandoned surfboard, I called his name again, a guttural scream that came from somewhere deeper inside me than I knew I reached.

I shouted one last time, "Jade!" No answer, no nothing. I dove down, wildly splaying my hands in front of me, hoping they would land on some part of him. When I found his leg, I began yanking him to the surface with me. I was surprised at how strong I felt under the water.

My lungs burned for oxygen, and as we crested the water's surface, my breath was almost a scream. Panting, I called to him.

The voice that replied was nothing like mine. Once his face broke through the water's surface, he calmly said, "I'm right here, Harlow. I'm not drowning, and everything is all right."

"You're okay!" I shrieked, grabbing him around the shoulders, while relying on the surfboard to keep us afloat. "What happened? I saw you wipe out, and then you didn't come back up, and God, I was so scared!" His relaxed composure had me confused.

"Don't be mad, okay, but I might have embellished the wipeout a tad."

I pulled myself to a sitting position on the surfboard, wiping the water from my eyes and the snot from my nose. I was sure he was in full hallucination from taking in too much salt water. "No, I saw you," I said. "The board was empty, and you didn't come back up."

An apologetic look swept across his face, but it was a look that also bordered on a smile. "I practically grew up in the ocean, and I

110

can tread water for hours. I could see you the whole time. I just wanted to get you out here."

"You jerk!" I screamed, pushing him away from the board. "I could have gotten myself killed swimming out here to save you!"

"Now, hold on," he corrected me, while swimming back to the board and pulling himself up to match my position. We were face to face, and our knees knocked together as the waves pushed through us. "You said you could swim."

"Yeah, I also said I didn't want to! You asked me to trust you not even an hour ago, and then you go and pull a fake drowning? I'm pretty sure you've already blown the trust part. God, why are boys so stupid?"

"You're right about my wanting you to trust me, but just hear me out." He put his hands out in front of him defensively. "Were you scared swimming out here?"

"Terrified!"

"Now, how much of that terrified time did you spend thinking about keeping your leg covered?"

"That's not the point!"

"Just answer the question."

As I breathed out an irritated sigh, my answer caught like a fish hook in my throat.

"Harlow," he said again.

I looked away before answering. "None."

"Okay, then. That's how much time I'm going to spend on it too. You didn't seem to hear me when I said your birthmark didn't matter to me. But it seems to be a very big deal to you. I just wanted you to truly understand how I feel about it, and maybe you could start to feel that way about it too." His fingers glided along my purple shin, over my knee, and to the creamy skin of my upper thigh. "You're beautiful, and this isn't a flaw. It's a purpose."

It was the first time I noticed the concave skin above his heart, the scars of something invasive and unnatural. He saw me noticing it.

"How are you so sure of yourself?" I asked.

"That's the thing with purpose. When it's clear, there's no worry about the unknown."

"Don't ever do that again," I demanded, though my anger had softened.

"I won't," he agreed. "Now, please kiss me."

Despite the heat of the afternoon sun, chills ran through me as we kissed. That day was one that I would cherish in the softest part of my heart.

Chapter 8

WE LAY UNDER THE SHADE OF OUR OVERSIZED UMBRELLA, ME in the crook of Jade's arm, his body aligned with mine, and Chiquita curled up and sleeping beside the beach bag. The ocean water had washed a thin layer of sea salt over me, leaving crusted swirls at random, whiter than the whitest parts of my skin. Drowsy breezes passed under the umbrella, fluttering the flimsy pages of the book Jade was reading. The turning of each page, coupled with the roll of the waves reaching the sand, was the only sound to penetrate the silence of our stolen freedom. It was a momentous morning disguised as an ordinary spring day.

With Mother's expectations tightly tucked in the forefront of my mind, I was the one who tried to ruin it. "Mother doesn't think I should see you. She says we aren't suited for each other. I'm supposed to be breaking up with you today."

He cocked his head in thought before he spoke. "That's excellent. Not the part about you not seeing me, but the part that implies that we're together, and that you're my girlfriend."

I hadn't expected a reply like that. "What are you talking about?"

"Well, now I don't need to convince you to break it off with your sort-of boyfriend. I'm glad, too, because I didn't have anything planned out for that speech. I was just going to wing it."

Still confused, I asked, "Aren't you the least bit upset that I basically can't see you anymore?"

His smile was reassuring. "Harlow, if you were breaking up with me, you wouldn't be lying in my arms right now. I'm getting the idea that you aren't used to breaking the rules. Don't get me wrong, I love that you have limits and morals, and if I'm the only rule you ever break, I promise your integrity will still be intact. But just to be clear, I was only trying to be funny about the Patrick thing. You're not going to see him anymore, right?"

"No, I'm not," I said with a grin.

He laid a kiss on my forehead, unconcerned about the next time we would see each other, or the time after that. The idea of being together, in a relationship, had been smoothly solidified without a fuss. Jade's blind trust in the evenness of life was a quality I wished I had myself.

As he went back to his book, I rolled over onto my elbow and asked, "What are you reading?"

He answered with a passage. "'I'd rather sing one wild song and burst my heart with it, than live a thousand years watching my digestion and being afraid of the wet.'"

"I have no idea what it means, but it sounds beautiful."

"It's you, us. It's a short story by Jack London called 'The Turtles of Tasman.' It's about two brothers who embody the opposites in life. One is a responsible man from upper-crust society who places a high value on things, the other a wanderer in search of a happiness that things can't provide."

"I have a good idea of which brother you think I represent, and I'm a little offended."

"You shouldn't be, because we're both searching for happiness."

For the sheer astonishment of his beauty, I kissed his inner arm, working my way across his shoulder and up his neck. I ran my finger along his arm, stopping to make swirls around each flower tattoo.

"What's the story with these?" I asked.

"They each represent a person from my life, a memory I hold. Pictures fade, but these will be here as long as I am, and I suppose I'll also take them with me when I go."

"Whom do they represent? Your family members?"

"Kind of. Remember the girls you saw at my place yesterday, pulling vegetables from the garden?"

"Yes."

"They'll both have a flower on this arm at some point."

"Why?"

"Because they don't have much else. And just like the brothers in the story, like you and me, they are searching for happiness too."

"I don't understand."

"It's why my mama looked at you the way she did, and why I'm really not supposed to say much else about them, or the ones who came before. Trust me, it can be a depressing subject, and I just want to continue to enjoy this day with you."

"Can I ask one more question?"

"Sure."

"Do you still have contact with any of the ones who came before?"

"Only one, but not much. She came to the homestead when I was still a little boy. She was wonderful, and I took to her immediately. My family enlisted her help with things around the house: cooking, cleaning, taking care of me, and running the shop."

"Was she pregnant like the girl I saw yesterday?"

He licked his lips and swallowed awkwardly, as if deciding on an answer. "Yes, she was. But because of her circumstances, she had to give the baby away."

"That must have been hard on her. I don't know if I could ever give up a child, no matter the circumstance. All I've ever wanted to be is a mother."

As I pondered the difficulty of that decision, my compassion must have been apparent.

"It was rough on everyone involved, but everything turned out all right. She was able to see her child grow up, even though it was from afar. It's probably the reason she took to me so well—there was some void that I unknowingly filled. She taught me about literature," he said, holding up his book, "and about art by painters long dead. She was an incredible artist herself. Her paintings were so vibrant, so full of joy. When you stood in front of one, you felt like you could walk right into the canvas and have no trouble becoming part of the art. She used to tear out pictures from art magazines and copy them so meticulously in her paintings, you'd never know it was a replica. It was very impressive. Everyone said so. She stayed on at the homestead longer than she should have, but I think she found her purpose with us."

"I'd love to see her work."

"Maybe you will someday."

"And this," I said, circling my finger around the scar tissue above his heart. "Is this depressing?"

"No, that's a miracle." He said it matter-of-factly. "A few days after I was born, I had to have heart surgery. Most babies are born with a hole in their heart, but within a few hours the body helps it close. Mine didn't, so the surgeon had to. It's also how my name came about. I'm told that Jade means hope and strength, and I guess at the time, we all needed just that. There's still a small hole in my heart; it's still broken. A surgeon can only do so much. The rest I'll leave up to love."

I rolled over on my back and groaned in disbelief. "No one talks like that. No guy I've ever met, anyway. How is it possible that I was lucky enough to meet you?"

He gently laid his chest on top of mine, the tips of our noses touching. "When are you going to start believing me? There was no luck involved in our meeting. I've been waiting for you."

"What about me? Will I have a flower on your arm one day?"

"No," he stated with confidence.

I smacked his arm in jest. "Why not?"

"Because…you get my heart."

I pulled his face toward mine, certain that I would never want anyone other than him. As the sun bled through a palette of colors that only sailors could know by heart, I lay in the comfort of Jade's arms, his voice reverberating against his chest as he introduced me to the words of Jack London.

Although I didn't give him everything that afternoon, I gave him more than I would ever give to anyone else. I gave him my whole heart, and he used it to mend his broken one.

Chapter 9

In the months that followed, I drifted on clouds that swept me from one place to another, always and eventually into Jade's waiting arms. The connection we had was powerful and profound. My heart had gradually defined itself by a longing that could not be swept away with the tides. Just the idea of him bloomed in every compartment of my mind, caressing all my senses—including some I hadn't even known were there, faculties that seemed to arise only now that I knew him. It had taken less than two weeks for me to fall for him, and for the rest of my life, I would be suspended in midair.

Despite Mother's attempts to push me closer to Patrick, Beth was one step ahead of her, clearing the way for Jade. However, the closer Jade and I became, the harder our togetherness proved to be. Mother wielded her powers at every chance she got. Had she given Jade the same small courtesies bestowed on the florist or the dry cleaners or even the neighbor she'd never liked, she would have seen what I saw in him. Jade wasn't some slack-jawed Neanderthal from a beachfront cave. There was depth to his intelligence, kindness in the way he conducted himself. He had all the expertise required to silently slide under the delicate ironwork fences of the magical Charleston gardens, so that most would assume he had always belonged there.

In the same amount of time as me, Beth had also been swept up by Jade. When together, they carried on like old friends. To be with these two people I loved most in this world made my heart full.

It didn't take long for Patrick to realize that he was on the outside of the relationship, and it was probably the only time in his life when he was on the outside of anything he felt he deserved. Our working relationship was strained. After years of finding myself on the outside, my empathy did not extend to the people who had intentionally kept others from finding a way in. My disregard for inhibitors like Patrick McDade and Caroline Coker was pointed and intentional.

His sulking lasted for a few weeks. Each time Jade's old truck rumbled to a stop on a side street near the gallery, Patrick would yell, "Bracelets is here!" The nickname he had given Jade pointed more to Patrick's personality than Jade's.

I loved it when Jade came to visit me at work. His knowledge of art was impressive, and he knew more than eighty percent of the clients who came in and actually purchased a piece. The woman from his past who had taught him about art had done a fine job of it. Whether pointing out avant-garde themes, praising some baroque ornamentation, or questioning an automatism in a particular piece, Jade painted his own canvas with words, and his was always my favorite piece. There were times when I was so enthralled by the way his voice drifted into my ears that I forgot to listen to what he was actually saying. Built like a man who moved heavy furniture, Jade commanded the room in stature, yet he still managed to fit amid the delicateness of the art. And he was just as colorful as some of the paintings.

Thanks to Savannah's suggestion that we have a dedicated space for South Carolina artists, a Ryan and Son's rocking chair sat front and center in a sunny window of the gallery. Patrick fought me tooth and nail on selling the first chair, but pair after pair, they began to sell, and then they were sold by the handful. Other than a self-centered bachelor like Patrick, I couldn't think of anyone who would only want one rocking chair. A lone chair on a porch or terrace said something about someone, and what it said wasn't very nice. Chairs were made for sharing, for pairs to take in the breeze in silence, battle the heat with a cool drink, or warm up together in good conversation. They practically sold themselves.

On days when he knew Jade would be stopping by the gallery, Patrick would morph into a shadow figure, lurking like a stalker in a corner. The obviousness of his interest was glaring, even though he tried to pretend that he was above such trifles as the two of us. As he pretended to do or be something important, he seemed to always have one eye and ear on our conversations. I assumed it was only a matter of time before Patrick got over his loss to Jade. Why he even considered me a loss in the first place was beyond my understanding. Considering what an impetuous boy he was, I did have reason to believe he would rat us out, or something even worse.

Over those months I spent with Jade, I became quite the little liar. Because of my sneaking around, I had made Beth quite the liar too. Mother would have had an aneurysm had Jade come to the front door to pick me up for a proper date, so I became good at fabricating after-work places and people I supposedly went to or saw. Had my lies been for any other reason than the dull ache of a love that only one man could soothe, my conscience would have gotten the better of me. What made it worse was that I didn't want to lie. I wanted to tell my family, his family, the McDade household, the boutique florist, and the baguette vendor on the corner of King and Queen Streets. As a matter of fact, I actually did tell her, and she gave me a celebratory lobster roll on the house. As much as I wanted to out us, the mistake would have had catastrophic repercussions. I couldn't imagine the heartbreak of losing him, so I traded my principles for passion.

The thing about trades, though, is that everyone has to give up something.

With the first semester of my junior year underway, my finance classes began to feel less mystifying. Mother had given both Patrick and me full responsibility over the gallery, and our roles during the daily operations organically became defined. His bruised ego aside,

Patrick and I did naturally work well together during business hours, and once he focused on sales, the gallery really took off. It seemed as though once a month, he was off on another quest to discover if the next up-and-coming artist was in fact that, or if the hype was too good to be true. Despite his shortcomings when it came to romancing a woman, Patrick knew art. He could tell if a piece was sellable within a minute, and he was even better at haggling down the price. A salesman in the truest sense, Patrick brought all kinds of life to the walls of my family's gallery, even the kind that others insisted wouldn't sell.

He knew that not everyone could afford a Jackson Pollock or a Jasper Johns—we couldn't afford those either—so he studied the trending market and focused on midlevel fame in the art community. Even though it had been Savannah's idea to dedicate a section of the store to artists from South Carolina, Patrick was the one who made the space flourish. In no time, he didn't need to travel to artists, because they came to see him.

"Ausby Fine Art, this is Harlow speaking," I said into the receiver.

"Clean up your brushes and clap off the lights, art girl. It's quitting time," Savannah replied.

"You do realize that I don't actually paint anything, right?"

"Whatever. Would you just go home and pack a bag? It's fair season, and I'm going to catch me a carney."

Since the fifties, the Coastal Carolina Fair had been bringing old-fashioned family fun to Charleston every fall. This type of fun was not meant for women like Mother, but my daddy never missed the opportunity to take me there. Acreage that lay vacant throughout the winter and summer months became a magical village in autumn, constructed in less than forty-eight hours. This was a place that childhood dreams were made of. From a certain distance, the carnival seemed calm, a kaleidoscope of colors that reflected against the river's surface, each night a beacon of lights blazing brightly. The makeshift city could assault your senses better than any, filling a thrill-seeking child with anticipation for days. Too much kettle corn would make you sick, the petting zoo might contaminate you with an infectious disease, and a rusty carnival ride held the possibility of slicing you into multiple pieces, yet these were the times of my childhood that I adored. Despite the appeal of the carnival, I hadn't planned on going without my daddy—not until Savannah called.

"How do I look?" Savannah asked as I opened my front door. She was wearing an outfit that was cut to here and slit to there.

I was shocked at the shortness of her black miniskirt, paired with the height of her leather boots. "Aggressive," I replied.

"Good. That's exactly what I was going for. I have a surprise for you. Let's go."

"No offense, but your surprises scare me. I never know if they'll end with ice cream or pornography."

She paused in thought. "Do they sell ice cream at the fair?"

"I think so."

"Well then, your night might end with both."

As we made our way to the entrance gate, I saw him waiting for me. "Jade!" I called out, running to meet him, to feel the sensation of him putting his hands on me. I wrapped my arms around his neck, pinning him in a kiss against the gate.

"Hey, baby," he crooned, sweeping the hair away from my face. That had become kind of our thing. It made me blush when he stroked my hair, excited when I smoothed his. "I'm so happy to see you."

"Surprise!" Savannah yelled, wiggling her palms like jazz hands for emphasis. Without once breaking her stride, she whipped out a camera from her purse and snapped a few pictures of us. Turning to continue walking backward, she added, "Let me know if you get to the ice cream. Have fun, you two!"

I asked him, "I take it Savannah put you up to meeting me here?"

"She called, but she only had to ask once. I'll go anywhere with you." Our smiles connected before our lips did. "Which ride do you want to get maimed by first?"

With our arms intertwined, we could have been the only two people at that fair. For all his tenderness, thoughtful disposition, and gentle nature, I couldn't understand why the people in my life refused to see what I saw.

With the wind at our backs and a fullness that could only be felt by two people in the rapture of love, we enjoyed everything the night had to offer. My daddy would have loved it, and he would have loved Jade, too. My heart dropped when I finally noticed the time.

"We should probably find Savannah soon. I'm staying the night with her."

"Why don't you stay the night with me?" Jade asked.

I pursed my lips, unsure of how to answer that question without hurting him. "Jade, you know the way I feel about you, but I feel strongly about sleeping with a man, too. I know it seems ridiculous, but I'm not ready. Blame it on my upbringing, but going to bed with a man isn't something I do. If it makes you feel better, you're definitely the front runner for the position." I laughed an uncomfortably fake laugh that even I didn't recognize. Not because my statement wasn't true, but because I wasn't in the habit of speaking to men about sex.

"Would you stay with me if you knew there would be no pressure for sex?"

"When I'm with you, I feel things that I've only heard other people talk about. I don't think I could trust myself."

"Could you trust me?"

Knowing the answer before I even opened my mouth, I smiled, and he did too, because he already knew.

He asked me, "Will you go somewhere with me?"

I answered him, "I'll go anywhere with you."

Chapter 10

I HAD A GOOD IDEA OF WHERE WE WERE HEADED, BUT THE NIGHT became even darker when he put a blindfold on me.

"Is this really necessary?" I asked, secretly loving his playfulness.

"Just a second, let me back her up," he said, throwing the Chevy into reverse.

When we finally came to a stop, Jade hopped out of the truck and began to make all kinds of racket in the back of the truck bed. I stopped trying to pinpoint his mischief and resigned myself to listening to the sounds of the waves instead. The door hinges squeaked open, and he slid his hand into mine, his lips against my cheek.

"Okay, steady now," he said, helping me out of the truck.

The sand, hot enough to burn your feet during the afternoon, now held a chill of the night. It brushed across the tops of my feet and between my toes. This was probably the most exciting thing I had ever done. Gusts of wind blew in synchronization with the crash of the waves—the ones on the shore, as well as those in my chest.

He pulled the blindfold off. "I have something for you."

The book was obviously old—no dust jacket, frayed binding— and it had a particularly musty scent that only came from the bowels of a library or used bookshop. Jade held the lantern near the cover.

"*The Call of the Wild*," I read aloud in the wavering light, "by Jack London."

"I think you'll like this story much more than the other. It's about a man in search of adventure, who finds strength in adversity, and then falls in love with an ugly dog—all things that suit you. There's an inscription inside."

I opened the book and turned the pages until I found what he had written.

Don't forget to look up.
Forever yours,
Jade

"It's beautiful, and I'll treasure it always."

Wrapping my hands around his waist, I wanted to hold on to this moment for as long as possible. I was smart enough to know that nothing lasts forever, but I had no idea how short some things actually were.

"Are you ready?" he asked. "Because this is the best part." He didn't wait for an answer before he turned out the light.

Seemingly closer to the earth than I had ever remembered it being, the moon hung like a portrait in the sky; the vast and endless darkness was the canvas on which it had been created. Once Jade turned the lantern's light off, the sky took over. When the light set, the darkness rose, both working in a conscientious alliance—the type of alliance I had yet to understand, yet I knew was the one I should look for. This alliance was love.

With the gentleness that I was becoming accustomed to, Jade took my palm and brought my hand to his lips. One by one, he lowered each finger, until only my pointer was left standing. The warmth of his smile engulfed me, and without so much as a whispered prompt, I remembered to look up. In that moment, we were as limitless as the sky, as inescapable as the tides, our only boundary the moon.

A feeling compelled me, and I took off toward the ocean. Unaccustomed to embracing spontaneity, I ran at a dead sprint. From a heavy cushion to a flat surface, and then into a body of vast possibilities, the sand and I changed form together. I heard his footsteps closing in, but then Jade blew past me and did a swan dive into an oncoming wave. Sweeping my legs out from under me, and then pulling me under, he shot me back up and out of the water, catching me as I came back down.

"I thought you didn't swim," he hollered as he broke the waves, pulling my waist against his.

"I didn't used to do a lot of things: swim in the ocean, sneak around with boys, stay the night in the back of a truck, and," I paused, intertwining my fingers in the warmth of his hair, "until you, fall in love."

A fury unleashed between us as he carried me to the shore. He pulled me on top of him on the sand. The wetness from our clothes suctioned them together, the sand chafing our skin as the waves stretched onto the shore, dispersing alongside us. His hand found the curvature of my backside, and he glided his fingers along the insides of my thighs. It was the moment I had most hoped for, and most feared. As I had expected, I didn't want him to stop.

His breath warm on my face, his eyes held an unmistakable hunger for me, and I would have loved nothing more than to be devoured by him.

"Let's go back to the truck," I suggested.

The vigilant moon lit the way. Jade wrapped my soaking body in a blanket. With the quickness of a Boy Scout, he lit a small bonfire near the truck, while I spread a stack of blankets across the truck bed.

"I'm freezing," he stuttered, his teeth still chattering from our romp in the waves.

I wrapped him in the blanket-cocoon with me, reliant on our fervency to warm us. His wet skin on mine sent an array of messages hurtling through me, and they all said the same thing.

Inside my body throbbed something long bridled, something ravenous, something unafraid. I dropped the blanket and peeled his shirt off over his head. The buttons on my shirt never once fumbled in his fingers as he looked deep into my eyes.

"We don't have to do this, Harlow. It's not why I brought you out here. I just want to spend time with you, to hold you without having to look over our shoulders. I'm not trying to trick you or force you to do anything you don't want to do."

"Shh," I whispered, putting my finger to his lips. "I want you, Jade, and I want you to have me. No one has ever made me feel like this, like I might explode if I don't touch you, rub you, feel you in my hands and between my legs. I want to know all of you," I said, glancing down at the bulge growing along his inseam.

"I can give you what you want without breaking my promise. Do you trust me?"

"Yes," I breathed, reaching a point close to desperation.

Upon my answer, he dropped his knees into the sand, grabbing handfuls of my thighs while pulling me to his mouth. His fingers squeezed my backside, as his lips worked their way up the insides of my legs. With an uneven mixture of conscious softness coupled with uninhibited desire, he worked his tongue like a giant pulse, nuzzling his lips inside of mine.

My stomach rolled in copious waves, intoxicated by the spreading thrill of the full-bodied sensations. Completely under his spell, I tilted my hips against his mouth, desperate to feel everything he could give me. There was a point when my body became un-belonged to me, when I was only a passenger on the spaceship that rocketed through my insides. I was arriving and departing on the same flight.

He bit his lip as he watched me live out the first-time throes of climax. A smile that I could almost hear flashed across his face. Jade was obviously pleased with himself, and with his performance. He had been the first to take me to new heights, and the look he gave me showed his pride in that mission. I lay back in the truck bed, trying to navigate the sensations that had taken me by delightful surprise. He crawled up beside me, burrowing his face into my neck, while lightly stroking my hair.

Shivering and sweating at the same time, my heart still beating in my ears, I decisively said, "I get it. I finally get what all the fuss is about." He chuckled as he left a trail of kisses on my earlobe, neck, and collarbone. "Jade," I whispered.

"Hmm?" he mumbled.

"That was unbelievable. There was a moment when I couldn't even speak. Is it always like that?"

"It's usually pretty good, but when you're with the right person, it feels like it can't possibly get better, and then it does."

"Jade," I said again.

"Baby," he pleaded, "that wasn't just magical for you. I have all kinds of heat running through me right now, and I'm trying my damnedest to get it to go back down, but every time you say my name, he wants to stay up. If you continue to whisper to me in that sexy voice, it won't be long before I can feel my balls in my throat."

"Oh," I replied, genuinely taken aback. Up until that point, I had been completely oblivious to the true meaning of the term *blue balls*. A grin materialized, along with a now-familiar feeling. "Jade." I whispered his name again, this time with an intention that was clear.

Guided by a moon so large and holy, I squeezed his sides and kissed his stomach. His eyes rolled back into his head as I slid my hand under the waistband of his wet and salty shorts. An involuntary gasp came out with his breath as my fingers reached the delicate skin of his erection. I had never been with a man, had never held him in my hands before then. It was more sensual than I had imagined. The silkiness of his shaft, the tenderness of his sack, which firmed upon my touch—this was my first journey toward a previously elusive happiness.

I had a grasp of what I was doing—I wasn't a complete prude— but his soft whispers of encouragement, his moans of my name, his confidence in guiding himself around my mouth: they were all said in a voice I had never heard, a voice that only his body spoke. All of it led me in the right direction.

"Harlow, look up," he beseeched me. "I want to see your face."

With my lips still pressed around him, our eyes connected, and his request proved to be exactly what he wanted, or maybe too much. With a sudden high arch in his back, his thighs tightened, and his fingers spread thick into my hair. He let out a moan that was surely for a job well done. Who knew that humans possessed this type of power together? The ability to take another person to such heights, to lift them, to hold them in these clutches, where words were only bystanders to touch. Before that night, the concept was almost as unexplainable as the moon. The deeper connection I felt with Jade was immediate, and it far surpassed anything I'd known before.

In each other's arms, our breath began to regulate together, under a sky smooth and black and blanketed with stars. We lay intertwined, as tight as a braid. It amazed me that two strangers made from separate cities, separate molds in life, could fit together as if they had been hand-picked and crafted of the most particular parts, all for the purpose of falling in love. Rolling onto my side, I pulled his arm across my stomach and around my ribs, tucking his hand under my chin.

The sea air seemed fresher, purer, changed somehow. I let out a sigh as I spoke. "I've never seen stars this bright before."

"They're always up there, but you have to get out of the light to appreciate them. The darkness is where you see them best. I take it you don't leave the city limits much at night?"

It was something I hadn't ever really considered. "No, I guess not. I told you I'm not in the habit of sneaking out. But I'm glad I did tonight. Let's stay here forever."

"As much as I would like that, we can't. I'm leaving soon."

Turning around to face him, I asked, "What do you mean? Where are you going?"

He slipped his arm under my neck and kissed me, chuckling as if he enjoyed my shock. "Don't worry, love. I'll only be gone a few weeks, four at the most. My dad and I go to Tennessee every fall, right before the first frost hits. We go to our farm that grows the oak trees for the rocking chairs we make. The first two weeks are for cutting and splitting, the second are for sowing. For as many trees as we cut down, we plant twice that amount. It keeps us in good business and conscience each year." He squeezed me in a hug, pulling me as close to him as physically possible.

"I'm going to miss you," I told him. "Four weeks will feel like forever."

"Forever feels like a very long time. We'll both be working hard with our heads down, and when I get home, we can finally look up." His eyes narrowed in on mine, seriousness furrowing his brows. "I love you, Harlow, and I would wait for you forever if that's what it took. I kind of feel like I already have."

"You don't have to wait anymore."

If I thought I loved him before, it was actually under that moon that I fell in love with Jade Ryan. Falling in love with him was like walking into the dark. The more time I spent with him, the farther I could see into the night.

As it turned out, it wasn't the kind of love that washes out with the tides or falls away with the seasons. It was the perennial kind of love that perseveres. It was the kind that drives you to madness and makes you rabid in the most beautiful way, a love that reaches deep into your insides and scrapes at your bones, leaving you complete yet exhausted. It radiated in my smile and seeped from my words, each breath an affirmation of the swelling in my heart.

It was the kind of love that lived inside of me and lasted, even after the relationship died.

Later, I would understand how short our time together felt. The loss of it was probably close to the feeling of forever. Deeply entranced by this love and naïve to the world, I had forgotten to look up.

PART THREE
THEN

Chapter 11

THERE WERE NO BALLOONS OR STREAMERS. SAVANNAH DIDN'T throw those kinds of parties. She did, however, talk me into letting some friends come over for a sunset swim to celebrate the last of the late autumn warmth. Unsurprisingly, Savannah broke her promise to keep the guest list to a minimum. She sucked at keeping her promises. Most college students ran in groups, and that's how they showed up to my house that night: droves of people, with armfuls of liquor.

Beth had taken Mother to an overnight antique show near Beaufort. They seemed to frequent that city more and more. As the evening went on, the partiers grew rowdier, and I liked them less and less. What I would have given for Mother to hurtle herself through the back doors and declare them all ungrateful and ill-mannered, ripping them enough for them to hate me and punish me by leaving the house. But I wouldn't be that lucky.

I had already found Savannah making out with some random guy in the bathroom, and then on the front porch. I wasn't even sure it was the same guy. Mother would have died if she knew Savannah was all over her proper Queen Anne home, doing the improper things that Savannah did. I didn't know if a bathmat could get herpes or a joggling board chlamydia, or if either of those would wash out of the carpet. Disinfectant would be a major priority after the party ended. Why did I let Savannah get me into these situations? I wanted to be home alone, pining away for my out-of-town boyfriend, not worrying about Savannah and sexually transmitted diseases.

She meant well, but more times than not, Savannah missed the mark. In fact, she tended to miss the entire target. Her egocentricity wasn't entirely her fault. I was sure that no one had ever shown her how to properly love before. I was probably the first person who hadn't given up on her, which may have been why she had stuck with someone as square as I was.

When she climbed up onto Mother's seventeenth-century matelassé blanket chest to dance for the crowd, I stepped in. Slurring and swaying, she made it clear that my role had turned from hostess to babysitter.

"Give me that," I demanded, swiping a purplish drink from her hand. "God, Van, do you always have to have eight million drinks? Why can't you ever just use some manners?"

Her words sloshed as much as the purple alcohol in the cup. "Manners are for people who aren't funny. Don't be mad, Low. I love you. I wanted to throw you a party, so you wouldn't be sad about your secret boyfriend leaving."

"Boyfriend?" I heard a male voice ask. I turned around to find Patrick nursing a beer. "I guess I shouldn't be that surprised," he continued. "You two are always falling all over each other at the gallery. It's sickening. But I thought Vivian raised you better than to fall for some beach rat."

Still holding Savannah upright, I replied, "Why do you think what I do is any of your business, Patrick? Why don't you be helpful, instead of starting a fight?"

"Hey," he said, lowering his voice and placing his hand on my arm. "I'm sorry, Harlow. I didn't mean that, but I have pride, you know. It's just that I thought we had something going, and out of nowhere you started seeing this Ryan guy. It hurt my feelings."

"Patrick, our families have been friends since before we were born. Don't you think it's a little too incestuous, you and me? Don't you want to see what's out there, who's out there, beyond

Charleston? I need to know that life has more than identical religions, schools, and ivy-covered fences."

He stared vacantly at me, blinking slowly like a mouth-breathing idiot. You would have thought I was trying to explain astrophysics. He proved my point, without meaning to.

"Look," I continued, "I never intended to hurt your feelings, and I'm sorry about that."

"Really?" he asked. "Friends?"

"Of course, friends. Now, can you please help me out by calming things down in here, so I can take her to get some air? I can't let Savannah get sick on Mother's Portuguese armorial rug. That tapestry costs more than her life."

A smirk curled his lip upward. "There she is," he stated in a righteous tone.

"There who is?" I asked, losing my patience.

"You can act like a saint, slumming it with the beach rat, but all of us here"—he pointed his finger to the people in the living room—"we're all stuck-up sinners South of Broad. You included. You should come to terms with that."

"Whatever, Patrick, just help me get these people out of here."

Savannah outweighed me by thirty pounds, and dragging her raggedy mess out the front door was a chore, to say the least. The drink I'd taken from her sloshed out of the cup and made ugly splotches on the wooden porch as we slowly made our way outside. She kept telling me she loved me, and I kept telling her to stop. When I sat her in the rocking chair, she listed to the side like a two-month-old pumpkin, eighty-proof alcohol pumping through her bloodstream. She was probably asleep on her feet before I ever sat her down.

The porch seemed to be the only place that wasn't littered with people. Inside, I heard Patrick telling everyone to start packing up, because the party was over. I couldn't believe he had thought beyond himself and actually listened to me for once.

I'd just gotten Savannah settled when I heard my name.

"Harlow," Jade called from the terrace walkway. His tone was one I hadn't heard before.

"I figured it was a waste of time to ring the garden bell. You can hear the noise from down the street. You're having a party?"

My first instinct upon seeing him was to run into his arms, but I had the distinct feeling he was mad at me. Confused as to what to do—we hadn't quarreled before—I froze.

"Hey, baby," I said. "What are you doing here? I thought you had already left for the mountains."

"I was sick about leaving you, and already missing you something awful. I wanted to come by and see you again. I didn't care if Vivian was here when I showed up, and I almost expected to have a battle with her about us. But man, I certainly didn't expect this. It seems like you'll do just fine while I'm gone."

The gravity of the situation jolted me. I put my hands out in a defensive gesture, but I had forgotten about the drink I was holding. "Wait," I said, "it's not what you think."

Even more surprise—although it was closer to a look of disgust—tensed his body. He stood rigid among the traces of delicate hanging garden flowers. "You're drinking? I thought you didn't drink."

With the cup still clutched in my hand, I tried to explain. "No, you don't understand. This is Savannah's. She's passed out over there in the rocking chair. I took it from her, so she wouldn't drink anymore. She was trying to throw me a party, so I wouldn't be sad about you being gone for so long, but things got out of hand. Patrick is kicking everyone out right now, as we speak." The moment I said his name, I knew it was a mistake.

That look was clear. That was anger.

"Patrick is here?"

"Jade, try to understand. I know this looks like I don't care about you leaving, but please, you know that's not true."

Patrick swung out of the screen door as he had a thousand times before. "Everyone's going to King Street. They'll be out of your hair soon."

"And how about you?" Jade shouted from the bottom of the porch steps. "Will you be gone soon, too?"

"Hey, Bracelets!" Patrick yelled back. He elbowed me in the side and hollered, "Bracelets is here," as if I hadn't noticed. "How about you head on off, back to your mountain town, and I'll worry about things here."

With a quickness that I never would have been able to stop, Jade rushed the top steps and threw his shoulder into Patrick's waist. The force knocked Patrick off his feet and sent him flying across the porch, where he crash-landed on his back. They wrestled on the floor, so tangled up that I couldn't tell a foot from a hand. Despite all my screaming, foot stomping, and demanding them to stop, those children kept fighting. It took Savannah waking up and leaning over the side of the rocking chair, emptying the contents of her stomach right next to where they were rolling around—*that* got their attention.

With my hundred pounds of force, I grabbed Patrick by the collar and shoved him inside, yelling at him to stay there. Jade looked at me as though I had just shot his favorite dog.

He stepped back before the hurt spilled out of him. "He's staying? You're letting him stay here alone with you?"

"No, I'm not. Please understand." My voice was that of a mediator, even and disarming. "I'm just trying to figure out what to do. I can't have two boys in a fistfight on my front porch. The neighbors will call the police and cause a world of trouble." I slid my hands down his sweaty arms, the tension in them palpable. "I don't know what happened here in the last fifteen minutes, but this has all just been a misunderstanding. I love you, Jade, I do. But you should go."

I hugged him, but our embrace was colder than a corpse.

139

He was clearly distraught, his words stopping and starting like a stalling car. "I shouldn't leave you alone with him. I shouldn't go." He pointed his finger angrily at the house, jabbing it in the air with each enunciated word. "He plays the part of the altar boy pretty good, but he is dangerous, Harlow."

"Calm down," I gently shushed him. Grazing my hand across his forehead, I let my palm come to cradle his cheek. He softly pushed his face back into my hand, and then put my fingertips to his lips.

"Do you trust me?" I asked.

"I'm sorry," he whispered, his breath blowing across the pads of my fingers. "I don't know what came over me, except that I hate that asshole. I just saw him with you, and I snapped, and Jesus, I hate those kinds of guys—I swore I'd never be one."

I took him in my arms, and this time the peacefulness registered between us. He nuzzled his nose into my hair, while I cradled my arms against his waist, both of us caught in a moment of wishful thinking that would never bear fruit.

"I love you," I said, one last time.

"I love you, too," he repeated back.

There was no fervent or lust-filled goodbye between us that night. I think the shame of how he had behaved stole any chance of that happening. And as I would soon find out, shame always outweighs desire.

Chapter 12

A STIFF BREEZE SENT THE PALM FRONDS CLAPPING TOGETHER, and the fallen leaves of shedding magnolias skated down the cobblestone street in somersaults. The rightful chill of the season had finally found our Holy City, and my shoulders hunched against the autumn nip in the air. With the descending daylight, the fringe of sunset dissolved into itself, darkening the sky like a chalkboard; white pinpricks of stars seemed hand-drawn by the thousands. Gaslit lanterns cast ornamental shadows in orderly rows, each house lit up in a way that could never be fully captured in pictures.

Despite Jade's wishes, Patrick stayed behind to help me clean up the house and take care of Savannah. It took both of us to carry her up the ancient staircase and get her into bed. As mad as I was at her for throwing an unnecessary and disastrous party, I couldn't help but smile as I covered her up in my bed. She was a mess, but she was my mess. She was going to owe me big time for this one.

With the house quiet again, I sat in my favorite rocking chair to take a minute to breathe and, in my own way, apologize to Jade. Like the dark stain that covered the rocking chair, his love had varnished my heart. I had hurt him, and knowing I had done that— even unintentionally—hurt me. My newness to relationships was my only defense, but I wasn't in the habit of disappointing people. Mother was another worry of mine. She'd wring my neck if she knew I had thrown a party. She'd do worse if she discovered that I had caved to Savannah's whining and peer pressure. Mother would never have caved; she'd never have had a friend like Savannah to begin with.

"Hey," Patrick said, taking a seat on the stoop beside me. He had a bag of frozen peas on the left side of his face. "I'm sorry about what happened, about all of it: the party, the alcohol, and the fight. I know you aren't cool with stuff like that, and I should have helped you, not made it worse. I brought you a peace offering." He handed me a glass of white wine.

"You know I don't drink."

"It's seriously like four sips of wine, and if anyone deserves a drink, it's you. You put up with a lot tonight, and this will help take the edge off. You'll sleep like a baby."

I didn't hate that idea. There was nothing I was looking forward to more than sleeping away this dreadful evening. I took the wine from him and smelled it, wrinkling my nose.

He laughed at the face I made. "It tastes a lot better than it smells."

I took a drink. Like Patrick said, I had earned it. "It's fine, I guess. I'm sure everything will be different in the morning."

We sat on the porch and sipped our drinks, the wind rattling the treetops above us. The quiet was a welcome change after the chaos of the party. After a long silence, Patrick surprised me with a question. "What do you see in him, anyway?"

I was so lost in the sound of the breeze, I had almost forgotten he was sitting there.

"Who?" I asked.

He rolled his eyes. "Jade. What's so great about him?"

I stopped to think, though I knew I could never sum up my feelings for him with just words. "Honestly, everything. But if I had to pick one thing about him, it would be his kindness." I turned to Patrick and caught his stare. "He's kind, Patrick. I'm not sure I need another reason to love him."

"Humph," he breathed, seemingly unsatisfied with my answer. I heard him repeat the sound under his breath. "Too bad you can't say the same for your best friend. I don't think she could be more selfish."

I had to agree with him on that. "Not tonight she couldn't. I don't know what it is, but I have some kind of weakness when it comes to her stupid ideas. She *is* quite persuasive. I just don't know how I get myself into these situations."

He laughed before answering. "Because you're a good friend, Harlow, not to mention a good person. You'd do anything for Savannah and, I'm assuming, Jade. You'd probably move mountains to help me, for that matter. You shouldn't beat yourself up about that. Most people know how to take, but only a rare few know how to give. You're one of the good ones, and you probably don't hear that enough around here."

"Aw," I said, my smile feeling bigger than it usually was around Patrick. "You know, you can be a real gentleman when you try. You should try more often. It suits you." I noticed the redness in his cheeks. "Oh my goodness, is Patrick McDade blushing over something little ole me said? Well, I am making history tonight." Broken and muddled, a thought hit me. "Hopefully Jade doesn't stay mad at me. I shouldn't have told him to go." I was about to take another sip of wine, but I realized my glass was already empty. He poured me another, which I drank in a surprisingly short amount of time. I turned to talk to Patrick, but the words that followed seemed to echo in my head. I wasn't even sure if I actually said them. "Did I drink all this?"

"Uh-oh." He laughed. "Maybe two glasses of wine was one too many." He scooped me off the porch steps, throwing my arm around his shoulder and setting me upright on my feet. "Come on, rock star, time to sleep it off."

My tongue felt fat inside my mouth, and I slurred the question, "Is this what wine does to you? I don't like it." With my eyes on the tips of his loafers, I now had to concentrate on moving my feet in sync with his.

His breath was hot in my ear. "Shh, just relax, Harlow. I'll take care of you."

Unable to make a try for the stairs—which looked much higher than I remembered—I mumbled for him to leave me in the carriage house out back. He shuffled me across the first floor, toward the back of the house. The carriage house had a shut-up heaviness to it, from its lack of use. Mustiness released from the comforter on the bed as he drew it back. The smell pulled at the inside of my nose as I lay down. I felt as though I had managed to get under the covers, but I couldn't feel my legs, and my eyes wouldn't stay open. My body felt detached, almost gone from me. I heard myself talking, but I couldn't understand what I said. A voice replied, the door closed, and then came the white noise of blackness.

Chapter 13

As I came to, there were panic-inflected voices whispering around me. The strong afternoon sun cast shadows through the plantation shutters, highlighting blurs of an untraceable figure moving around the room quickly. Her hands touched my bare arms and legs gently, with soft strokes. My head screamed when I opened my eyes, as though poison-dipped arrows had been shot into my ears. Curling into a knot that was likely to rip me in two, my stomach rejected my own smell. I leaned over to vomit, but only sound came from my throat. I felt a deep pain in my groin. My chest and hair hurt, and my thighs were sore. The room tilted and swayed; I would likely have tripped, if only I could walk.

"We're going to get you some help, Harlow," Beth assured me. "Just hang on." Her words started and stopped, seemingly choking her as they came out. I could tell she was trying not to cry.

Confused by my jumble of thoughts, by the waves of blackness that intercepted my vision, and by the pain running up and down my insides, I whispered, "Why do I need help?"

"Oh, honey," she lovingly replied, stifling her tears.

My back lay against the headboard of the bed at an awkward angle, my hair in a messy pile above my head. A haze covered my vision like a blanket of fog, though the colors of things slowly morphed into focus. White shiplap walls held pictures of hand-drawn birds, while the beige sheer netting above the four-poster bed fluttered, a fan circulating the air above me.

Despite the spotting darkness, knickknacks and gold accents on floating shelves flickered in the wavering light. As Beth hurried around me, Mother, with her brunette coiffed hair and blazing red lips, remained unmoving in the doorway.

The thought came to me slowly, as if it were a test question I hadn't studied for. Yes, I realized, I was in the carriage house. *Why am I in the carriage house?*

As my hand went to my head, my eyes looked down to my body, and the scene was something that my brain refused to absorb. My involuntary shaking was immediate, and the panic came hard from somewhere deep inside me. My teeth vibrated together in reaction. Bile from a hidden corner of my stomach rose up. I swallowed and swallowed and swallowed again. I felt as though I couldn't get air, but I desperately wanted to breathe.

What was I looking at? Whose body was attached to my eyes? Why was vomit across my chest and blood covering my thighs?

I wanted my body to work, but everything felt forced. My eyelids didn't function, and my legs were unable to run me away from myself. Around my lower half, a pool of chestnut and crimson had soaked into the white sheets, leaving behind gelatinous globs too thick to penetrate the bedding. Still wettish to the touch, smears of it had dried across my thighs and coagulated in my pubic hair. My hands—and everything they touched—left a cardinal trail, a calling card of sin. Moments were only played in fast-forward, and I couldn't think, couldn't process the information fast enough. I had awoken to a crime scene—my own crime scene. My eyes darted around the room, desperate to anchor on something concrete. They settled on Beth. She took my face in her hands.

With a soft but firm voice, she said, "Look at me, Harlow. Look in my eyes. Don't look anywhere else. Just look at me and breathe; breathe with me."

My words finally came, only they were spoken in sobs. "What's happening to me?"

Beth kept my eyes trained on hers, but the panic in her voice was growing. "The doctor will be here any second. You just keep looking at me, and we'll just keep breathing together."

The pain from the afternoon light, which snuck in when the doctor opened the door, blinded me into involuntary submission. Beth had said he was there to help me, but my insides rejected his hands on my skin, and my gag reflex retaliated with every whiff of his woodsy cologne. When the warmth of his sweaty fingers found the insides of my knees, I heard someone scream, but I couldn't feel it. It took me a moment to realize that the person screaming was me.

In a thick and official voice, he said, "I'll give her something to calm her. Hold her down for me."

Despite my flailing, a prick went into my arm. A concoction of blackening heat spread throughout me, and I was relieved for the darkness to find me. Only a place so soft and forgiving would soothe my fears. It was a place I could turn to for comfort and learn to hide within, and over the next nine months, it would be a place I frequented. This darkness would become the place where I thought I could escape the world, but as it turned out, it was the place that prepared me for it.

Chapter 14

OVER THE NEXT WEEK, I BARELY MOVED. MY MIND WAS STILL fuzzy, and my body ached in places that I didn't know could hurt. Although the space around my heart hurt more than the space between my legs. Once Beth got me situated in my room, I didn't go back into the carriage house—ever. I didn't do a lot of things that I used to do. I would never finish college, my birthmark would eventually go back undercover, and I would sleepwalk through the next twenty years of my life. While my life had seemingly stopped, other people kept on living theirs, a lesson of the tides within me. Time waits for no one, and with each revolution of the clock, that became more apparent.

Our old house echoed with secret conversations. I heard them talking, always talking, and usually about me. Mother and Beth had a constant conversation going about my well-being. When one paused, the other interrupted, each with her own ideas of what to do with me, or how to get me out of bed. Not used to an unmanageable daughter, Mother was at a loss as to how to control someone who couldn't control herself.

It was only three weeks before my breasts became sore, and then I started throwing up in the morning hours. I'd like to think it was a valiant effort between my soul and me, working together to purge my insides toward a clean slate. That wasn't the case, though.

There were moments when I would get a residual whiff of Chanel Nº5 and know that Mother had been on the third floor. I suspected she was deciding on how to redecorate my room once she had shipped me off to the Total Disappointment Center for Delinquent Daughters. Not one for the patience of emotional nurturing, Mother had grabbed the situation by the throat and strangled everyone involved into submission. It was what she did best.

"Get out of those disgusting sweat pants, and get in the car," she ordered one afternoon, while towering over my usual spot in bed.

"I don't want to go anywhere," I mumbled.

"You don't have a choice in the matter." Her tone was absolute.

Since Mother usually got what she wanted, in only a matter of minutes, Beth and I were in the back seat. I couldn't remember the last time I had seen her drive, and so intent on a destination. When she pulled into the neighborhood drugstore, I understood why. *McDade Pharmacy* lit up the dashboard in neon letters. As the light spilled in through the windshield, tears instantaneously spilled over the rims of my lashes.

"Why are we here?" I cried.

She replied with a coldness rarely experienced in the Lowcountry. "You know why. Go in and get a pregnancy test." She held a folded twenty-dollar bill in the air, only touching the corner as if the money to buy the test were as contaminated as I was. "Just get it over with, so we know once and for all."

"Please, don't make me go in there," I sobbed.

She turned around and pulled her dark shades to the bridge of her nose, revealing a raw and readable gaze. Her scowl seemed to suck away all the oxygen from the back seat of the car, and I suddenly felt as though I couldn't breathe.

"I'm not the one who put us in this situation, so I'm not the one who should have to go in. Get moving." The words were malignant, her tone sharp.

There were fifty corner markets in Charleston. She didn't even have the decency to take me to another drugstore. Her sympathy extended only as far as her hand reaching into the back seat. I was a twenty-year-old girl who was scared out of her mind. I needed the warmth of a mother's hand and the assurance that in that moment, I was loved. I got a twenty-dollar bill instead.

Beth took my hand as we exited the car. She walked ahead of me, and the automatic doors opened before us. The blast of frigid air-conditioning did nothing to cool me. I think it purposefully avoided me. Mrs. McDade was standing in the front of the store, the bulky shoulder pads of her suit seeming to swallow her neck. She stared a hard glare at me, frozen the instant I contaminated her happy and family-friendly store. Mr. McDade's reaction to my presence was the same. Neither of them spoke. Apparently the rumors had arrived before we had.

Beth gave me a gentle nudge and said, "Go stand over there by the carpet cleaners. You'll be hidden by the partition, and anyone who walks in here won't see you. I'll go get the test."

When Beth approached the counter with two boxes in hand, Mrs. McDade began to cry, openly sobbing as the register beeped with each scanned box. The cashier seemed as paralyzed as I was. It was as if those beeps were confirming Mrs. McDade's deepest fear: the great Patrick McDade had once again been swindled by a girl who was obviously trying to nail down her eligible catch of a son. I don't think her mind could have envisioned any other scenario.

When the total amount showed on the register screen, the cashier placed the boxes in a plastic bag.

Tear-soaked and nearly hyperventilating, Mrs. McDade screamed at Beth and me, "Just go, both of you!"

Beth nodded her head to Mrs. McDade and then gave me a nod, signaling that it was over. But it wasn't over; it was just getting started.

Both pregnancy tests confirmed what we had all suspected. I was knocked down and knocked up in the same punch.

Mother and Beth didn't seem to understand how to get me to accept the news they continued to give me. Playing good cop, bad cop, they took turns sitting on the foot of the bed, forcing me to listen to results I did not want to hear. Their forthright repetition of the words *pregnant* and *pregnancy* seemed as inconceivable as a baby. I sunk low into the covers and curled into a fetal position. It struck me that something as small as a speck could be so giant, so mighty, so capable of causing such grief. A wholly unreal number of tears streaked my face; a grisly white roar howled in my ears. If only I could kill a word.

I was pregnant, and yet I couldn't remember ever having sex.

The vastness of this news and what it meant for me—and for the people who surrounded me—felt unbearable, crushing, and infinite. I turned out the lights and curled back into bed. I let the darkness absorb all of me, hoping it would take the baby inside my belly with it. What I slipped into was beyond depression. This was a free-fall plunge into a blackness of repulsion and despair that took far more of me than I had ever imagined I had to offer.

Chapter 15

THE LETTER CAME ON A WEDNESDAY AFTERNOON. I HELD IT against my cheek until the warmth from my palms began to smear the ink on the envelope. It took hours before I brought myself to open it, and even then, reading it felt like a betrayal. His words were painted with delicate strokes, his love for me frequently and beautifully expressed. Jade was coming back soon, and I would have to tell him how I had ruined our lives.

On the day of his arrival home, my mood was wretched. I was caught between wanting to get it over with and wishing it would never happen. The scenarios I allowed myself to oscillate between were on the extreme ends of fantasy and reality. One moment I envisioned us as an old married couple, having gotten through this small blemish in our lives. The next I pictured him saying all the things—when I was truly being honest with myself—that I deserved to hear. Even though I couldn't remember doing it, I had spread my knees and let Patrick inject me with his poison. However that night had unfolded, there was nothing I could say or do to make that fact untrue.

"You're up!" Mother exclaimed with an unusual amount of pleasure in her voice. "Come and sit," she added, motioning me over to the kitchen table. "Beth has made a beautiful breakfast for us this morning. You must be starving."

"What's wrong with you?" I cautiously asked.

"What do you mean? I'm just inviting you to have breakfast with me."

"That's what I mean. Why are you being so nice? Did you have a neighbor evicted or something?"

She shook her head as if I were full of nonsense, not truth. "Don't be ugly. Eat your waffles. Remember, you're eating for two now."

I wasn't sure if her comment was out of complete and oblivious self-centeredness, or if it was an excellent rejoinder to my previous dig. One could never tell.

"It's nice to see you back in appropriate attire. Is Patrick coming over?"

I couldn't believe she had mentioned Patrick. I hadn't spoken to him since the night of the party. The night Jade had told me Patrick shouldn't be there. The night I lost what was only mine to give.

"No, not Patrick. Jade. He's home from Tennessee, and he's coming over. I have to tell him."

She folded her newspaper and set it aside on the table, trying to give her best impression of a caring mother. "We won't discuss the fact that you went behind my back when I told you not to see that boy. I'll do you that favor. That's in the past now, and this is for the best, Harlow. That boy is from a different life than yours. He was never suited for you, not like Patrick."

"You're acting like Patrick and I have been dating for years, and I've just received this dream proposal from a man I love. I don't even remember sleeping with him."

"I find that hard to believe. Opening your legs to a man before wedlock is hardly something you forget. Patrick is an excellent match, and once we get past this initial awkwardness, things will be fine."

Awkwardness? Is that what we're saying this is?

She continued, "We'll have a wedding bigger than this town has ever seen!"

I almost choked on my waffle. "Wedding? I'm not marrying Patrick."

Her fingers spread like tentacles across her monogrammed placemat, and vermillion splotches instantly rose to her cheeks. Her words were pointed and threatening. "Oh, yes. Yes you are, Harlow Ausby."

I jerked myself out of the chair, the force of the motion knocking it over behind me. "You're not going to tell me who to love!"

Her eyes narrowed, and her voice growled low, "Love has nothing to do with it."

I met her tone with equal conviction. "You're not going to tell me who to marry."

She matched my movements as she shot up from the table, her chair toppling over too. The clatter surprised me; I hadn't known her to move that fast. Her voice switched to a snarl. "I don't need to make that choice for you. You signed the marriage license with that bastard child in your belly." With intimidating quickness, she came around the table, grabbing my shirt collar and yanking me toward her. "You have the opportunity of a lifetime here, and I refuse to let you screw it up!"

Not bothering to hide the mockery in my voice, I screamed, "Marrying Patrick McDade is not the opportunity of a lifetime! Maybe it was in your lifetime, but I don't want your life!"

When her palm connected with my cheek, it knocked me backward. I stumbled over a chair, eventually landing on my backside against the curio cabinet. The genuine shock of the moment left me speechless—until I said the first thing that came out of my mouth. "I hate you. You're the worst mother alive!"

Without missing a beat, Mother replied, "Good, I'll be sure to thank you in my speech."

HE CALLED THE MOMENT HE GOT BACK. THE EXCITEMENT IN his voice made me feel morning sickness all afternoon. After all our sneaking around, my telling him to come to my house to see me gave him a hope so false that it bordered on a lie. Before Jade, I had done everything asked and expected of a society lady in training. I had all but excised cross words and ill manners from my life at home, and when I did venture out into the world, I never went bare-faced or bare-skinned. Excessive obedience hadn't permitted me to break one insufferably tedious rule in my unbending and dutiful childhood. My only act of defiance was falling in love. My only crime was of the heart. All those years, and all that exorbitant compliancy: it was all for nothing.

Although it was close to winter, the air felt thick enough to stick in my throat and choke me just for breathing. Maybe it wasn't so much the weather as it was the fear. As I waited for Jade, a curtain in the dining room window would shift, catching my eye enough for me to look over. A shadowed figure paced back and forth behind the plantation shutters. Beth was waiting for Jade with me. Through the window, she attempted to smile at me, but the smile never reached her eyes. At that moment, I felt as though she was all I had.

When I buzzed him through the heavy garden door, I had to steady myself against the porch railing. Waves roiled inside me, taking my life and my future further and further away. He picked me up and swung me around, laughing in his joy to see me, to hold me again. For seven seconds, he was completely oblivious to the fact that I was about to kill half of the goodness inside him. It was when I started to uncontrollably sob that he began to figure it out.

"Harlow, what's wrong?" he asked, the panic in his voice rising. "Look up, baby. Tell me what happened. Tell me what's wrong."

A guttural voice ripped through me, shredding my heart as it came out. "I'm sorry" was all I could say through my pain-laden tears. Over and over again, "I'm sorry" were the only words I could utter, yet they did a colossal injustice to how I actually felt. I rubbed my face against his shirt, touching his arms and hands and trying to fill up on a lifetime of him in the next sixty seconds.

He smoothed my hair and kissed my forehead, rubbing my back. "What's wrong? Why are you crying?"

The permanence of what I had to tell him struck me, and as if the garden bricks were being yanked out from under me, I lost my footing. My legs too weak to hold up my shame, my knees buckled, and I began to fall. Jade's hand went to my elbow, and he held me like a rag doll as my feet dragged beneath me, refusing to function. He gently sat me on the porch steps, the fear palpable in his eyes.

"Why are you sorry? Please, just tell me. You're scaring the hell out of me!"

I just blurted it out. "I'm pregnant!"

The look on his face was heartbreaking. I saw him trying to do the math, trying to add up an equation that had no solution. "No, you can't be. We didn't have sex."

I didn't have any other words, so I said them again. "I'm pregnant, and I'm so sorry."

He still looked confused, as if my statement were debatable. "No, you're not."

I nodded. Yes, it was true.

He stood up. His eyes became expansive, and his hand swept through his hair. He paced in the garden, before abruptly halting.

"What?" It came out as only a breath, like an involuntary exhale after being punched in the gut. His arm stretched across his stomach, clutching his side tightly, as if his insides were in danger of spilling out. "Oh God, no, Harlow. What have you done? What did you do to us?" He doubled over, still keeping his insides intact. Tears covered his face when he stood back up.

"I'm sorry, Jade, please—"

"I waited for you for so long, waited for us. I loved you. I trusted you!" I watched the thought hit him. "It was Patrick, wasn't it? You slept with him!"

"I don't remember doing it. You have to believe me!"

"Bullshit! It was the night of the party, wasn't it? I saw you, Harlow. I saw you with a drink in your hand. You think I'm some idiot who uses my hands because I don't have a brain?"

"No, I don't think that. I would never think that about you. Please, you know me!"

A hardness came over him, and he backed away from me, slowly making his way to the terrace door. "I don't know you, and I don't want to know you."

Honesty is supposed to make you feel better, as though the weight of your admission frees your soul—even if what you've admitted is something terrible. I had just confessed my terrible, and after saying it aloud, the atrocity made me gag. My terrible wasn't followed by some form of relief. In fact, my admission only made the weight of terrible sink lower into my belly, where it snuggled alongside the even heavier weight of an unwanted baby.

After the noise of his truck faded into the distance, I moved myself back to our chair. It was the first time I had ever seen this type of pain before. To know I had caused it was beyond any shame I had experienced, and it was the first of several times when I wanted to die. Not because of a man, or a broken heart, but because I realized that this was all there was to life. I had spent my entire twenty years following society, Mother, and God, and it had gotten me nowhere.

Chapter 16

BETH TOLD ME THAT I WAS DEHYDRATED. I DIDN'T EVEN FLINCH when the needle went into my arm. My condition must have been bad, bad enough for Mother to call Savannah's home. Only a certain level of hell would have forced the hand of Vivian Ausby. Lava must have oozed from the receiver when she dialed the number. I was grateful she had called Savannah over.

"Hey, girl," Savannah whispered into my ear. "How are you holding up?"

Had there been any tears left, they would have surfaced, but I had cried myself empty.

Pulling the fruit out from behind her back, she said, "I brought you a pineapple."

Somewhere deep inside, I'm sure I found that funny.

"Too soon?" A long sigh accompanied her next stupid statement. "Sorry, I went straight for the joke; it's what I do. When I told you to sleep with him, I didn't think you'd actually do it. Not the best time to start listening to the dumb stuff I say."

In any other situation, her sick humor would have made me laugh. She knew it, and I knew she was trying to cheer me up.

She dropped the pineapple and lay down next to me in the bed. "I've been trying to get ahold of you, but this is the first time Vivian would let me see you. I'm sorry I wasn't here for you sooner."

My voice came out as a whisper. It might have been the only volume I had left. "It's fine. I just wanted to be alone."

"Yeah, I get that. Do you want to tell me what happened that night?"

"I've been lying here day after day, asking myself that same question. Maybe I gave it to him, maybe he took it from me. I don't know the answer. It doesn't matter.... Maybe it's better I don't know, don't think about it, and push it as far back in my body as I can. Maybe if I shove hard enough, it will take this baby."

She got quiet, and Savannah was never quiet. A chunk of time passed before she spoke again. "I feel like this whole thing is my fault. I never should have told you to sleep with him. You have no business going to bed with a man, not one from around here, anyway. None of them deserve you. But the party, the party was definitely all my fault. I'm so sorry, Low. I don't know how I'll make it up to you, but I promise that someday I will."

"It's not your fault. It's not either of our faults. I was born to this life, and you were thrown into it, and it will never change. That's just how it is."

"Listen, I know you feel like you can't go on, but you have to. I simply won't allow you to just fade away. We're going to get through this, because you won't feel this bad forever, I promise. I'm proof that you can survive anything. My mother yanked me up from everything I knew and moved me to a city that's wound tighter than a screw's ass. I've survived because of you. So you can expect the same from me in return. Beth and I will be with you every step of this...well, this shitty turn of events. You may not want to hear this, but there is a bright side."

I pulled a face at her.

"You get the chance to be everything to someone—even if it's not who you intended." She leaned over and kissed my cheek. "Harlow, you're the kindest person I know. You're compassionate and organized and smart, and you know all the correct silverware at a place setting, plus those stupid rules of fashion that I'm always messing up. Most importantly, you know the best of everything that Charleston has to offer. Your heart was made for mothering, and above all else, it's what will make you an excellent mama."

Without reply, I turned my eyes back toward the wall, my cheek still smashed in the pillow.

"But before any of that happens, you need to take a shower, because you stink. This room stinks. Jesus." She smiled, and for the first time in a long time, I smiled too. "Now, if you get your ratty ass up out of this cesspool of a bed and take off those heinous pajamas, I'll give you a surprise."

"I don't like your surprises, and I don't want to get out of bed," I mumbled.

"You liked the last one, and you'll want to get up for this one, too."

Begrudgingly, I sat up and swung my feet onto the floor. "I did like your last surprise. It was the best night of my life."

"I know, and that's why I brought you this." She pulled a picture out of her back pocket.

The sight of him—even in print—took my breath away. It was the picture Savannah had taken of Jade and me at the fair. He had his arm around my shoulder, and my hands were wrapped tightly around his waist. The lights of the Ferris wheel were the perfect backdrop, but none shone brighter than us.

I clutched the picture to my chest, as if that would allow me to step back into that night.

She smiled at the happiness she had brought me. "I thought you might like that. Hurry up and shower, because the rest of your surprise is waiting outside."

"What do you mean?"

"Did you think I would just lie down and let you suffer? I'm known for causing trouble, and I have to protect my reputation. I'm probably already going to hell. At this point, it's either go big or go home, right?"

I had no idea what she was talking about.

"I went and got him. Jade is outside, waiting for you. He loves you, Harlow, and you love him, so why don't y'all just kiss and make up already? Screw Vivian and Patrick and anyone else who says you two shouldn't be together. I'll admit that I don't know much about love, but if I ever do fall in love, I'd want it to look like what the two of you have."

———

FACING HIM AGAIN WAS HARDER THAN I INITIALLY THOUGHT IT would be. When Savannah told me he was outside, all I could think about was getting him to forgive me, getting him back. But when I saw him leaning against her car, it was as if I had a chemical cleansing of the soul. He had created a whole new world for me, and I had a responsibility to protect him from my own tormented new world.

After weeks of torturing myself with only thoughts about myself, I felt as though I was finally stepping out of my own way. For the first time since life's haze had blinded me, I could finally see. I did love Jade—I knew that to be truer than gospel. I also knew what loving him meant. I knew that letting him go would be my one chance to love him harder.

"Jade," I said, coaxing him to look up from the ground, "thank you for coming." He was kicking something nonexistent against the curb. "Will you walk with me?"

Wordlessly, we started toward the Battery. High Spartina grasses waved under the Spanish moss, seemingly transcended by the sunlight, moving the briny air around us. Two boats sat far out toward the Atlantic, just specks on the horizon. The stale breeze gave off the pungent scent of pluff mud, a telltale sign of low tide. How could something so revolting be so enduring? The competing scents of magnolia and confederate jasmine comforted me, and the familiar stench of the marsh mud made the conversation seem bearable. As we climbed the cement stairs, I felt him readying himself for our exchange.

As I leaned against the seawall, I kept my voice as even and straightforward as possible, and then I began my partial truths and half lies. "I'm going to marry Patrick. For everyone concerned, it's for the best. I will be a mother, Patrick will do whatever he was going to do anyway, and you can live your life without me in the way—"

"I want you to stop," he interrupted me, looking hard into my eyes.

"I'm sorry, but it's been decided."

He grimaced, and it felt as if the space between us were swelling, even though neither one of us had moved. He acted as though he hadn't heard me. "I want you to stop waiting for your life to happen. This is one of those moments, Harlow. If you go along with this, your entire life will change, and not like it did when you met me. We both know that marrying Patrick isn't who you are, or the life you want." His hands cupped my cheeks, and he pulled me to him. My headstrong resolve was no match for his lips on my face, his hands in my hair. With a panicked desperation, he begged, "If you need me to tell you that I forgive you, I do. I'll say whatever you want me to say. I just want to be with you." My hiatus of tears had ended, and my face was soaked in my confusion. "Marry me, Harlow. Marry me, and I promise you I'll love that baby, and I'll raise it as my own."

A manic and desperate kiss flowed between us, and for a fleeting moment, I believed the fantasy of his proposal. In the same brief span, I think he believed the delusion of my acceptance.

"Patrick's family would never let that happen. He would never agree to that."

"He or she?"

I stepped back. "I don't understand."

"You know exactly what I mean. Vivian. You're going to spend your entire life letting her make your decisions for you. You're going to take the easy way out, because you're too damn scared to stand up to her!"

"That's not fair."

"Fair?" he cried. "Are you kidding me? Do you think we're talking about fairness? Is that what you think this is? Do you think standing in front of the woman I love, begging her to marry me, is fair? Do you think it's easy to come here and face you? The way your mother has looked at me like I don't matter, the way she's talked about me—in front of me—like I wasn't there. Not to mention forbidding me from seeing you. To her, I'm just a blue-collar nobody, with a carpenter father and a bleeding-heart mother who can be bought off."

"Bought off?"

"This!" he screamed. He pulled a ripped-up check out of his pocket. The name on it was Vivian Ausby; the amount was fifty thousand dollars. "This is how much control you have over your life. This is how much we are worth. I may be cheap, but I'm sure as hell not for sale."

Disgust plunged so deep inside me, I felt as if my feet had swelled. I had to sit down on the Battery wall, for fear of stumbling over myself. "I didn't know she did that. I swear to you, Jade, I didn't know."

"I hadn't planned on raising a baby who isn't mine, but I'm willing to do that, because I want you. I want to be in this life with you. Don't think for one second that I think any of this is fair. That's life, though, and it's not always going to be fair."

He kneeled in front of me, grabbing my hands and putting my fingers to his lips. His eyes squeezed shut; his face said everything I didn't get to hear. His breath on my fingertips traveled all through me, and my objectivity melted away in the heat of my heartbreak.

"I have a hundred reasons to walk away from you, but all I need is for you to tell me to stay." He begged me as if he were haggling for his life. "You said you'd go anywhere with me. Here we are, and this is where I'm asking you to go."

This man was too good for me. He deserved his own life—one unattached to an Ausby—his own child, his own wife. To know that this man and his goodness were in the world would make bringing a child into it a little easier. I didn't deserve him, and he certainly deserved better than me. With a sound as soft as tearing paper, I answered him.

"I won't do that to you."

"Well, that's my choice. You don't get to decide who I love."

That was a sharp slap. It was the same thing I had once said to Mother. "No. Your whole life would become about me."

"It already is, Harlow!" His tears had started to spill. "I love you so much that I think it's killing me." He grabbed my hands and put them back to his face. "You love me. I know you do, and that love will last longer than time, go further than this life, because it's forever."

"I know that! Don't you think I know that? I'll have plenty of room for regret. But tying you to me, to this family, or to this baby won't be among those regrets."

"Don't do this." He whispered the words with palpable pain.

"I'm not a stupid woman, Jade. I know that what I feel for you only happens once. I'll never stop loving you, and the best way to show you is to let you go. It's about the only thing I can do."

"You don't have to do this. Please," he begged again, "don't do this to us."

With the only shred of composure I had left, I told him for the last time, "I love you, and I'm so sorry."

He sat down next to me, heavy and still on the concrete wall. With his elbows resting on his knees, his head collapsed into his hands. Tears fell in fat tendrils as he sobbed out the words, "Okay, that's all I've got. That's the best I can do."

I touched his face, sweeping his hair across his forehead and out of his eyes. Losing a love like this one was a pain that had teeth, and the silence that swallowed us was something close to a death.

A lifeless kiss passed between us, one almost as dead as I felt inside. I left him on the seawall that afternoon, in hopes that his love for me would turn to hatred—anything that would make going forward with his life easier.

I walked home alone. I climbed the house's ancient staircase, not bothering to take off my shoes. I drew the curtains, and then I climbed into bed, into a darkness so deep, it would take years to climb out of.

Chapter 17

ON THE DAY THE GRAPEVINE FASHIONED A NOOSE, THE McDade family paid us a visit. When I forced myself to go downstairs and greet them, I discovered that a wedding had been planned, and the future of my baby was next on the list. I had never felt like less of a person in my life.

Patrick's face, I was surprised to see, was a mangled mess.

"What happened to you?" I asked, shocked at the array of colors around his eyes.

He looked at the floor before answering. "I was mugged."

The adults went straight into a tizzy, speculating over the culprit. Each talked over the next, further enlarging an already big story, while Patrick continued to stand there, looking at the ground. Beth leaned against the doorway, her arms crossed sternly over her chest; the height of the antique corbels made her seem small. It was clear that she refused to participate in this shotgun catastrophe.

Mr. McDade purposefully cleared his throat to give Patrick the floor. If I hadn't been so numb about the night we apparently slept together, I might have felt sorry for him. Usually comfortable in his own righteousness, on this day, his chest did not puff, and his eyes did not gleam. Only a boy stood in front of me, a wilted and sorry little boy who had been shamed into obedience and was terrified of his future. This boy was supposed to be my husband, my child's father. My doubts about this boy were vast and thorough.

Mr. McDade was the type of man who did not doubt his own authority. He cleared his throat again, but this time the sound seemed more threatening. Patrick took a deep breath and stepped toward me. He didn't bother to take a knee, and I didn't care to ask him to.

"Harlow, considering our current circumstances, I think it best to get married. We already work together, and coincidentally, the business could stay a family gallery. I know this isn't what we had planned for ourselves, because life had a plan of its own, and now we have a baby to consider. I'm sure that over time we can learn to love each other, and I know a marriage will make our families very happy. So, what do you say?"

He held out the ring without asking me the question, which was fine, because I didn't want to hear it. Over the years, it would be something I held on to: the fact that he hadn't actually asked, and I hadn't answered. But since I had no specific gift for rebellion, we acted as though he had requested, and I had accepted.

"Hear, hear!" Mr. McDade cheered before Patrick had even taken my hand.

The whole time, I just stood there, frozen to the spot. Patrick slipped the cold metal ring onto my finger. It might as well have been a chain.

———

AS THE MONTHS STRETCHED, SO DID MY STOMACH. DESPITE MY reluctance, this baby was on her own schedule, and she would wait for no one. As the days ticked down, I noticed myself beginning to nest.

Even though I refused to attend any bridal showers, Vivian took it upon herself to register at all of the most coveted stores in Charleston, signing my name as the bride-to-be. The women at these shops swooned over her position as mother of the bride, and Vivian didn't ward off their admiration. I'm sure she didn't tell them that her daughter was pregnant or only twenty or not in love with the groom, or that she was in love with an entirely different man. I'm sure there was plenty she left out of the picture she painted of our glorious life South of Broad. It was a day she had waited for, her moment, her only moment. As I lived in my own denial, Mother had created a fantasy of her own, one that allowed her a glimpse of happiness.

Patrick and I had a small ceremony at the courthouse. The bright spot of that undesirable afternoon was Mother's miserable face. She got no glorious wedding, no bridesmaids or groomsmen, no showcase for her beauty—only an ordinary cake and a knocked-up bride. Beth offered to stab Patrick with the cake knife, and there was a part of me that truly thought she would do it. Her ability to make me laugh in spite of my despair was something that no one else even came close to having.

Patrick had moved into the main house, Mother into the carriage house—which was just as lavish. The intrusion of a man—let alone a husband I didn't love—took some getting used to. He was meticulous and orderly and detached from our life together. On the nights when I could escape into the darkness, into the fantasy of finding Jade again, I accepted Patrick's advances and pictured Jade's face while Patrick sweated and grunted on top of me. It was the type of sex that I had been taught was expected of a wife, the kind that a wife submitted to out of necessity, not the kind I had been shown that night on the beach. On the nights when I couldn't stomach the charade, I found Jade anyway. His memory was in the comfort of our rocking chair, his something to remember him by.

The gallery was a refuge for Patrick—for both of us—and I was never sad to see him go in the morning. He threw himself into his work, and I worked hard not to think about throwing myself over the second-floor piazza. Not that I would have done it, but even trying would have been a waste of time, as Beth never left me alone. I had told her that spending time with me might drive her mad. She replied that she couldn't think of a better way to go insane. I needed someone—she knew that—and I was glad she was that someone.

"How will I ever breathe again?" I asked her on a not-so-good day.

"Shallow at first, and then one day, you'll take a deep breath, inhaling all of the goodness around you. You'll cry when it hurts, laugh when it's funny, and love deeper than you ever imagined you could. When it comes to your child, your soul is bottomless."

"How do you know?" I asked.

"Even though she is a part of him, she is a part of you too. By instinct alone, you'll give her the very best of you."

I could only hope she was right.

━━━━━━━━

DOWNTOWN WAS CHANGING. VACANT HISTORICAL HOMES WERE being bought up and turned into hotels and bed-and-breakfasts, and gradually, as Charleston beckoned more tourists, so too did it beckon the artists who discovered our little gem of a gallery shining in the French Quarter. Patrick had an extraordinary eye for art. He scored big on some influential artists, and after turning on the Southern charm people seemed to revel in, he made the gallery a huge success.

Atlanta, Chicago, even New York: all vied to be first in line to purchase pieces from our new collection. Patrick, as it turned out, was the enterprising businessman he was supposed to be, and he played the part perfectly. That *aw shucks* Southern drawl was an unassuming mask that disguised his lying blue eyes. As the money rolled in, I rolled up, tighter and tighter, bearing down for this baby.

I passed through the days like a shadow. The only noticeable difference between them was my belly. Truth be told, I thought a miracle would save me, red and thick like on the morning I had awoken to find that my virginity had disappeared. If ever there was a moment for God to step in, it was now. I prayed He would take her before she was born. But praying for her death to the God who had given her life tangled and squeezed me in confusing sorrow. I can still taste that guilt to this day.

———————

WITH ORANGE WISPS AND PORCELAIN SKIN, MY BABY WAS PERFECT. How could something so innocent start from something so wicked, I wondered. Evie McDade clenched her fists and emptied her lungs with a cry so mighty, my own tears fell. As the doctor put her to my chest, she turned her slits of eyes to me in recognition. She knew me, and although I hadn't thought of it before, I already knew her too. It was the only moment in my life when I can remember the world stopping and time standing still. It was also the day when I became grateful for unanswered prayers.

Her energy, I quickly learned, was extraordinary. She slept hard, woke early, and ate at a rate faster than I could produce. In those early months, as well as through the years, Beth was a godsend, never wavering to exhaustion, and always quick with the love that kept her gingers afloat. That Mother rarely spent time with Evie left me at a loss. Yet Beth's compassion for a granddaughter who wasn't her own lifted me, and I felt that we could not be dropped.

For a time, I tried to swim upstream, but after only a few years, my arms became tired, my legs weak, and my heart a nonparticipant in the game. The barrier between Patrick and me was thin at first, but it thickened with the years, until I finally surrendered to it. Love can push you in ways you never knew you could go—mine was forward. Even on the days when I thought I had nothing left, my love for my daughter gave me a little shove and kept me moving.

From a certain angle, we were picture perfect. The wife, the husband, the darling redheaded baby girl—two old families from Charleston, merging in wealth and power. I think we played the

170

part perfectly. The only thing lacking between us was what would have made the illusion real, but neither truth nor love could be conjured from thin air, and neither Patrick nor I was willing to work for either of them.

Was I happy? Being a mother made me happy, and when I was with Evie and Beth, I was happy. The hours spent with those two gave me pure and uncompromised joy. Wife, mother, homemaker, peacemaker: I became what I was raised to be. When Evie turned five and started elementary school, the days became long. I thought I missed her—and I did—but really, I missed myself. The days gave me enough time to wonder. I had more of a choice in my life than I had initially led myself to believe. I know that now. But it was easier to blame Mother than to take responsibility for my choices. I'd told myself that I was doing Jade a favor by pushing him away, but he had been right, and I was just scared. I thought that if I just kept my head down and did the work, I wouldn't miss looking up. I was right for a time, but eventually the truth found me.

I tried to wish Jade out of my mind, but he was always there, waiting for me in the darkness. More and more frequently, I pulled his memory up into the light. I didn't want to let him go, and as the years went on, I wasn't able to. The summer I met Jade, I was old enough to be educated, but still young enough to be ignorant. He was a part of my past, and my inability to let him go made him a part of my present. I couldn't imagine a future that didn't hold at least the idea of him.

I'd be a liar if I didn't admit to asking myself questions with no answers through the years. What would it have been like if I hadn't gotten pregnant, if I hadn't had her? What if she hadn't come with Patrick? I hated myself for those thoughts, but I had them. I often thought about the life I'd left behind, but as the years passed, one thing became clear: I gladly would have traded my life for my daughter's. Unlike the blaring purple birthmark that ran down my leg, Evie wasn't my flaw, but my purpose.

PART FOUR
NOW

,

7:00 a.m.

A drizzling rain tapped the windows just beyond the slanted shades of Mother's hospital room. Three hours of sleep was five too little, and my body instantly protested upon waking. Whether it was because of the finality of the divorce, the refracturing of an already broken heart, or the gala looming ahead of me, just swinging my legs out from under the covers pulled my body in a way that it didn't want to move. I always dreaded waking up from my dreams—the only place Jade came to me. Sideways, backwards, made up, and real, I could count on him to show up and meet me there.

Still comfortable in the fantasy of Jade Ryan, I struggled to hang on to the memories of us. Yet the more I opened my eyes, the more the fantasy evaporated into the daylight. The tighter I tried to hang on to each memory, the harder they were to grasp. My memories of the dream—flimsy and vague—slipped away.

Usually a creature of dutiful habit, I took a moment to realize that I wasn't going to start my fourth decade in another fruitless mental state. This wasn't an ah-ha, explosive decision. The thought just came to me, and I accepted it. It was strange, yet ordinary. Once the notion struck me, my body moved just fine.

Beth lay motionless under the weight of sleep, and I envied her dream state. Quietly, I grabbed my purse and eased the door closed, happy to let her rest. The gala would take a toll on us both. At least one of us would be rested.

With the Ashley River in my rearview, I made my way home. The earlier rain was now a distant memory, the fog had lifted, and a windshield sunrise highlighted the morning tides along the harbor. I relished driving through the peaceful city, before the traffic coagulated. I enjoyed the stillness of this Charleston. It wasn't often that you caught her sleeping. Charleston is a city of many masks, and this was the most beautiful of them all.

Color bled from every angle of the city. It reflected in boutique storefront windows, it overflowed from the orderly flower boxes that spilled lemon cypress and blue-tinged violas, and it was even in the rivers where the Ashley and the Cooper collided. Sunrise in Charleston was a moment time wanted to hold, and sometimes I understood why.

I sat in my car long after I had put it in park. I had gone through these same motions thousands of times in my life, and I had taken every one of them for granted. Selfishly, I had always assumed that my car would be parked on this street, that the porch would hold the rocking chairs I couldn't stop buying, and that the doorbell would sing only to me. The shame of losing the home that had been in my family for generations was beyond what I could accept. Had I been more of a participant in my own life, maybe I wouldn't have screwed it up so badly.

I opened the front door to the smell of divorce and betrayal and lessons in sin. As I placed my purse on the entry table, I saw a Birkin bag I recognized. She was there. Lexi Pratt had stayed the night in my family's Queen Anne home. Her fingerprints were probably all over the handrail. I bet she hadn't taken her shoes off before climbing the stairs, either.

Patrick strung together a display of disgusting snorts and hacks so loud that I heard them clearly from downstairs. They were there. I was there. I panicked, so I made coffee. I told myself that it was for me, but I wasn't kidding anyone. It wasn't in my nature not to share. Obviously.

Each floorboard groaned under the weight of Patrick's footsteps coming down the stairs. I heard him tying a double knot in the belt of his robe, something he had done every morning since the first one I had woken up to with him. I hated that sound.

Not one to show his emotional cards, only a slight eyebrow raise indicated his surprise at finding me in *his* kitchen.

"Harlow," he stated, taking the mug I had gotten for myself and filling it with the coffee I had made. "I told you the house wouldn't be empty until the weekend. You can come back and pack your things then."

"I can't believe you let her stay here, Patrick. Mother isn't gone yet. Her body isn't cold, but yours certainly is. I would appreciate it if she didn't come back here."

"Well, Harlow, I couldn't give a shit about what you do or don't appreciate. We're divorced, and all of this belongs to me now. You can thank your bitch mother for that. Jesus, you're so pathetic. She cut you out of her will, left you absolutely nothing. That's how much she cares about you. If I want to have thirty women stay the night here, and if I want to sleep with every last one of them, it's my business. You are no longer my wife, and this is no longer your house."

"How dare you. You've humiliated me for years in front of our family and friends. You parade around town with Lexi Pratt—and God knows who else. You were supposed to become a fine man, but standing in my house, telling me to get out so you can make room for your next girlfriend, you are nothing you were supposed to be. You are nothing but a disappointment."

"Wait just a second there, darling," he snarled. "I did what I was told to do. I never wanted to marry you, any more than you wanted to marry me. One night changed our entire lives. I've done my time, I've served my sentence, and I've paid more than what I deserved."

"I should have loved myself with the wasted effort I put into you and this disastrous marriage. I gave up the love of my life to make us a family."

"Should've, could've, and would've. You do what everyone tells you to do, and even that you seem to screw up. Give me a break with the Jade Ryan speech. It's been twenty years, Harlow. You don't even know him anymore. You don't even know who you are, and you never did."

I was floored that he had spoken to me that way, though what he said didn't surprise me. He wasn't entirely wrong, and he wasn't finished, either.

"You even managed to fuck up fucking," he continued. "For the time that we dated, you shot down my advances, but only a few months with Jade Ryan and you were ready to give him everything I had worked for. He didn't even have to try to get you into bed. You were happy to give it up to him when you thought he was with you in the carriage house."

A chill ran down my spine. "I don't know what you're talking about. Jade and I were never in the carriage house. I haven't been in there since…" Suddenly I couldn't breathe. The thoughts that took ahold seemed to strangle me. Tears filled my eyes, as if my body knew why I should cry, and my mind had been waiting on permission.

I knew what he had done. I had always known what he had done. I was just too ashamed to admit it to myself, until that moment with Patrick in the kitchen.

"Save your pathetic schoolgirl act, Harlow. You said some pretty raunchy things that night. Now that we're divorced, a little tip: your next husband would appreciate that kind of enthusiasm in the bedroom. Having sex with a corpse tends to make a man stray."

"You bastard!" I screamed, dropping my coffee mug to shatter on the floor. "You raped me. How could you do that?" As though a strange fit had come over me, I couldn't stop blinking. With each thought, my eyelids shuddered and my face twitched, as if a seizure would help me find the right words. "You did that out of spite because I loved someone else?"

Lightning flashed in his eyes, and thunder raged in his voice. "I took what was mine, what I had worked for! You came onto me like some fucking maniac, more than happy to give it up. Our families wanted us to be together, and I was the one who made sure that happened."

"You put something in that glass of wine. You drugged me!" The thought swiftly hit me, almost knocking me over. "And you drugged that tourist, that girl in high school. You raped her, too. How many times have you done this? How many girls? Jesus Christ, Patrick, you're an honest-to-God criminal. I'm going to the police. You're going to pay for what you did."

His eyes blackened like two stones, and his anger registered in the snarl that set upon his thin lips. "She wanted it, and so did you. I gave you everything over the years, and you didn't appreciate a goddamned bit of it."

How could I have let this go for so many years? I was just as disgusted with myself as I was with Patrick. What would my daughter think of me? How could I ever face her? Patrick had laid me down that night to make sure I never stood up to him again, so I'd know my place. He just hadn't counted on making a baby.

I looked at him with more than perfect hatred. "You took something that was only mine to give. You took something that was meant for someone else. YOU STOLE MY LIFE!"

"I did what you asked me to do!"

"You're blaming me? I didn't know what I was saying. I was drugged! You're a criminal and a sociopath. You're sick! I feel so sorry for Evie."

"You're the one who turned her against me."

"No, Patrick, you did that all by yourself. There's only one rule in parenting, and it's very simple: show up. You never did."

"How could I, when I've always been the one to keep everything together? I brought your family's gallery back to life after Vivian started blowing through money we didn't have. I paid the bills, bought you that Lexus, all the clothes, the parties, the private schooling for Evie. Who the hell was going to pay for all that? Not you, pining away for some fucking carpenter."

"God, Patrick, don't you think I could feel it? Feel that on some level, something was wrong between us? I was never going to be anything but a corpse in your arms. I've spent years blaming myself for that night, hating myself for hurting Jade. You're the most awful person I've ever met, and I can't believe my daughter has the misfortune to share your genes."

He picked up his coffee mug and took a sip. Though he would never admit it, I knew he was contemplating my rightness, acknowledging the truth of what I had said.

He seemed to shake off any remorse that had the potential to penetrate him. "It doesn't matter now. That was forever ago. The house, the business, the money—all of it is mine. As far as what happens to you now, I couldn't say, because it's not my business. But from where I'm standing, you're fucked."

I took off running toward the stairs. Deciding what to take wasn't hard, when nothing belonged to me anymore. There was only one thing I wanted inside that house, and it was hidden away in the top drawer of my dresser.

When I pushed the bedroom door open, Lexi jumped, pulling the covers tight to her chin. Her face was covered in tears, and unwashed mascara from the night before had created a black mask across her cheeks. It was apparent that she had heard our conversation.

"Did you get all that downstairs?" I asked her. "Scared? Yeah, you should be. That was a nice little preview of your future. If I were you, I'd get as far away from Patrick McDade as possible, as quickly as possible. Otherwise you'll end up with a baby in your belly and no recollection of how it got there."

She burst into a sob when I mentioned a baby. My only assumption was that there was already one in there. I pitied her and the life she had wasted on Patrick, the future she would waste even more. Naked in my bed, she continued to cry as I wildly threw clothes out of the drawers, careless as to where they landed.

Patrick came bounding up the stairs, yelling, "Don't listen to her, Lexi! She's a liar. I love you!"

"Where is it?" I screamed at Patrick. "Where is my picture?"

He sat on the bed trying to console Lexi, but she kicked and punched him away through the covers, screaming at him to never touch her again.

"I burned that stupid picture!" he finally yelled at me. "Threw it in the fireplace and watched the heat eat away your stupid smug faces."

That picture of Jade and me had gotten me through some incredibly hard times. Even though the color had leeched away from the edges, and the hairline wrinkles had turned into deep creases, I still saw it as though for the first time, every time. It had become a part of me, and it was a crushing blow to know that part of me was gone.

While Patrick and Lexi continued to argue, I shoved some clothes into a bag. I scanned the closet and grabbed the first dress I saw. It would have to do for the gala.

There was only one place that made me feel as good as that picture did, and it would take me twenty-four minutes to drive there. Not that it would make any difference now, but he had to know the truth. I had spent twenty years under a blanket of guilt, and it was time to throw it off.

8:00 a.m.

JUST BECAUSE I WAS SOFT DIDN'T MEAN I WAS STUPID. THERE was eight grand in our joint bank account—plus more in another that I apparently didn't have privilege to—and I took all of it in the form of hundred-dollar bills. He had everything else, including a new family, and I didn't suppose he would make a stink about eight thousand dollars. Besides, that was pocket change compared to what Mother had left him in her will.

As I processed the totality of our disastrous marriage, an inkling of guilt reared into my thoughts. *I should have stopped him that night. I should have stopped this marriage before it ever started*, I scolded myself. But then I quickly redirected with a new voice that I hadn't heard in some time, maybe ever. *No, I'm not doing this to myself anymore. Not ever again. I'm done breaking; I might not even bend.*

If only for today, I decided to let the fault lie with others. Patrick said that he had done his time with me. So had I, with the burden of guilt. As I walked out of the bank with a duffle bag full of cash, the rebellion washed over me, and for a moment, I thought some of it might have actually seeped in.

Back along the Ashley River, the traffic was at a standstill. The sun was now high, yet the city streets were still slick from the rain-soaked morning. I took a moment to really look out over the harbor, and my heart fluttered inside me like the breeze against the tides. It was as if I were seeing this world for the first time. Maybe going to see him was a fool's errand, but that wouldn't stop me from running it. To understand that our past was unchangeable was one thing, but to know that it wasn't entirely my fault was something completely different.

As I crossed the last bridge into Folly Beach, the scents of the Atlantic rose like a saltwater gospel. The Charleston bustle shifted into the slumber of Folly. Air was easier to breathe, shade stretched a little farther, and the sun's passage seemed to slow. People moved there either to forget or to be forgotten, and the pace of life was so measured that it was possible to do both.

The long dirt road welcomed me, as it had so many times before. Some of my most valuable lessons had been learned at the end of that dirt road. I parked the car in the empty gravel lot. The store didn't open for another thirty minutes, so I got out and walked around.

The main house hadn't changed in twenty years—and neither had the smells. The scents of lemon varnish and sawed wood enveloped me, and I could feel him there. His hands on the small of my back, his breath easy in my ear. I noticed that I was smiling.

A shadowed figure turned the sign from closed to open inside the general store. The porch protested as I made my way up the stairs, and the bell on the door gave a friendly ring upon my entrance. The morning light shone in through the double-paned windows, highlighting shelves of miniature rocking chairs in a rainbow of colors. Baskets of hand-picked vegetables sat in orderly rows, each with a two-for-one or five-for-three tag attached. A box fan whirled to life in a distant room, threatening to drown out the sound of coins being dropped into a register. I was the only customer in the store.

She seemed to be the one thing in the store that time had grabbed ahold of. Her brow was much more furrowed, her hair now a thick pad of silver. Although she had aged—we both had—she still commanded a presence that her homestead seemed to respect. My heels announced my arrival at the front desk, but she didn't look up.

"Hello," I said. "I'm sorry if I'm intruding, but the sign said that y'all are open."

"We are." Her voice was even and unenthusiastic.

"I'm not sure if you remember me, Mrs. Ryan. My name is Harlow McDade."

Her sight remained unmoved from the task of filling the register. She still didn't look up as she spoke. "Oh, I remember a lot of things, and I certainly remember you."

My hands began to sweat. She made no attempt at friendliness. She didn't even lift her head as she continued, although her eyes met mine. "I remember plenty about you. You're the reason I don't have any grandchildren, and why my son doesn't have a wife. You're the reason he stayed here for so long, and you also happen to be the reason he's now gone. I couldn't possibly forget you, Harlow, although I wish I could."

Her words were sharp, and standing in front of the counter, I felt like a child taking a lashing for stealing candy, or something equally bad. Shrinking in confidence and stature by the second, I didn't know if she expected me to reply. I was confused and ashamed, and I didn't know if I should turn and leave or continue to take my punishment. I did what came naturally and reached into my bag of Southern guilt; I went straight to the apology.

"I'm sorry, ma'am. I didn't mean to cause your family harm. I loved your son."

Placing her hand on the counter, she then looked ready to fight. "Yeah, well, you sure do have a funny way of showing it. Is that how y'all do love South of Broad?"

"I should go."

"Yes, you should go. You should go and never come back. What you did to him was unforgivable. Had Beth raised you, none of us would be in this position, but Vivian Ausby and her hoity-toity, rich-bitch attitude ruined you—just like she tried to do to Beth, and everyone else who comes out of that holier-than-thou city."

I had no idea what she was talking about. "I'm sorry? You must be mistaken."

"I don't make mistakes, and my memory is long and wide. Go ask your mother."

"I can't do that. She's dying. She's been in a coma for weeks."

"I can't say I'm sorry about that. She certainly made her own bed, and it's only fair that she die in it. But I'm not talking about your grandmother, Vivian. I'm talking about your mother, Beth." Although her delivery was methodic, her face contorted, as though she had unleashed a secret that had torn and clawed at her insides to get out.

I backed away from the register, unwilling to absorb her words. She didn't know what she was talking about; she couldn't. My hands fumbled with the doorknob. I couldn't get out of there fast enough. I opened the door with such force that it violently hit the opposing wall. The once-cheery bell made a dying sound as it fell from the hinges and dropped to the floor. The air was thick in my throat, and my mind swirled with a thousand memories as I walked back to my car. I didn't know which were real, or whom to believe. I got in but just sat there, unsure of my ability to drive.

A knock on my window made me jump. His face displayed an embarrassed sorrow, and he motioned for me to roll down the window. When I just sat there staring at him, he opened my door. His voice was gentle, and the sight of him made me miss my daddy.

"Harlow, I'm Walter Ryan, Jade's dad. I'm not sure if you remember me."

"Of course I remember. You look so much like Jade."

"Yeah, we get that a lot. I'd like to show you something, if you'll come with me. I have something that belongs to you."

On autopilot, I got out of the car and followed him toward the side entrance of the staining barn. A group of teenaged girls intently watched us as they ate breakfast together on the screened-in porch of the main house. Another girl filled drinks with one hand while carrying a baby in another. Every belly at that table was filled with much more than food. They were all young, and they were all pregnant.

Mr. Ryan walked me to a free-standing structure no bigger than a shack. Like everything on the property, it was well built. He paused before unlocking a dead-bolted door. The slight shaking of his head suggested he had plenty to say, but his silence told me how unsure he was of the starting point. Crinkles appeared at the corners of his green eyes; they were identical to the ones I had fallen in love with as a girl. Jade was certainly his father's son, and just being near Mr. Ryan made me ache for my time spent with his son.

"I'm sorry about what my wife said back in the store. She's hurting, and you were a perfect target for her pain."

"I don't understand."

"I don't suppose you do, but it's probably time that we finally start talking about it. I think it's the only way for any of us to heal."

"Yes, sir," I agreed, although I had no idea what I was agreeing to.

A suctioning sound escaped with the opening of the door, and the doorway exhaled a sigh of air-conditioned mustiness. As orderly as the shelves in the general store and workshop, the room held racks of paintings. Beautiful and ornate hand-carved wooden frames sat in uncluttered rows against the walls. Each painting was held steady by wooden dowels, so the frames wouldn't topple over like dominos if one were to accidentally shift.

Moving farther into the space, I ran my finger along the edges of the frames. I was desperate to pull one out and look at the painting it housed, but too mannerly to overstep my bounds. I nervously waited for an invitation. Walter Ryan must have sensed my anxiety. It was the first time I saw him smile.

"Do you know what this place is?" he asked. "Yes, it's a woodworking factory," he continued without waiting for a response, "and yes, we make rocking chairs. But do you know the real purpose of the homestead?"

I thought back to the girls I had seen picking vegetables the first time Jade invited me there. Although that was twenty years ago, they were the same type of girls who sat outside this hidden art gallery, eating breakfast.

"Jade once told me there are girls who stay here because they have nowhere else to go. They work at the homestead in exchange for a warm bed. He never told me more than that, though. Now that I'm seeing it for myself, I assume these girls are the real reason for this place."

Nodding in agreement, he said, "That's right. The homestead didn't start out that way, but this is how it's changed over the years. Despite what you encountered today, my wife's heart is suited for much more than rocking chairs. She will always love her son, but the girls who come and stay with us are her heart. They come here with nothing but shirts on their backs and babies in their bellies, and with the right amount of care and financial stability, they go on to begin their lives. But for my wife, they never really leave. She remembers them all, and she feels as though they become a part of her."

I thought of Jade's tattoos dedicated to the girls who had stayed there. Going by the amount of ink on his arm, this place had held many girls, many hearts. "That's a very noble quality, Mr. Ryan," I replied, "but I don't see what that has to do with me, and why your wife thinks Beth Chaney is my mother."

He paused again, rubbing the thick beard around his jawline. "Well, because she is. Besides being your mother, she is also an alum of the homestead." He moved down the narrow pathway of picture frames, stopping at the back of the room. The veins popped from his leathered hands as he gently slid a portrait out from between a set of dowels.

All he had to do was turn it around. After that, no words were needed.

The painting was oil and acrylic on canvas, the brushstrokes barely visible, and the likeness exact. The subject was a three-year-old ginger with all the time in the world; her only concern was how to get that wooden swing to go higher. Her dress was covered in white smocking, and the sunset behind her was the color of fresh blood. It was painted more intricately than the real photograph, the one visitors commented on, the one Jade had said was beautiful—the one that still hung above the credenza in the vestibule of my family home.

There was a signature in red paint at the bottom, against the beige strokes of tall winter grasses. When I inspected it more closely, the tears came with a vengeance. Bessie London was the artist of that beautiful painting of me. From my obsession with a book I had been given twenty years ago, by a man I had never stopped loving, I knew that Bessie London was Jack London's wife.

And I knew the curves and flows of that signature. Beth was the artist of this fine painting, and she had taken the alias Bessie London.

The day at the beach came roaring back to me, our conversation as clear as it was when Jade told me. Beth was the woman who had taught him about art, who had helped raise him and introduced him to the stories of Jack London. I was the baby that had grown in her belly and was then given away. All those times Jade told me he had waited for me, that he had loved me his entire life—those weren't just the admissions of a lovestruck boy. He was being literal. Jade had known me before I was even born. My mind swirled with conjured images, and every beat of my heart felt like a tiny explosion inside my chest. I thought I might pass out.

Walter Ryan put his hand on my arm comfortingly.

I stuttered, "I don't even know what to say. Obviously, this is a shock to me. Are all these paintings by her?"

"There used to be a lot more, but she sold most of them."

My interest was piqued. "To whom?"

"A man came to the homestead one day years ago, asking for her. We don't take kindly to uninvited strangers—our customers are close to family—but he said he knew you and promised he could bring you and Beth together again. He also wanted to buy some of her paintings. Beth left that same day to go back to Charleston, and then got a job working for Vivian not long after—most assuredly, to be with you."

"Can you tell me why Beth was here to begin with, or who she was running from?"

"I think that's a conversation you need to have with Beth. I've already said too much. You can tell her that I'm keeping her paintings safe for her."

"Thank you, Mr. Ryan. I will." I turned to go, but I couldn't leave without knowing. "Mrs. Ryan said that Jade doesn't have a wife, but I know for certain he's married."

Walter looked at me with the wisdom of age and the gentleness of a father. "In Jade's case, a marriage license is created with a signature of the hand, but a wife comes with the signature of a heart. There's a big difference between the two."

"Do you know where he is, or when he'll be back?"

"Harlow, he won't be back, not this time. I don't suppose he'd make the same mistake twice. You'd better be going; I need to check on my wife. But the painting is all yours. It always has been, and you're welcome to take it with you."

As he put the picture in the back of my car, he said, "I'm sure I've caused you a bit of trouble, but even secrets this deep don't always stay buried." He paused before he spoke again. "Before you do anything rash or say something to Beth that you can't take back, you should know that she always loved you. She loved you enough to give you a better life, and for her that meant surrendering to the terms of it. Please, give my love to Beth, and tell her how happy I am that you two found each other."

"I will. Thank you for telling me, Mr. Ryan. I don't know how I can repay you."

"You just have a happy birthday, and we'll call it even."

10:00 a.m.

THE CLOUDS HAD BEGUN TO GRAY AGAIN. THE WEATHER seemed as mixed up as I was. But on my drive back to the hospital, I refused to accept the impending darkness. Through sheer will, I forced my way through a lifetime of unstable memories. As the clouds swallowed the late-morning light, Charleston looked different now, altered somehow. Though perhaps what had changed was me.

I parked my car in long-term parking. I had to see the painting again. Unveiled upon the opening of the tailgate, the colors exploded inside the car's dark interior. The painting had been created by hands of immeasurable talent. Hands, I supposed, that I was part of, and that were part of me. I wasn't who I thought I was.

Glancing back into my memories and freely rummaging through the thoughts and feelings of my half-self felt like a violation. Even though I had surely created those memories, were they even mine? Did they still belong to me? My mind was trapped in a half-told truth, my body in a semi-lie. All that I had known to be true, my foundation, my core: Because it was a lie, was I a lie too?

Beth sat on the edge of Mother's bed, a banker's box beside her. As I entered the room, she dropped the pictures she was holding back into the box. She turned to look at me, and the wideness of her eyes was telling of her fears. Like a scared little rabbit, her shoulders were slumped, and her bottom lip quivered. She braced herself for the unknown. We both did.

"I went to the Ryans' homestead this morning."

"Yes," Beth said. "Walter Ryan called me. Harlow—"

I put my hand up to stop her. "Right now, it's my turn to talk."

She nodded her head in submission. Her eyes filled slowly, but her expression remained braced. She watched me scan the paintings around the room.

"Did you paint all these pictures?" I asked. "Is that why they're here?"

"They were done years ago, but yes, they're my work. It was part of Vivian's wishes to have them here with her at the end. She thought they would force me to tell you the truth."

Waist-deep in Mother's antics, I had assumed that Beth was the keeper of the secret, not the enforcer.

"What is the truth?"

Her voice was strangled, and I wasn't sure if she was actually breathing. "I'm your birth mother, and Vivian is your grandmother, my mother. I have bite marks on my tongue from every time I wanted to tell you, and for a time it was all I could think about. The longer I waited, the harder it became, and eventually I knew I would just hurt you by telling you. So I resigned myself to wait for this day, your fortieth birthday."

The chaise I had slept on the night before was still covered in wrinkled sheets. I sat down in the middle of the chaos to think.

"Why today? What's so special about me turning forty?"

She handed me an envelope. The handwriting across the front was unmistakably Mother's. "This will explain so much, answer so many questions you might have."

"I don't want to read about my life in a letter! Wasn't forty years enough time to think about what you'd say to me? Don't you think you've had long enough with the truth? Why don't you start with that—with the truth? With why. With how. With all the information that makes up a person, the story that tells them who they are and where they came from. Don't you dare pawn this off on a letter. I'm worth more than that paper, and I deserve the truth."

By the time I had finished scolding her, Beth was in the throes of a shoulder-shaking sob. Sputtering word fragments, mixed with deep breaths and hitches in her throat, tumbled out in an unrecognizable mess. Despite my anger, my heart hurt for her. Watching someone come undone of their own doing was difficult. She was still Beth, still my confidante and cheerleader. I moved next to her and took her hand. It was the same hand as yesterday, as the day before that, as the one I had always remembered.

In the most intrusive but delightful way, the thought hit me. As a young girl, night after night I had prayed, watering the seeds of my prayers with tears, with hope, and with the purity of a delicate heart. Where there had been the shadows of Mother's coldness, there had also been the warmth of Beth's light.

All these years, Beth had been the answer to my prayer. I had wanted a mother exactly like her, and the truth was, I had one. Maybe the journey wasn't the exact one I would have chosen, but she had been with me all this time. *Why is that something to feel bad about now?* I wondered.

Wiping her eyes with the sleeve of her shirt had left a trail of black under her lids. She looked so ridiculous that I couldn't help but stifle a laugh.

Confused, she looked up at me and asked, "Why are you laughing?"

I corrected her. "I'm not laughing. I'm holding it in."

"No you're not. I can clearly hear you covering a laugh. This isn't funny."

Her getting mad only made me laugh openly.

"Stop!" she cried in confusion, throwing her tissue on the floor with force. "This is serious, Harlow. I lied to you for a long time."

I pulled in a deep breath. "Thank you," I said. "I needed that laugh, as well as the truth. And I've always needed you."

The tears that filled my eyes came not from sadness but joy. A life that I felt had gone wrong had suddenly righted itself. And although some things ended that day, the second half of my life began. To her surprise, I pulled her close to me and hugged her hard, holding her tighter than ever before. For forty years, I'd been searching for the feeling of rightness that came with her embrace, the feeling you could only find in the arms of your mother.

A continuous smile spread across both of our faces, followed by a deep sigh, and then the same giggle.

Beth spoke first. "You can ask me anything. I'll tell you everything you want to know."

"Okay," I said, readying myself with a slow blink and another breath. "Daddy will always be my daddy. No matter the circumstances, I refuse to think of him any other way. But who is my biological father?"

Beth seemed to smile at the passing image of his face in her mind. I knew that smile. It was one I had so often, thinking of Jade.

"He was a wonderful boy—but just a boy. We were so young. He was the love of my life, but he died right after we found out that I was pregnant with you."

"I'm sorry. That must have been hard for you."

She patted my hand with a faraway look in her eyes. "Yes." She nodded. "It was hard, but I'm grateful for the time we had together, grateful for the gift he gave me: you."

"How did he pass?"

"It was an allergic reaction to wasp stings. Can you believe that?" she asked, though she didn't wait for a reply. "It was during the spring, and he was hosing the pollen off the porch of a neighbor's home. He destroyed the wasps' nest, and the wasps took his life. So strange. Such an ordinary thing, to get stung by a wasp. It was an accident, just a stupid accident. Despite that fact, he was still gone, and I knew I wasn't what was best for a child."

"How did you end up at the homestead? I thought it was only for girls in trouble, girls running from something."

"Oh, I was the definition of trouble. I ran all right, but funny thing about that was, I never could seem to get away from myself. It's probably the reason I always liked Savannah so much; she reminded me of myself. It's also the reason that I respected you more than I ever let on. You're so much stronger than I ever was."

"What do you mean?"

"People can act evil, but that doesn't mean there isn't any good in them. Vivian used to be a whole lot sweeter in her younger days. I'm the one who made her hard. In her defense, she just wasn't ready for me. She came from a time when parents weren't questioned, and rules weren't broken. I think she was nineteen before she ever sassed her own parents. She had no clue that the earth could create a child with such will, such independence, and the stamina for both."

"You're always so composed. It's hard to imagine you so reckless."

She threw her head back in laughter. "Lord, I was, though. Vivian and I have always been opposites. She was like you before my teenaged years: quiet, mannerly, and always beautiful. But I just didn't want what she wanted. I didn't want to be told who I was going to be. Like a typical teenager, I thought I knew the world, and the parts I didn't, I wanted to go find out about. I didn't get very far, though. It turns out that you need money to see the world, and to have a baby at eighteen years old. I tried to come home, but it didn't work out."

"She didn't let you stay there?" I asked intently.

"Oh, goodness, Harlow, it was quite the opposite. She did everything in her power to try to make me stay, but I didn't much care for rules, and I didn't have any intention of following them." Beth looked hard at me. "It was all me. I'm the one who screwed up, because that's what I did best. We all make choices in life, and the hardest part is living with them. I chose to give you a better life, and I had to surrender to the terms of that choice. I always screwed everything up. I wasn't going to let that happen to you.

"I knew about the Ryans' homestead from one of Vivian's charity projects. Her cocktail ladies-who-lunch friends held an auction to raise money for those girls. With me being pregnant, she made me go with her to deliver the proceeds check. She thought she would be teaching me a lesson in gratitude; she just didn't realize how quickly I learned. I fell in love with the place, and also with the little boy who ran amuck there."

"Jade," I whispered, not even needing to ask.

"Yes," she said, smiling through her answer. "That same day, I told Vivian that I wasn't going back to Charleston. I was an indignant and selfish girl, and I ruined things, Harlow. I ruined people, ruined relationships, and I couldn't ruin you too. I knew the best thing for you was to be raised in Charleston by your grandparents, who had a grand amount of love for us both. Trust wasn't something I had in myself—not with someone as important as you. Vivian and Daddy wanted to tell you the truth several times, and they tried everything in their power to get me to come back. Daddy opened the art gallery in hopes that it would entice me. After being shot down so many times, Mother went her own route. She purchased the Ryans' homestead when they defaulted on their mortgage. At first I thought Mother bought the homestead out of viciousness, but now I think it was the only way she knew how to stay connected to me. She did the wrong thing for what she thought was the right reason. She's owned it all this time, and Mrs. Ryan has never forgiven her for it."

Of course.

"That's why Mrs. Ryan was so cold to me," I said. "I remember the first time I met her, she couldn't get me off her property fast enough. She probably thought something entirely different was happening that day. She didn't hate me—well, maybe she did—but she was definitely scared of me. I suspect she's just been waiting all this time for the other shoe to drop."

Beth looked at me. "It's scary to live with such a secret." Though her words were small, they felt giant.

"Yes, ma'am," I agreed. "It is."

"I need you to understand something. Just because I gave you up did not mean that I didn't love you. I cried myself to sleep for months, driving myself mad, wondering if I had made the right decision. As I watched you grow, through the pictures and videos Vivian sent me, I knew I had done right by you. I never could have given you the life you deserved. So I went to school concerts, dance recitals, even your high school graduation, but always in the shadow of the crowds. In your younger days, I took Jade with me to give him a new experience. As you got older, though, he began asking to come with me, and I couldn't have stopped him from seeing you even if I'd tried."

She grinned as she spoke of the past. The memories surfaced in the sparkle of her eye, the depth of her smile.

Her story soaked into me. I pictured the images and adopted them as my own truth. It was something to be old enough to be told the story of your life, the one that happens before your memories insist on something entirely different.

The colors in the paintings lined against the wall enveloped me and wrapped me in warmth, just as Beth had on the day I was born, as she always had, even from afar. In contrast to the starkness of Vivian, a misunderstood woman, Beth had brought color to my life. I got up to examine the art more carefully. Turning the smallest canvas around in my hands, I inspected its back. Forgeries are scandalous, yet not uncommon. With talent, any piece—like all of these in the hospital room—can be forged into an astonishing replica. I never would have been able to recognize these paintings as fakes. But when you know what to look for, the back of a painting is as distinguishing as DNA.

Nothing stood out to me. Not that that was surprising, though. I'd spent most of my time at the gallery in the office, dealing with debits, credits, all things boring in nature. Patrick was the one who…

"Patrick," I gasped, whipping around to face Beth.

The letter she had tried to give me was again in her hand, languid against her fingers. "You need to read this," she said.

Across one page and then another, I read Mother's message about me, about Beth, and surprisingly, about Patrick, all handwritten on two ordinary sheets of paper. The first was a letter of apology. The second was a document of intent. My tears fell in soft wisps. People had gone to great lengths to make sure the Ausby home still held some secrets, but the time for secrecy was over. We were starting fresh, starting over.

The document stunned and tore me, solidifying my misunderstanding of her. Although Mother was still the woman who had tormented our relationship with cut eyes and cross words, I now understood that pain had been behind her viciousness. The pain of a loss is something that scabs, scars, and may temporarily subside, but it never fully heals. I knew about that type of pain. To know we shared it was something of a comfort, even if it was only two sheets deep.

"Is this why you two were always going to Beaufort?"

"Not at first, but after a time, yes. Within the art community in Beaufort, Vivian had met a man who struck her fancy, a lawyer by trade and a lover of art. Their relationship was innocent enough, but through the years she opened up to him, and he gave her solid legal advice. She trusted him, and so did I. Vivian knew how shallow the wading pool in Charleston was, and she wanted to make sure that her legal plans never got into the wrong hands. It was the only time in her life that she wanted in with someone from *off*."

Even if she did fancy this man, he wasn't from Charleston, and on some level that would always matter to her. The image of Mother courting a lawyer whom she most definitely would have considered inferior to her South of Broad roots struck me something funny. The image must have struck Beth too, because we both burst out laughing.

Beth wiped her laughing tears and sighed, "He was cute as a button, and I know he loved Vivian very much, even if she didn't allow herself to love him back the same way. You asked me why this day. Well, because that's what the terms of the contract stated. Before I came back home to work for Vivian, she made me sign my name to a promise that our secret wouldn't go past your fortieth birthday. And now you know that Patrick has a contract of a different sort.

"Patrick has known about our arrangement for some time now. But he wouldn't have gotten a dime if he ever told you the truth. Since the truth seems to entirely escape him, I don't think he ever really had a problem keeping it. To this day, I still don't think he's read the contract Vivian gave him in its entirety. His judgment of Vivian's intelligence was grossly miscalculated. Too stuck in that head-of-the-household nonsense, he'd never imagine that a woman could outsmart him. She did, though, and so did you: you got Evie."

I clutched the letter to my chest, hoping that sheet of paper could give me the same breath it had taken away. I soaked up a brilliance far greater than I had ever perceived living inside Mother, and I easily grasped her plan. I knew her tentacles stretched, but until then, I hadn't fully understood the depths to which they plunged.

All the while, this woman of coiffed hair and red lips, of harsh words and Chanel N°5, of wielded power and deep thought, lay motionless in an ordinary bed. The life she had lived, and the plan she had made, were finally coming to fruition.

12:00 p.m.

BETH AND I SAT AND TALKED AS WE ALWAYS HAD, ONLY NOW, I saw myself when she looked back at me. She told me stories of her time at the homestead, how they had narrowly survived Hurricane Hugo, and how her art had flourished in a place of such beauty. I wasn't hesitant to ask questions about Jade as a child, and she relayed every memory that happened to pass through her mind.

Hormones and self-righteousness, love and hate, and the light and dark that bind mothers and daughters together: they have twisted pathways and venous networks, and they are just as separating as they are cohesive. When times are good, the friendship flourishes, but when times are strained, the hurt can create such shadows. If you don't choose to stand in the light, all the shadows from each broken word will grow to be larger than both of you combined, until all that's left of the relationship is darkness. When Beth came back into our family, she brought all the light with her.

"Aside from Vivian, there is someone else you need to hear out," she said. "I think you should go upstairs and talk to Savannah again." She held one hand in the air, one over her heart. "I swear, I don't know what's going on with her and Jade. I lost the privilege of knowing his personal life long ago. But something's just not right there."

I had lost that right, too. "Mr. Ryan mentioned something about that. He was vague, and I was already beyond grateful for the information he had given me. It didn't feel right to push for more. He said that Jade had left the homestead."

"No," she said with disbelief. "He would never leave that place. He loved it there."

"It's not my business, hasn't been for a while now. I can't imagine him moving Savannah, though, unless it's to another hospital. She's so frail. Aside from hospice home care, I doubt she would survive anything else."

It was again my turn to make things right, even if I hadn't made them wrong. Or maybe I had. I wasn't completely sure of any memory at this point.

"I don't know if I can see them together," I continued. "Knowing they're married is one thing, but watching it play out is something entirely different."

"This thing, this journey we're on…No one has the right answers. The only thing I'm sure of is that life is good because of the people in it. You have to love like there's no possibility of a broken heart—even when you have one."

"Yes," I agreed. "I'll go up there. At the very least, she needs to know that I forgive her. I wouldn't be able to forgive myself if I don't."

"Harlow," she said, "do you recall what I asked you last night? About remembering the day you met me? A famous author once said, 'The two most important days in your life are the day you were born and the day you find out why.' Today, I can say that I was part of both, and that pleases me to no end."

I smiled. "Jack London said that, right?"

"No, that was from Mark Twain. I read much more than just London."

I leaned over to hug her again, and the words just came out, as naturally as water flows downstream. "Thank you, Mama."

We looked at each other in surprise. No matter what had happened in the past, it had still gotten us here, gotten me to this day, and that was the best gift either one of us would ever get.

2:00 p.m.

Had it not been for the machines at work, the room would have been graveyard silent. It was as if they were an intrusive third party in our intimate space, making her every breath audible, but barely. The machines weren't the only unwanted visitors in the room. A medicinal smell hovered over Savannah, something chemical, something raw, something cold. Thinness ate away at her, leaving veins to climb her body like overgrown ivy. In my time with Daddy and Mother, I had learned a great deal about death and dying. Death is very much alive. It's a living, breathing heat that swallows you from the inside.

As I sat down next to her bed, her eyelids fluttered without opening. She appeared to be grappling with an internal torrent. I hoped she dreamed as she lived: wildly, unapologetically, and always in color. I loved and hated every bit of her personality all at the same time. Savannah had the ability to be that conundrum, to make you love her and hate her within the same breath. Staring down at her then, I chose to love that about her.

The afternoon light that came in through the shades was muted and warm, and the pictures of her family that littered the desktop seemed almost as much a part of the room as the monitors alongside her body. Savannah had always lived in the moment, even when inevitability loomed. I had never known her to look back; the water in the harbor was the only sense of the tide behind her.

She stirred before she awoke.

"Savannah," I whispered, hoping not to startle her by my presence.

She turned her colorless irises toward me, seemingly blinking my face into focus. "Hey," she whispered in sleepy words, "you came back."

"I did. I hope that's okay. You didn't tell me everything yesterday."

"Well, no, but you didn't really give me a chance to tell you. You didn't give Jade one, either."

"No, I didn't, and I'm sorry about that. But I'm here now."

She pressed the button on her remote to bring the upper half of the bed eye-level with me. She took a moment to gather herself, just staring into space. "Low," she finally started, "despite our break, we've been friends for a long time. I know I've put you in some pretty compromising positions in the past, but do you really think I would steal the love of your life?"

I answered with silence, because when it came to men, well…

She waved her hand away. "Never mind, don't answer that. I slept with Patrick all those years ago because I'm selfish. I admit that. I wanted to be wanted, and at that moment, he wanted me. Were y'all married? Yes. But you didn't love him, Harlow. You've never loved him. I'm not saying what I did was right, because it was so very wrong, but I didn't do that with Jade. He wasn't something I wanted, but something I truly needed."

"How did you end up at the Ryans' homestead?"

She took a deep breath before answering. "I was pregnant with Penny, impregnated by a stellar choice of a man. You know how I always pick the gentlemen," she added, winking at me. "He didn't want a kid, and I knew that. Mama was sick, Lexi was, well, Lexi, and I didn't know what I was doing. I didn't have the first clue about being a mother. Hold on to your hat." Savannah squeezed my hand. "Vivian was the one who told me about the homestead. Believe it or not, she had really nice things to say about the place. I knew you'd spent time out there, and that gave me a level of comfort. Of course, I knew Jade, even though I hadn't seen him in years—not since you two…" Her words trailed into an awkward pause.

"Anyway," she continued, "Mrs. Ryan took me in and showed me the ropes. She helped me get my feet wet with mothering, and I thought that would be the end of that time of my life. As it turned out, cancer would be the end of my time. Penny was only three when I was first diagnosed. Mama was nearing the end, and there was no way she could take care of the both of us."

"Your mom had plenty of money. Why didn't you use the lottery winnings to pay for someone to take care of you?"

"I did, in a way. Penny has spent most of her childhood at the homestead—certainly the part she remembers. She's learned about compassion, hard work, service, and love. She wouldn't have gotten those same lessons from revolving nannies and hospice nurses at my mom's house. She needed the homestead; we both did. Mrs. Ryan adored Penny, and she welcomed us back with open arms. I was happy to pay rent, and to financially help keep it going. I owe her everything."

The way people kept describing Mrs. Ryan made me feel as though, except for Mother, I might have been the only other person she hated.

"Jade and I saw each other every day. We ate dinner together, went to the movies, hiked trails, and took Penny to the beach. I kept thinking that I had beaten the cancer, that any day, Penny and I would be back on our own, but the cancer kept coming back. Jade helped so much after my diagnosis, advocating for experimental drugs that insurance wouldn't pay for. I wouldn't be lying here had he not, and despite how you must think I look, I'm in pretty good shape for the shape I'm in. He's my family; he's always treated Penny like his own daughter. He's a wonderful man."

I felt myself wishing she would skip over those details. I then immediately felt guilty. Ridding myself of this ridiculous Southern guilt, slowly but steadily, was going to take some time.

"Here's the part you aren't going to like…. I could have easily fallen for him. I mean, you'd be a fool not to. Besides the fact that he's impossibly handsome, his kindness is so pure that it makes you question your own. We would have been so easy together. The only problem with that scenario is that I would have spent the rest of my life talking to him about you."

My heart twisted inside my chest, causing a lump to form in my throat. "What?" The word came out smashed and desperate.

"He loves you, Harlow. He's always loved you. And he'll spend the rest of his life loving you. I know him, and this is like nothing I've ever seen. He's loved Penny with that same loyalty, too. I wanted her to have a mother *and* a father. She's a good girl who didn't ask for any of this, and despite all of it, she deserves to be taken care of. I brought him a contract, and he agreed to the terms. We're best friends—that's all we are. Nothing more." She looked at me, seemingly confused that I had little reaction. "Feel free to applaud. Don't hold back," she teased.

She couldn't rely on humor with something as important as this. "What kind of contract did he sign?"

Is this what Mrs. Ryan meant about Jade being married but not having a wife?

Savannah replied, "A contract that would give everyone everything they've always wanted, and one to ensure that Penny would have one parent, with the possibility of two. I wasn't going to leave her with Lexi. Don't get me wrong, I love my sister, but a man will always take center stage in her life. Boyfriend after boyfriend…there was no way I would let Penny grow up in the middle of those men. Jade was already a father figure for her and, as you already know, a fine man.

"I love him dearly," she continued, "but not in *that* way. Not in the way that you love him. And don't try to deny it. I saw the way y'all saw each other, as if both of you had a secret you desperately wanted to tell. I made sure to take notice. You have to talk to him, Low. He's all torn up about your fight in the hallway. He's waited

205

for you for so long, and I think he expected things to happen much differently yesterday."

My heart scrambled and bobbled; her words fumbled around inside me. A new sense of panic arose, a feeling as if I had botched some crucial assignment. I had spoken to Jade the night before with words that came from pain, said with teeth and talons. The same words Mother would have certainly used.

Jade might have left because of me, and I didn't know how I was going to tell Savannah. My feelings about him were one thing; I had lost him before, and if I had to, I could do it again. But there was a child involved, one who could have a dad. I would have given anything to spend one more afternoon with my daddy. If I could help it, I wouldn't let that happen to Penny.

The weight of my mistake sank me to my knees. We were about to take another bad turn. I felt it in the stillness of my hands, the shallowness of my breath, and the upturned quirk in her mouth.

"What?" she asked, looking at me perplexedly. "I thought you'd be happy to hear all of this. At the very least, I was sure you'd be relieved that Jade married me out of duty, rather than love."

"I do appreciate you telling me, because you didn't have to. You don't owe me anything. I don't know how to say this, but I think I really messed up this time."

"Why? What'd you mess up?"

"I went to the homestead this morning, and Mrs. Ryan was really ugly to me. She said all kinds of things, mostly about how I ruined Jade and ran him off. She said he wasn't going back to the homestead, and Mr. Ryan agreed. I think I really screwed things up for you, and I'm so sorry, Van. Please, forgive me." I clenched my jaw and gritted my teeth, waiting for her reply.

She furrowed her brow. "Now you've put me in a terribly awkward situation. I kind of have to forgive you; I'm not really in a position not to. Otherwise I'll probably go to hell. I'm trying to be super nice these days. The dying thing, you know?"

Confused and a little horrified, I gasped. "What? Why would you say that?"

"I'm kidding! Jesus, you have got to lighten up. Look at me, Low. Don't you go feeling sorry for me. Don't do that. I've lived my life on my own terms, and I have no regrets. You understand?"

I nodded in agreement, unable to speak.

The skin on her hands was paper-thin. Her fingers felt like silk sheets sweeping across my arms, as she stroked my shoulder and relaxed into a sleepy smile. "Jade just needs some time to work out the details. He'll turn up, probably when you least expect it. So don't worry yourself. Is Evie in town for the gala tonight?"

"How'd you know about the gala?"

"Please," she said, rolling her eyes, "the city is growing, but not as fast as the gossip. Everyone we know knows about the gala."

"No." I sighed. "She's not coming. At this point, if I want to see her, I pretty much have to go to her. Patrick and I haven't done the best job of making a home for her to come back to. We're like two ghosts haunting the same house. She's a busy college student, though, and I get it. She's living her life, and I wouldn't want to hold her back."

"You miss her, don't you?"

"I do—terribly. I miss her needing me. As mothers, we spend eighteen years raising our babies into women, and one day, we're just supposed to let them go off on their own. I was just a baby when I had her, so she raised me as much as I raised her, I suppose. Anyway, enjoy your time with Penny. She is a delightful little girl. I promised her yesterday that I'd pay her another visit sometime soon. I'd love to get to know her better."

Savannah smiled with all her teeth, as a tear ran down her cheek. "She is more than I ever deserved, and I'm lucky for the time I have left with her. You keep that promise to her, okay?"

"Pinky promise," I said.

Apparently cancer made even the most sedate tasks exhausting, because Savannah was no match for the weight of sleep. "I'm just going to rest my eyes. Stay and sit with me a minute, okay?"

"Of course. I'll stay as long as you like. I'm grateful to have found you again."

She was out before I finished my sentence. It felt strange to know this Savannah. Savannah the mother, the one who put others first, the Savannah who could hardly get out of bed, much less terrorize the town. I couldn't help but picture that feisty girl with short skirts and cheap lip gloss, who slept with whomever she wanted and had no regrets. That hardened girl couldn't possibly know how weak the world would eventually make her. If cancer had taken that fire from her, then it was my responsibility to carry her torch. And if carrying her torch meant burning this city down, I wouldn't hesitate even for a moment.

5:00 p.m.

WHEN SHE STEPPED OUT OF THE BATHROOM INTO MOTHER'S hospital room, it was as though I saw my future as well as my past. The hem of her gown kissed the floor, and the beading made a swishing sound with each step she took toward me. The brightness of her hair had faded with age, strokes of gray replacing it, as if she had painted them in with the smallest of brushes. Her dress was the color of fire, and her lips matched. She was a classic beauty, a type of exquisite that captured the essence of Old Southern elegance. Charleston praised a certain kind of beauty, the kind found in the delicate ironwork of ornate fences, the soft ivory arches of a magnolia blossom, and the strength of keeping a decades-old secret. The kind of beauty found in Beth Chaney-Ausby.

"You look amazing. I don't even know what else to say, but wow!"

"Oh, stop, you're embarrassing me." Beth gathered the train of her dress, waving it back and forth to flutter against her calves, while admiring herself in the full-length mirror. "But you're right," she added with a giggle. "I do look good. There might be some sugar left in this shaker after all."

"Let's hope that's not all that's left in your shaker. We have a very big night."

"The paintings are on their way from the homestead to the Sugar Mill, and I slipped the driver some extra cash for his secrecy. Not that I had to. He has less than glowing reviews of his boss, Patrick. But with the future of the gallery so unstable, I wanted him to know that the Ausby family cares about him. I hope he isn't out of work for too long."

"We can make sure that doesn't happen," I said. "Are you ready to do this, to give this town a show they've never seen?"

"If you're talking about the gala, then yes. But if you mean the way people are going to swoon over you in that showstopping mini, then no. Because no one will even recognize you, honey."

"In the mess with Patrick this morning, I just grabbed a dress from the closet, not realizing it was Evie's. My birthmark shows, I know. You don't think it's too short, do you? Mother would have a fit if she saw me in this."

"All the more reason to wear it. You're ravishing." She took my hands in hers. "We've taken a windy road to get here, but I'm so proud of who you've become. With no help from me, and certainly none from Vivian, you've done this on your own. You come from a long line of strong and uppity women, Harlow, and there is no better time for those traits to serve you than now. I hope you realize how useful that strength is. Now, do you have your speech ready?"

I glanced over at my purse sitting on the bed, the note cards peeking out beyond the clasp. When I first read the speech Mother had written for me to give at the gala, my initial response was utter disbelief. To have the ability to create such a meticulous and diabolical plan left me a little terrified, but mostly in awe. Not being the one in her sights was a welcome change.

"I have it," I replied.

"Okay, present time," Beth exclaimed, softly clapping her hands together in elation.

"Don't you think we've already reached the threshold of excitement for one day? I don't think I can take any more surprises."

"Don't be a party pooper," she said, batting away my comment with the flick of her wrist. "It's just something I threw together." She reached under Mother's bed and pulled out a package that had been wrapped in burlap. It could only be another canvas—the size was a dead match. "I hope this brings you as much joy to look at as it did for me to paint for you. I love you so much. I always have. Happy birthday, Harlow."

"Oh!" I gasped as the cloth dropped to the floor. My fortitude was no match for the flood of emotions. It was my picture with Jade, of us at the fair, only it was now a piece of art.

Waving my fingertips in front of my eyes, I blubbered, "Don't you do it, don't you make me cry. I already have my face on, and it will be a total mess if you make me cry. Patrick told me he burned the picture. Did you paint this from memory?"

Surprised, she replied, "He didn't burn it. It's taped to the back of the canvas. See?" The masking tape made a soft tearing sound as she pulled my picture off my new favorite piece of art. "I had to take it from your drawer and hope you didn't notice, so I could keep the painting a surprise."

Gathering myself with deep breaths and blotted tears, I lightly touched the canvas. It was a replica of the photograph, yet it was more beautiful than the real thing. "Thank you," I said. "This is the best birthday present I've ever gotten. It'll be hard to let it go."

"You just got it; why would you have to let it go?"

"Who knows what will become of us after tonight? We don't even have a place to live at the moment, and we need as much money as possible. Without a doubt, this painting will sell at the auction tonight. We have to show the art community the talent they've already invested in. I don't want you to think I don't love it, because I do. I just love us more."

"Whatever you want to do, I'll support you. That said, we need something to mark the occasion. Aha!" she called out, walking around the foot of Mother's bed to her nightstand. She picked up Mother's bottle of Chanel N°5 perfume.

Stretching my arm across the bed, I grabbed ahold of Beth's hand and Mother's.

Beth started again. "Let's not get emotional. Vivian would hate that. Maybe just a few words. Ahem. We love you, Vivian."

"We do," I repeated, unsure of what that love was, but certain it was somewhere inside me.

"Tonight is for you."

With three squirts of the perfume, forty years' worth of memories were magically unlocked. A ticker tape of pictures ran through my head all at once, and with the smell of her signature scent, I felt her there with us. Despite the hardships between us over the years, no one could ever deny that Vivian had a strong sense of self, an even stronger sense of direction, and an absolutely clear route to get there.

As the mist of the iconic fragrance floated across three generations of Ausby women, I felt prouder of my roots than ever before, however tangled they may have been.

5:30 p.m.

THE EARLIER CLOUDS HAD EVENTUALLY GIVEN WAY TO sunshine. The weather still couldn't decide. The humidity assaulted us with a thickness that made it difficult to inhale. Our driver arrived at the hospital precisely at five thirty to whisk us away to the annual—and probably the last—Ausby Art Gala.

In past years, no matter the venue, the cars had lined up to stretch farther than parking allowed. Since Mother had friends on the city council, street closures were no problem, traffic cops were readily provided, and all of Charleston's upper echelon turned up.

When we pulled into the circular drive of the Sugar Mill Plantation, a small line of cars waited ahead of ours. Mother had picked this venue for its sheer embodiment of Charleston. The mill's history stretched back to the first shots of the Civil War. It had survived Union blockades, foolhardy business ventures, several hurricanes, and one earthquake. It had been burned down and rebuilt. Like us, it had withstood the beauty as well as the darkness of life in the Holy City.

Set against the Ashley River, the lichen-streaked brick structure towered above the sailboats in the Charleston Yacht Club. Rows of orderly masts in high tide made a picturesque backdrop in the harbor. The evening sun burst its final blazing rays, seemingly admiring itself in the windows of the historic building. The lingering light dappled the writhing trunks of old oak trees, and year-round Spanish moss clung to the branches like the thrown confetti of a perpetual party. This scene was among the many reasons that I believed the Lowcountry was one of the most romantic landscapes on earth.

When we were next in line for valet parking, I took Beth's hand in mine. "All these years, I've known you as Beth Chaney. What made you choose to go by that last name?"

Beth grinned a seemingly impossible grin as she answered, "Chaney was Jack London's real last name."

"Of course," I replied, her answer evoking my own smile.

Ten years, months, even days ago, I wouldn't have recognized my own strength. On this night, I felt as though I had been born for this, as if my whole life—and what I had assumed were unanswered prayers—had been leading up to this one night. A sense of peace washed over me as the valet opened my door. Despite the business that lay ahead, I felt as though I could finally relax.

Usually with an event of such prestige, the list of attendees was well thought out yet still held room for some necessary ne'er-do-wells, who didn't make much of an impact whether they showed up or not. Politicians, critics, avid art buyers, and old money were the first to open an invitation from Mother—the right guests of influence to fill the ballroom. B-listers were invited to feel special, and also to make sure the C-list—the people who desperately wanted to attend—heard about the grandness of the party for days to come. Event staff was meticulous about verifying each guest before they entered the front doors, by requiring a hard copy of the official invitation.

Butlers dressed entirely in white circulated the room, offering strong liquor and delicate canapés, and a three-piece orchestra played as we made our way through the chatter of pleasantries. As I introduced my companion as Beth Ausby, I reveled in the looks I received. When Beth came into my life, it had given me great pleasure for strangers to mistake her for my mother. How could they not? I like to think that on some level, I knew we belonged together, even if I didn't know the depth of that truth. Now I also realized that maybe some of those people weren't surprised. Among the ones who had truly known the Ausby history, my introduction was met with grace and kindness.

Despite the gossip that flowed South of Broad, blue blood flowed too, and secrets of that caliber were held tighter than family. Born into a borough where some salivated for gossip, I may never know how Vivian managed to keep Beth's true identity a secret from me. Maybe Vivian had sweetly asked people to keep her family matters private, or maybe it was more of a stern suggestion. With what I now knew, I suspected that her request looked a lot like intimidation, and that it came in the form of blackmail.

We made our way over to a longtime friend of the family, the newly retired police chief of Charleston. He thanked us for the invitation. Before she fell ill, Vivian had had a long talk with him. Although he had never purchased a piece of art from the gallery, he always received an invitation to the gala. Sometimes Mother had her priorities straight.

The atmosphere inside the Sugar Mill swirled with curiosity about the evening's events. People offered uplifting thoughts and prayers for Mother, but what they truly thought had nothing to do with her health. The gala was far less crowded than in years past; that, I could tell, confused our guests. I couldn't help but smile at that. Despite the whittled guest list, this *was* the year that everyone would talk about.

After-dinner drinks and dancing would take place in the tents, while dinner service and the auction were to commence under the pressed-tin ceilings of the grand ballroom. Cocktails and hors d'oeuvres in hand, people mingled within the prewar stucco and brick walls, admiring the history, as well as themselves. A trio of stringed instruments drowned out the pointed clicks of sky-high stilettos against the wide-plank hardwood floors. The night was off to a smooth start.

Across the room, I caught sight of Patrick brownnosing the mayor, while Lexi stood awkwardly to the side of their surely

215

engaging conversation, looking out of place. I knew that position well. I also knew why the shading in her face had a green tinge. When she noticed me, I gave her a courteous nod. She gave one back, and Patrick rolled his eyes. He looked down at my uncovered leg in disgust, tensing as I approached their circle.

"Mr. Mayor," I began, curtsying with my greeting, "thank you for coming tonight. As always, it's an honor to have you here."

He gently took my hand and kissed my palm, twirling me a bit. "Harlow, I wouldn't miss this. My, you are a sight this evening. And that dress!" His gaze turned serious. "I want to thank you for the generous flowers and sweet card you sent my wife. It really helped lift her spirits."

"I appreciate that, but the thanks go to Mother. That was all her doing. How is your wife? Is she feeling better?"

"Much better, thank you. And Vivian? Is there any good news there?"

"Only that she isn't in any pain. We're keeping her comfortable for now, letting God take the course that He sees fit. Thank you for asking about her, though. I'm sure she misses not being here tonight."

"I'll bet she does," the mayor agreed. "God does have His own plans for us, and I'll pray for her to find comfort in His hands."

"Yes, sir, He sure does." I took Patrick's arm. "If you don't mind, I need to steal this one away from you. We're about to start the dinner service, and he needs to make the welcome speech."

"Please, go right ahead."

Patrick added with slimy schmoozing, "Tell your wife that I'll be praying for her recovery. We'll finish our conversation in a bit."

As the mayor walked away, Patrick leaned into my ear. "Jesus, Harlow, is your skirt short enough? How did you know his wife was sick, anyway?"

"I know lots of things you don't. And believe me, Patrick, after tonight, no one will be talking about my dress."

216

He cuffed my arm with a strong grip, slightly jerking my ear closer to his mouth. "You better have put my name on that get-well card. I don't want to look like an idiot."

I turned and smiled at him, smoothing out his lapel and straightening his bow tie. "Oh, darling, you don't yet, but you will."

"What the hell does that mean?" he asked.

"It's time for your welcome speech," I redirected, gesturing toward the stage.

Still behind us, and still not part of the group that mattered, Lexi leaned stiffly against the marble-topped bar, watching Patrick make his way to the podium. She was by far the most beautiful woman in the room, yet she was also alone. I supposed some things never changed. Unapproachable girls grew into unapproachable women, and the ones who made men their priority grew up to be alone. I didn't hate Lexi Pratt; I probably never had. What I did feel for her was pity. If only recently, I had come to understand that it was Beth, Evie, Savannah, and even Mother—the women in my life—who had brought fullness to it. I was sure that Lexi couldn't say the same.

I stepped back to where she was standing, and I made an offering to be that kind of woman for her. "Hello, Lexi," I said. Her eyesight darted around the floor. She looked confused, a little terrified. "You look very nice this evening."

She paused before she spoke, but even then, she was hesitant. She finally brought her sight to mine. "Um, thank you. So do you."

"How are you feeling?"

Her voice became nervous. "I'm fine. Why?"

"Morning sickness was relentless during my first trimester, and I couldn't keep anything down." Her eyes bulged. "Soda crackers and sparkling water with a lemon were the only things that settled my stomach. Don't get me wrong, you still look beautiful, but you also look like you might not feel well. I just thought the suggestion might help, in case you're having a hard time finding something that doesn't upset your stomach." I gently patted her arm. "Okay, good talk. I'll see you later."

Like a deer in headlights, she remained wide-eyed as I walked away with even more pep in my step than when I had arrived.

When the hors d'oeuvres grew sparse and the aperitifs heavy, Patrick took the stage. He clinked a silver spoon against his glass to silence the murmured chatter. Only when he had every aristocratic eye in the room upon him did he begin his speech.

"Gentlemen, ladies." He winked when he mentioned the ladies and got a cheap laugh. He was an alley cat among the storied streets of Charleston, and he roamed so often that he had made himself a joke. Only, he had no idea as to who would get the last laugh.

"As always, I want to thank you for coming to my event tonight."

I rolled my eyes. *As if he did any of this.*

"We're all here to celebrate the art that enriches our lives, but personally, I'm celebrating for another reason tonight."

I watched a smile grace Lexi's lips and then quickly turn into a scowl. She must have thought she was the most important thing in Patrick's life, especially since he was officially divorced. She must have also thought his announcement would be about his love for his unborn child. She had no clue about the depths to which Patrick loved only himself. Yes, she would surely need someone in the coming months, someone like I had.

"As you all know, my beautiful mother-in-law has been fighting for her life. If we know anything about Vivian, it's her strength of self, her eye for art, and her love of family. These are her core foundation. Although my time as an official member of the Ausby family has recently ended, I was fortunate enough to be a part of it for two decades. I learned a great deal about art, as well as business, from Vivian. Apparently she considered me quite the student, because she has left Ausby Fine Art solely in my care. For you, our current clients, as well as potential clients, the structure of the gallery won't change a bit. I've personally dealt with every piece of fine art bought and sold through the last twenty years, and you can continue to expect the same fair and honest service over the next twenty."

Oh my God, what an idiot.

"All of this is courtesy of Vivian Ausby. So let's raise our glasses tonight to one of the best. To Vivian," he saluted.

"To Vivian," the audience repeated.

8:00 p.m.

Neither Beth nor I sat and ate with the rest of the guests. While they dined on freshly caught redfish and tarpon, hormone-free filet mignon, and roasted oysters, our tastes were centered on the arts. Behind the maroon curtain at the front of the dining room were the auction items. Each year, Mother chose a noble and dignified charity to receive the funds collected by the auction. This year was different, though. Patrick had refused to donate pieces from the gallery, making himself and his business the sole benefactors of the auction.

This was no time to be nervous; time was something we were losing. This wasn't an antiquities auction at Sotheby's. Although our guests believed they were bidding on pieces by Kinkade and Dupré, the only originals on auction that night were by the artist Bessie London, master forger.

After taking a look from behind the curtain, Beth said, "They're clearing the plates. You better get out to the tents to confirm they're set up."

I passed through the dining room and headed outside to check on the progress. The last of the evening light had muddled, leaving the sky a picturesque painting of its own. Every derivative of the color red lay against the horizon; their reflection in the river doubled the intensity of the sunset. The undulating water against the pier and the songs of the bullfrogs at dusk made my heart swell. There was a sense of home in those songs, a place I knew I would never leave. The peacefulness provided me with a moment to just be.

A lingering combination of confederate jasmine and blackwater tannins rose into the evening. The tents lit up the field, shining like two moons rising from the high Spartina grass. I took in an unadulterated view of the Ashley River beyond the venue.

I didn't hear the footsteps approach behind me.

"If there's time, I have a last-minute donation to the auction," I heard him say. He placed something heavy on the ground beside him.

I would have known his voice from any, but the possibility of being wrong made me hesitate before turning around. With the twinkle lights above us, Jade Ryan looked as though he were part of the night, someone created entirely by the stars. Dressed in a tuxedo, he seemed like a different person. It did something to me immediately, as if my whole body had been asleep and was just now waking up. I think a small part of me died just from the sight of him.

"I could tell you that the chair is a birthday gift, but from the backlog of rocking chairs you've ordered over the years, I don't think you have room for any more."

His voice was soft and nervous, and his words sounded as though he had rehearsed them on the way over. I was so happy to see him that I almost went blank. I couldn't think of what to say. The longer I waited to speak, the more uncomfortable he looked.

"Harlow, please, say something."

With undisguised disbelief, I finally said, "You're here."

He smiled, shoving his hands deep in his pockets. "Where else would I be?"

"I don't know. It's just that your parents said you had gone, and that you weren't coming back. I didn't know if I would see you again."

"I'm not going anywhere. I've already waited this long."

I wanted to run to him, to hold him, to rest my face in the warmth of his neck. I wanted him to want me. I wanted Savannah's husband for myself. How would I ever be okay with that? How would anyone be okay with that?

His silence was expectant, so I said what I was thinking, what I thought he was desperate to hear. "I know about all of it. I came to your homestead to see you this morning, but you were already gone."

"You came to see me?"

"I know it shouldn't matter after all these years, but I needed to clear my name."

"I don't understand."

"I came because I needed you to know that you were right about Patrick that night." He knew the evening I was talking about. I could see it on his face. "I did sleep with Patrick twenty years ago, but only because he took advantage of me. Although I always knew that night was never right, I found out only this morning how wrong it actually was. Patrick finally admitted what he did to me. He drugged me. He raped me." Jade's eyes found the ground. I felt as if I was hurting him all over again. "So I came to your place this morning, and while I was there, your dad showed me the paintings. Later, Beth confirmed what he had told me. She told me about her, and about you too. I know she's my mother."

His shoulders slumped with relief and what seemed like sorrow.

"Harlow, I'm sorry about all of it. I don't know what else to say."

"You were right about Patrick. You were always right about him. I'm sorry I was too naïve to believe you. As you know, Beth is a wonderful woman, and she was already a mother to me. Now it's just official. I love her, and I always have; there are no bad feelings there. I'm glad it's finally out, and no one has to keep secrets anymore. It must have been hard on everyone, you included."

He stepped toward me, hesitating yet still closing the space between us. The way he looked at me, he saw more of me than I had even seen of myself. It was the same way he looked at me in my dreams.

"I also talked to Savannah," I continued, "and I know about your arrangement. I'm sorry I didn't give you a chance to explain last night. I always knew you would get married—you have every right to be happy—I just didn't think it would be to her."

The muscles in his jaw tightened; his full lips became thin. "If not Savannah, then who? I've only ever asked one person. Who was I supposed to marry, Harlow?"

His comment was meant to elicit a response that I wouldn't give. Not then. "I don't know. It was just hard, though, seeing you two together, even after all these years. I lost myself for a minute, and I got a little crazy. I apologize for that."

"Please, don't." His tone wasn't accusatory, and he let out a sigh. "Don't apologize for anything. The first time I had to see you with someone else, I went a little crazy too."

Perplexed, I asked, "Who did you ever see me with?"

Cocking his head to the side, he raised his eyebrows as an obvious answer to a stupid question. Patrick's black-and-blue face all those years ago flashed across my mind.

My eyes bulging, I gasped. "No! Patrick said he was mugged. You did that to him?"

A little smirk appeared, slightly raising one cheek. "The only thing I stole from him that night was his pride. I didn't give him even half of what he deserved, but I'm not proud that I beat him up. Well, I guess I was then, but that was a long time ago. It never made me feel better. It didn't change anything. It still didn't get me you."

Whether it was because of the grass beneath my feet, the thickness of the scented air, or my pulse pounding hot in my ears, I could feel something shifting inside of me. We were done with pretending to have a normal conversation. The space between us now small, I found my hand suddenly in his. I closed my eyes yet didn't move away, as if I could hide standing still, as though shutting my eyes would make me less guilty of wanting this man for twenty years, wanting him more today than when he was mine. I had to remind myself that he was someone's husband.

His skin smelled clean, his breath of bourbon, and I could tell I was fighting harder than he was. He seemed to waver on his feet, leaning into me like a punch-drunk boxer. His breath came warm against my face, as he put his hands on my cheeks, touching his forehead to mine.

His whisper was soft in my ear. "To talk to you and touch you, to be this close to you and not kiss you—it's killing me."

"You're married, Jade." His breath caught as he inhaled his name from the air. "Despite what she says, I think Savannah does love you. I won't do that to her, hurt her in that way."

He let go of my face and stepped back, wrestling with a flash of anger. "What about me? I've been in love with the same woman my entire life. And it was fine when I was younger, because I was completely naïve about what time does to people. Even though you were real, you were still a figment of my imagination, a fantasy that I hoped to eventually make true. I didn't know that waiting for you would be the goddamn marathon of my life. But now…"

His words moved me, but Savannah's image stuck with me. How could I know the depth of love that women bring into your life, and then turn around and stab one of them in her dying back? "I won't," I whispered.

I felt the length of twenty years pass between us, while at the same time realizing how quickly those years had been chewed up. The moral confusion sat in my throat and pinched my breath. We were talking about us, about the love that had lived inside me for longer than I cared to recall. It was happening, and I was letting it pass me by.

His sigh was long, and he squeezed his eyes closed before he spoke. "For two women who haven't spoken much in ten years, y'all sure do know each other pretty well." He pulled a small square of folded paper out of his jacket pocket. "She knew you'd do this, put your own feelings aside and stay loyal, even when she wasn't. She told me to give this to you."

He handed me the note as though it were a child's permission slip.

Good or bad, Savannah had always been able to change a mood quicker than a gust of wind. A smile took over my entire face, and I think I laughed out loud when I read what she had written. Plain as day, I could hear her voice echo throughout my head as I read her words: "Jesus, Harlow, just fuck him already. No regrets!" *Savannah always knows how to embarrass me at just the right amount.*

Jade's eyes were trained on me, as if he could see right through me, and obviously he did. His voice turned serious again, but without the desperation this time. Sweeping my hair away from my face, he said, "I can't let you go, Harlow—not this time—and I don't want to. Don't you dare try to convince me—or yourself— that you don't love me. I know you do, because I can feel it, and I can see it. I saw it twenty years ago, and even more yesterday. I see it right now."

He pulled me to him by the base of my neck, braiding his fingers into my hair, sealing our lips together, and finishing what we had started twenty years ago. His kiss moved all through me, the inside of his mouth warm, the strength of his body a home for mine. If God had taken me in that moment, I would have considered it a successful death.

It took me a moment to notice that we were swaying together, even though the only music was coming from inside. I laid my head against his chest, inhaling his goodness and not wanting to break away, needing to truly put an end to something twenty years too long. Guilt, often fear, sometimes anger, usually remorse—these were the unfortunate emotions that had the tendency to cling to me. Enter hope. This hope was something new.

"I have to get back inside," I said. "Beth will be wondering where I am. Will you come with me?"

"I've always told you that I'd go anywhere with you. It's the only place I've ever wanted to be."

9:00 p.m.

THE WARMTH OF HIS HAND RADIATED IN MINE. I KEPT GLANCING at him, memorizing his features in case I woke up from this beautiful dream. Each time I looked up at him, he was already looking back at me. His expression held a mixture of worry and peace. I don't think he wanted to wake, either. I squeezed his hand to prove that we were real.

Inside, polite murmurs had turned into liquored-up laughter. Alcohol, indubitably, plays a large part in the success of an auction. As I took in the well-lubricated crowd, it pleased me immensely to see people enjoying themselves and each other's company.

Beth greeted us at the door with open arms, hugging Jade's waist tightly. "You found each other," she crooned.

"He was never lost. He's always been right here," I said, patting my heart. He leaned down and kissed me again. "I have to work, but make yourself comfortable at the bar," I told him. I noticed Lexi still standing alone. "Go stand by Lexi, but not too close. I don't want to have to dig her talons out of you."

"There has never been anyone but you."

Oh Christ, I can't even think straight around him.

Scanning the room, I eventually found Patrick. With his back against the wall and a group of ladies around him, his flirtation was ridiculous. He managed to touch every one of them as he spoke. The arm, the waist, a twirl of the hair—he commanded their affection with skill. *Idiot.*

I left Jade to nurse a drink in the crowd, taking Beth's hand in mine. As we passed through the conversations of unsuspecting guests, I gave a purposeful nod to our friend the retired police chief. The traffic cops from earlier had been promoted, and they stood at his heels attentively.

The crowd quieted as we took the stage. Before I began, I found Jade in the audience. His smile anchored me—and propelled me forward. I had every right to feel anger toward Patrick, but I wasn't celebrating what was about to happen. There had already been enough hurt, enough pain for all of us. I just wanted to get this over with and get on with living my life, instead of running from it. My hands were shaking as I took in a breath.

"Hello," I began, trying to find my voice. "My name is Harlow Ausby." *Ausby. It's been a long time since that name has felt good to me.* I saw Patrick look up. "I'd like to thank everyone for coming, thank the staff who helped to put on an incredible event, and especially thank Patrick for making this night so exciting." I looked directly at him. "I'd like to thank you for being here." Patrick looked confused by my generosity. "As you know from years past, we hold an annual auction to help raise money for a charitable donation. This year proves especially important."

The curtain drew open behind me, showcasing five exquisite pieces of art. A collective gasp funneled through the audience. Some were so drawn to the beauty that they were compelled to stand up and move toward the stage to get a better look. The elderly in the crowd covered their eyes with glasses, bringing into focus what some art lovers only dreamed of seeing. Had these paintings fallen into the hands of an average civilian, they may never have known the value of what they held. While not Picassos or Renoirs, the pieces were more than modestly valuable, by artists both scholars and collectors would recognize. They were the kind that people in the know snapped up, and that's exactly why they had been chosen for the auction. The room was set ablaze with excited chatter.

"As you know, Vivian Ausby's connections within the art community rivaled even those of many artists themselves. She was never afraid to go after what she wanted, and she hardly let anyone stand in her way. Tonight is no different. If you would all take a look at your auction paddles, you'll find a number engraved on the back."

The audience complied, curious, I could tell. Patrick was moving slowly toward the stage.

"My friends, that isn't just a number, but a year—a year when you bought a painting from the Ausby gallery." He moved a little faster. "Your patronage is why you were invited this evening. You've been loyal and generous, and we're going to do our best tonight to repay you for your business. You'll all have a chance to bid on these works of art. It's my honor to introduce you to our auctioneer, Mr. Shirley."

The auctioneer, though a little drunk, took no time in diving in.

Patrick had positioned himself at the corner of the stage, looking confused about what was happening. He tugged at his collar as if it were choking him. As I stepped away and let Mr. Shirley drive up the bids, Patrick grabbed ahold of my hand, yanking me farther from the microphone. Hard to miss in any circumstance—he was a head taller than most of the guests—Jade immediately came into view. He pushed his way over to us through the crowd.

"What the hell is this?" Patrick growled in a voice darker than new asphalt.

"It's an auction," I replied. "Don't worry, you'll make plenty of money."

As Patrick let go of my arm, I held up a hand to Jade, stopping him from coming closer. His eyes were wild, and I think he would have loved nothing more than ten minutes alone with Patrick, but he listened to me. He stopped right where he was.

With a love of narrowing the field and goading the desperate—or just plain egotistical—into thinking they would win much more than a piece of art, Mr. Shirley played with the women and toyed with the men. He always got the sale—and his commission. Exasperated cheers followed each purchase. The Kinkade gone, the Dupré taken, and the Von Amerling the first to go—butts were out of seats and paddles were in the air. Amid all the excitement, people began to fan themselves, spreading a seemingly holy spirit around the room. The women cackled like hens, while the men blotted sweat with monogrammed pocket squares.

The plan was working.

The crowd was exhausted by the time Mr. Shirley came to the last piece of art. The painting wasn't revered, nor were its subjects famous. It was of two people—kids, really—holding on to each other, the lights of the Coastal Carolina Fair shining behind them. Voices became quiet as Mr. Shirley began with the opening bid. Despite what the bidders thought, this was the most valuable piece of art in the collection, and it was our lifeline to the future. Panic rose within me. If someone in the room didn't find the artistry in this painting, I didn't know how we would move on.

"Three thousand dollars," a voice called out from the audience.

Everyone turned to see who would place such a price on something so unknown. No one knew this beautifully rustic stranger, his credentials, or from what gallery he hailed. All they knew was that he thought the piece was valuable, and maybe they should too.

I smiled at him with a full heart, mouthing the words, "Thank you."

Jade mouthed back, "I love you."

"We have three thousand," Mr. Shirley called out. "Do I have four?"

One by one, paddles began to go back into the air. Though this tight-knit art community was small, its ego was priceless. Patrick was grinning in the corner, completely unaware of his soon-to-be-cemented infamy. He knew those paintings weren't originals, and yet he stood by and let money trump morality.

The woman with the winning bid cheered when the final lot closed. She had won the painting of Jade and me, and she was willing to pay ten thousand dollars for it. In all, we had auctioned almost two hundred thousand dollars of art. I took center stage again.

"My," I exclaimed into the microphone, "that certainly was exciting! Congratulations to all our winners! I can assure you that this evening, your drinks are on the house." Collective laughter ensued. "Now comes the portion of the auction that you truly won't believe. Believe me, I had trouble believing it myself. We will not take any money from you fine people tonight, but you're all welcome to take home your paintings." The chatter arose. "You see, this was more of an unveiling than anything else. It's with deep sorrow that I regret to inform you that you've been lied to. Not just tonight, but for years. The date on the back of your paddle represents the day that Patrick McDade sold you a fake."

People backed away from him as Patrick rushed toward the stage stairs. The fraud was on him like a stench, which our guests could now smell. If the chatter had been excited when they thought they were buying something valuable, the outrage was thunderous when they found out they'd spent thousands on worthless art.

Patrick bullied his way toward me. "Calm down, folks," he yelled, grabbing the microphone from me. "This is all a mistake that will get sorted out. Harlow is just upset that our divorce is final on the day that she's officially old." He jerked my arm, pulling me from the podium. "What the hell are you doing?"

"Since you're clearly delusional when it comes to the truth, I'm telling it for you. I know what you did. I know you bought Beth's paintings at the Ryans' homestead and passed them off as originals to unsuspecting clients."

He jerked my arm again. "Ouch," I cried out. "You're hurting me."

The cops moved to the stage. A terrified look washed over Patrick, who realized he was being cornered by a crowd that was ready to swallow him—and cops who were there to arrest him.

Doing a one-eighty, he put his hands on my shoulders, begging in the most pathetic way. "Harlow, don't do this. You can't let this happen to me. You're my wife, for God's sake."

"Not anymore I'm not. We were married, but I was never truly your wife. You ruined my daddy's good name, your family name, and your daughter's."

His fingernails dug into my skin as he growled at me. "You think you're so smart, but you're in just as much trouble as I am. You own half of this crime, and I'll make sure you suffer as much as I do!"

"Oh, darling, a small and shallow man told me just this morning that the house, the business, the money—all of it is yours. I don't own any of it. Remember that?"

The reality of the situation was pressing down on him, squeezing sweat from every pore of his face. I hoped he was picturing Vivian's face in his mind. Now that his ego had started to shrink, it left room for his imagination to wander. I suspected his thoughts were turning to orange jumpsuits and metal bars, maybe the karma of a midnight rape.

"I can't go to jail. I'll never make it in there. You have to help me, Harlow. You have to tell me what to do. What should I do?"

I repeated what he had said to me earlier with relish. "As far as what happens to you now, I couldn't say, because it's not my business. But from where I'm standing, you're fucked."

With his hand held high, Patrick screamed, "You bitch!"—right about the time that Jade's fist connected with the bridge of Patrick's nose. His feet came out from under him, as Jade jumped on top of him. The scene was vaguely familiar. Jade hit him repeatedly, so hard that I thought he might kill Patrick. Behind each blow was the anger of lost time, the devastation of a broken heart, the violation of a crime, and the heartbreak of a stolen womb. I was relieved that the police intervened, because I don't think Jade could have stopped hitting him even if he'd wanted to.

I held Jade against me, his breath coming in hard blows, the sweat that speckled his button-up shirt wet against my face. "Just breathe. It's okay now," I said into his chest. "It's over."

"There was no way I was going to let him hurt you, not again. I still love you so much, Harlow, and I've waited so long to tell you that," he said, breathing the words into my mouth, breathing the life back into me, and kissing me as if we were the only two people in the room.

As the officers dragged Patrick—a pathetically sobbing mess— away, the room erupted into chaos around me. I motioned for Beth to join me at the podium. Beating on the microphone—which had been live through the entire ordeal—got people to start to quiet down.

"People, people, please," I begged. "Everyone just calm down! If you will all take a seat, we'll figure this out." Displeased groans rumbled through the room as the crowd obeyed. "I can assure you that each one of you will leave here tonight satisfied. If we can't reach some kind of resolution this evening, I promise to spend every day working on a plan to make you as happy as the day you walked out of my family's gallery with what you thought was an original piece of art. In the back room, we've set up a business center. You'll be able to speak with knowledgeable appraisers, who can tell you the value of the original, as well as a fair price for the forgery. Mrs. Luann Wolfe from Windsor Art Appraisals flew all the way in from New York to help."

Mrs. Wolfe stood rigid in the arched doorway, her large-framed glasses seemingly shrinking the size of her face. Upright and clad in black, she looked like someone who drank tea instead of coffee, ate late and never had a problem getting a reservation, and rode only in the backs of cars.

"She'll be staying in Charleston all week, and she's happy to work with you one on one to find a fair remedy for your situation.

As far as tonight's winning bidders, Mrs. Wolfe has already evaluated each piece, and she is happy to speak with all of you. I can assure you, we won't leave here tonight until everyone has had ample opportunity to speak with these fine appraisers.

"I understand that some of you may be inclined to contact your lawyer, and your notarized documents will be essential in recouping lost funds, as well as for financial restitution. If you feel that's your best course of action, the Ausby gallery won't stand in your way.

"Now, you must be wondering about the pieces you own. I'd love to tell you about the artist." I motioned for Beth to come closer. "Although each one of you owns a replica, you also own an original." The people just stared at us, so I continued. "Beth Ausby created these paintings some years ago, when she was naïve to the loose morals of people willing to do anything to make a dollar. Long ago, Patrick McDade bought these paintings from her, and then he proceeded to sell them to you as originals. Most of the pieces sold by the gallery over the years *were* originals—I don't want you to get the wrong idea—but once we found out about the fakes, we knew we had to do something. As devious and illegal as selling fakes is, all of you have to admit that Beth's talent is undeniable—that's why you believed in the authenticity of the pieces. In case no one was keeping track, the sum of the bids for just five of her paintings was close to two hundred thousand dollars. You don't have to like it, but you must see the value in them."

The guests who had been duped looked anywhere but at me. I suspected that their shame equaled their anger. But the woman who had bought the painting of Jade and me smiled brightly across the audience. At least one person was happy with her purchase.

"As far as the hand-carved oak frames, they're made by a local family, the Ryans," I continued. "Mrs. Wolfe has a separate appraisal for those. Jade Ryan is a wonderful and honest man, and I invite you to speak with him about his craft." I gestured for Jade to take a bow, but he just stood awkwardly at the side of the stage.

Someone was nice enough to clap, and luckily a few others joined in.

"Once again, thank you for coming tonight. I know you were brought here under false pretenses, but once Vivian Ausby discovered the fraud that was happening in our gallery, she quickly came up with a plan to rectify it. Since she can't be here herself, it's my job to beg for forgiveness. We're willing to do whatever it takes to make this right, even if we weren't the ones who made it wrong. Please, try to enjoy the rest of your evening. Thank you."

Taking in a deep breath, I let the calm begin to wash over me. People dispersed to different corners. To survey the room was something spectacular. Some gravitated to Jade, cornering him with questions. Others headed straight for the appraisal room to speak with Mrs. Wolfe. I supposed that those were the ones whose egos had been bruised the most; we would likely be hearing from their lawyers. The people who gravitated to Beth, the art lovers in truest form—those were the ones who made me smile. They saw the value in their pieces, the value in her, and I felt certain we would hear from them again.

11:00 p.m.

WITH EVEN THE LINGERING GUESTS GONE, THE SUGAR MILL was empty once again. I kicked my shoes off under the table and slumped down in exhaustion into a ridiculously overpriced rental chair. Although the excitement of the night still buzzed in my ears, the paddle fans in the arched ceilings created the only actual noise in the ballroom.

Jade and I had put Beth in a cab back to the hospital for the night. Despite her vernal spirit, her age had started showing as midnight closed in. Before even leaving the Sugar Mill, Beth already had several commissions. And because the woman who was willing to pay ten thousand dollars for Beth's most recent piece wasn't charged, she had commissioned Beth for three more. As Beth hugged us goodbye, her smile was fuller than I ever remembered seeing.

Jade sat down in the chair next to me, resting his jacket across the back. He patted his lap, smiling an impossible smile, gesturing for me to sit with him. I was happy to oblige. Wrapping my arms around his shoulders, I put my face against his, inhaling all of his goodness and appreciating the moment with him—just being with him. I wasn't sure how long we sat in that comfortable silence, but I was sure that it wasn't long enough. Considering the time we had already wasted, the rest of my life with him wouldn't be long enough.

I began to kiss his cheek, gently working my lips to his ear. "Jade," I whispered. He didn't answer, and only closed his eyes and bit his lip through a smile. "Jade," I whispered again, knowing exactly what I was doing.

"God, that sounds so good. Harlow, you know what that does to me, and I think you might be doing it on purpose."

"If I were meaner, I might just be playing with you, but I really do have something to say."

He pulled his head back, giving me a questioning look as I took a document out of my bag. "I have something for you," I said, handing him the envelope.

From surprise to disbelief, his expression underwent several transformations as he thumbed through the pages. Placing them back on the table, he said, "You don't have to do this. I want to be with you no matter what happened in the past. You don't owe me anything."

"I know that, and I appreciate your saying so. Even though I would have done the same thing, this wasn't my call. Vivian is the one who transferred the deed to the homestead back to your family. This was all her."

He swiped his hand through this hair, shocked at yet another turn of events. "I don't even know what to say. This is just...it's everything. At least it will be to my parents." He laid his palm on my back, and as his eyes turned serious, he said, "Thank you. Thank you so much for this."

His hand slid up into my hair, and he pulled me to his mouth—not with aggressive desire, but with the gentleness I had known all those years before. He kissed me as if for the first time, and it was good enough to be. Even though I was now forty, loving him made me feel like a young girl again.

"I'm proud of you," he said. "I'm proud to know you, Harlow."

"What? Why?" I asked, confused and a little embarrassed.

"You stood up for yourself tonight, stood up for your family, and you did the right thing. I don't know if you would have been strong enough to do that twenty years ago. You amaze me. You really do."

"Yeah," I agreed, "I amaze me too. There's something I've been wondering, though."

"What's that?"

"The first day we met, you brought a rocking chair up to my front porch."

"Yep, I remember. I picked that one special for you."

"With all the secrecy about Beth being my mother, why would she bring you to my house? She had to know how dangerous us being together was for her secret. Why would she risk it for a rocking chair?"

He smiled before he spoke. "I didn't give her a choice. I wanted to meet you so badly, and I was done taking no for an answer. She knew she could trust me, though. I had never given her a reason not to. I am sorry that I had to lie to you to keep her secret."

I let out a relaxed sigh. "It's all right, but no more apologies—from either of us. Let's just get out of here. I think I've had enough for one night. I've got to get out of this dress."

He smiled at my comment, and I playfully rolled my eyes.

"I think that's the best idea I've heard since I walked through the front doors, and that's saying something, because I've heard a lot of good ideas tonight."

I started to laugh, but a thought struck me. "Wait," I said, holding my hand against his chest. "This was an invitation-only party, and the guards at the front even checked *me* to make sure that I had an invitation. How did you walk through the front doors tonight?"

He reached into the inner chest pocket of his tuxedo jacket and pulled out an envelope. The lettering was handwritten in gold calligraphy, and it was addressed to Jade Ryan.

Not only had he been invited, but he finally belonged. The look on my face showed him my surprise, not that he hadn't already figured it out.

"After seeing you in the hospital room, and then the argument we had in the hallway—when you seemed surprised to see me here tonight, I realized that you hadn't invited me. I was finally so close to you—something I've wanted for so long. I felt like it was slipping away again. Don't get me wrong, I'm grateful for the invitation from Vivian. I know how hard it is to swallow that amount of pride; it's enough to choke you. But there was a part of me that hoped it was you reaching out to me after all these years.

"It wasn't my first choice to show you the note from Savannah, either. I wanted you to want me over anything, at all costs, but when you said you couldn't be with me, I couldn't take any chances. I was willing to do whatever it took to bring you back into my life. I was—am—desperate for you, Harlow. I want the beginning of my day to start with you, for it to end with you beside me, and to love you hard through the middle."

I tilted my chin up and kissed him, and I could feel the smile on his lips. It felt good to open that part of me again, to lean over that edge of abandon. There was a hint of that free fall I had felt with him so long ago, only now it didn't feel as reckless. It felt more like a purpose.

"No regrets," I said. "Let's go."

"Are we going any place in particular?"

"I have one in mind. Do you still have the Chevy?"

"I certainly do. Are you planning to do something in the back of it?"

"Maybe I am. Maybe I'm just curious."

"I didn't think you were that type of girl, not on the first date anyway."

"Technically this isn't a first date. And I do a lot of things I didn't used to do."

With a big grin, he asked, "Like what?"

"Sneak around with boys, stay the night in the back of a truck, and sleep with someone so quickly."

With the laughter of an inside joke and the precious memories rising from our past, those small moments felt huge to me. But I knew the best ones were yet to come.

12:00 a.m.

THE SOFT GLOW OF THE RADIO DASHBOARD CREATED OUR OWN manmade moon. Stars that were spun by the thousands across the black sky gleamed in patches through the slow-moving clouds. Even though I could only sporadically see them, I trusted they were always there. Much like the clouds, we were slow and easy this time on the beach together. We didn't rush, bound by the patience that twenty years of separation required. Those lost years were an accumulation of hurt and pain, of joy and youth, but mostly of time. Time was the one thing we thought we had lost, but in his arms, I realized that something that valuable could never be gone. On that night, we well understood the preciousness of time.

Once again, Jade had put his Boy Scout skills to work, and the heat from the small bonfire warmed the night air around us. On a blanket in the sand, with my hips nestled between his legs and his arms wrapped around my body, we talked, and then we didn't. The quiet between us was just as loud as the conversation, and it was a feeling we both understood, a language we both spoke. Every so often, I felt him squeeze me a little tighter. I knew it was his way of making sure that the night was real, that he hadn't conjured our togetherness in a dream.

The melodic rush of the waves meeting the sand lulled me into a peacefulness I had never known, and my tired body fought hard not to cave into the rhythm. An unattractive yawn came from deep within me, the day managing to catch me once I had finally stopped running.

I felt his silent chuckle through the vibrations in his chest. "What?" I asked. "Are you laughing at me?"

Openly laughing now, he said, "Kind of. I'm just thinking about the times we came out here, and you making a big stink about not swimming. Then randomly, you take off in a dead sprint to the water and shock the hell out of me. I probably never said so, but it's one of my favorite memories of you."

"You never told me that, but you also didn't have enough time to. I'm glad you're telling me now. I've thought about that night a thousand times. I've thought about it so much that I don't even know if I'm remembering it right."

"Hmm." He sighed, placing his lips on the top of my head. "I'm sure you remember it just fine. I know I do. It's something I'd never forget. You aren't going to run down there again, are you? I don't think I have the energy to chase you this time."

I paused to think about that question, then, tilting my chin up, I kissed him. He smiled, because he knew.

I turned around in his lap, swinging my legs to straddle his waist. "You won't ever have to chase me again. I'm done running."

I cupped my palms to his cheeks and felt the strength of his jaw lean into them. I kissed him slow and long, my hands sliding in and out of his hair, matching the rhythm of our tongues. His mouth was warm and skilled, and my skin pebbled upon his touch. He laid me down on the blanket in the sand, sweeping my stomach with the tips of his fingers, gently, purposefully, just enough touch to break me down, while patiently waiting to go further.

As I pulled his shirt off over his head, I kissed his lip, his jaw, the contour of his neck, my tongue following the pronounced ridge that gradually dipped into the depression above his chest. His back was long and muscular, and my fingers caressed the deep rivets along his spine. He pulled me down to him with a quick but gentle jerk of my hips, slipping his lips against mine before parting my mouth with his tongue. Dissolved with pleasure from throat to waist, I pushed my head back, a divot in the blanket cradling it like a pillow. Farther and farther down he went, touching all of my skin. With only wisps of kisses, Jade was able to put me back on that flight to the place we'd gone only once before.

The stars our audience, the fire our light, I could see only the top of his head moving slowly as he took his time, as if he had studied and specifically chosen the placement of each kiss on my stomach. His beard brushed against my breasts, the hair long enough to feel soft against the delicate parts of my skin. My palms spread out across the curvature of his shoulders like a cat in full stretch, digging into the unsteady rise and fall of his back.

His hands came to life, and his fingers slid inside of me, flexing and curving, crooking to send my hips in their own rise and fall against the strength of his hands. I pushed back into him, wanting all of him. His attention on me proved to be too much, and I could feel his arousal growing against my leg. I wanted to hold him in my hands and claim him as my own. The power of our patience weakened, and we were moving harder, seeking pleasure, both of us becoming more desperate for what only the other could give. A deep moan came out of him as I took him in my hands, his eyes squeezing shut, his mind lost somewhere in this moment.

He laid himself on my stomach and spread me wide, but suddenly stopped to sit back on his heels, looking me over. A seriousness took over him, the kind that can only be found at the juncture of deep love and great desire. It was a look that every woman should get from someone at least once in her life.

He swept his hands along my thighs, filling his fingers with skin, only stopping to kiss my knees. He paused, again with that look, that greed that's only captured in the weakness of the person who brings you to your knees. An unadulterated need that, until that moment, you hadn't realized was such an important thing in your life. In that space of time, it takes ahold of you, erases the world around you, funnels you down until he is all you see, and all you could possibly want is more of him.

Looking down at me, he mouthed, "I love you," as if it were the only answer to all the questions of life.

"Jade," I whispered, and was met with a seductive smirk.

With a feather-light touch of his fingers gliding between my thighs, I took him in my hands and opened my hips. Absolutely nothing on this earth enthralled me more than the sensation of him slowly sliding into me, deep under my skin. I arched my back, my mouth opening in response to his touch. I called out his name in breath and whispers, my voice trapped somewhere between my legs. He was, somehow, both tender and rough, pressing forward and holding back, on top of me, around me, inside of me. Something fundamental collapsed in my brain, exploding in colors of deep blues and ecstatic greens. I succumbed to the flames between us, of his heat and his fire, all of it exploding inside me.

We lay under the stars, truly satisfied, in each other's arms. I kept asking him to tell me he loved me, and he kept wanting to hear me whisper his name. They were words that would never die in my mouth or tire in my ears. He stroked the skin on my arm so delicately, and I listened to the rise and fall of his chest. I wasn't sure how much time passed; it wasn't my concern. We found our purpose out there on the beach, as detached from our past as the moon from the waves.

Breaking our silence, he said, "You know, she picked me because of you. Did she tell you that?"

"Who did?" I asked, laying my head back on his shoulder to watch his mouth move.

"Savannah. After she got sick, she knew there was no better person to mother Penny than you. Once we got to know each other again, she knew I wouldn't love anyone else. I made that clear. I suspect she thought the same about you. I think she figured that going through me was the best chance for Penny to have you. It was you all along. I was just a bonus in the scenario."

"She wants me to raise Penny? Why wouldn't she have said something to me?"

"She didn't need to. She had a plan, and you know how stubborn that woman can be."

"What if we had never found each other again? What would she have done then?"

"Honestly, I don't think that ever crossed her mind. She just believed it would happen. I think it's part of the reason she's held on for so long, fought so hard to keep up with the cancer. She needed to know that she was right about us, and I think she wanted to be there to see you and Penny together, to see that love for herself."

"I had no idea," I said, shocked but grateful that Savannah would trust her only child to my care.

"She's made a few comments here and there, but I could always tell she was shoring up her plan and checking things off her list. When you and Penny met, and she got to see you two together, I think that strong-willed part of her was finally able to relax. Besides Penny, you're her favorite person in the world, Harlow. You're mine, too."

That kind of love filled me with something that words could never articulate, something that could only be felt inside a person. "I'd be honored and love nothing more than to care for Penny."

The stars shone down on us like iridescent rain, and as our breath regulated with the crash of waves, we fell into a restful sleep, into a dream that would surpass the night, the day, the year, and the decades. Because even when we awoke, the dream of being together would never end.

PART FIVE
LATER

THE DEATH

SHE TOOK HER LAST BREATH ON A WEDNESDAY EVENING. HER body had withered to an astonishing ninety pounds in that hospital bed, as if death weren't satisfied with only her soul and was trying to take all of her with it. We gathered in the space around her bed, our elbows on her unwrinkled sheets, our hands on her body, the softness of our words meant to float up with her spirit into the sky.

Though her body was no longer heavy, the void that she left behind was. Her death moved my heart in a way it didn't want to go. So much time we could have had, memories we could have made. The unfairness of life was insufferable. The people who visited spoke largely of that; comfort was too often wrapped up in suffering. I hoped there was some truth to that—that there was comfort even in the darkest sorrow—but I didn't consider it to be gospel. I had known a time of suffering, and I couldn't recall one single comforting thing about it, except escaping it. Maybe that's what her death was—nothing more than a great escape.

She was unapologetic and set her words in stone, she was rebellious in the most intelligent ways, and her legacy would live on in her daughter, in all of us. She was softer than she let on, and more fragile than she cared to admit. Her love for her daughter made her surrender to terms that she never would have chosen, but then did, if only for the sake of love. Although I had missed so many years of loving her, it was my solace that in the end, I did.

It was a great privilege of my life to be with her when she passed, to hear her last breath, to feel the spirit break free from her body, her eyelids fluttering with the force of its escape. I surely felt it pass through me, and I hoped that some of it decided to stay.

I don't think we're meant to keep such secrets. With each passing day, passing year, the layers of resin wrapped up in secrets harden inside us, balling up into something that eventually weighs more than we do. I couldn't imagine that someone could stand at her weight of untold truths, much less breathe. There's a freedom in honesty, even if that truth isn't what we want to hear. We need it to lighten our steps here on earth, and to keep us weightless when it's our time to fly. Gravity doesn't exist among the stars.

I stayed with Mother until her arms began to cool, until the blood that once pumped furiously inside of her began to still. Like the tides that continuously moved with the pull of the moon, so did the Ausby blood flow through my heart. I had the best and the worst of her inside me, and for the first time in my life, I didn't consider that fact to be an unfortunate one.

THE LIFE

"LET'S GO!" I YELLED, MY VOICE BOUNCING OFF THE PLASTER walls and funneling up the ancient staircase. "Last day of school, and you don't want to be late!"

She sounded like a herd of something large barreling down the staircase. For a seven-year-old girl, Penny had the ability to make the commotion of ten men. As she jumped from the third-to-last step, she deposited herself with a *thud*, the tap shoes she'd chosen to wear making a racket in the entryway. Her hair looked as though she had traveled miles in a convertible, a windblown rat's nest that I couldn't believe had happened in her sleep.

"Oh, my," I exclaimed, turning her in a circle to inspect the mess. I picked her up and showed her our reflection in the hallway mirror. "I think we need some work up top. What do you think?"

Penny shrugged and said, "I think it looks great! Who cares what other people think?"

I laughed at her honesty. She was so her mother's daughter—her father's, too. Her right arm was covered in stick-on flower tattoos, the birthmarked skin around her elbow left bare.

"You have a lot going on here. How about if you let me brush your hair, then I'll let you choose the dessert for your lunch. Deal?"

She stuck her hand out to shake mine. "Deal."

"Okay, back upstairs you go, to get the hairbrush. And don't forget to brush your teeth while you're up there."

Her feet were already moving before I'd even set her down.

After I went back into the kitchen to finish Penny's lunch, Jade wrapped both arms around my waist and squeezed, burying his nose in my hair and inhaling my smell. He pulled me close to him. I hadn't heard him come in behind me.

"Hey, baby," he crooned, turning me around and kissing my face.

I was gross, hadn't showered, reeked of coffee breath, and was still in my nightgown. My face still had the sticky remnants of my nightly slathering of Vaseline. As he took my overly moisturized face in his hands, the look he gave me almost made me blush. Even in my morning mess, he looked at me as if he were seeing me for the first time. He brushed his lips softly against mine, and then harder, opening my mouth with his tongue. Had I not come from women with such strong willpower, he would have liquefied me with that kiss, with all of them.

"Oh, no," I said, pushing him away. "We have a busy morning and a lot to do today, which doesn't include that. You just keep your hands where I can see them and your tongue in your mouth, buddy. Otherwise…" I kissed him, matching his passion, letting it fill me until we had time for more. "Otherwise," I began again, composing myself, "I'll be a fool for you, and I won't get anything done today. Jade," I whispered into his neck.

He stepped away from me. "That's not fair. We were playing an innocent little game here, and then you started playing dirty. I'll remember that. I've got to watch out for you Southern women."

Penny came tromping into the kitchen. "Daddy!" she hollered, jumping into his arms.

The side door into the kitchen slammed closed. "Mother!" Evie yelled, a grimace on her freshly woken face. "What's all the noise?" she demanded to know, twirling her red locks around her finger and waiting for an answer. "I can hear y'all from the carriage house!" My sullen and sleep-deprived daughter was home from college, bringing her laundry and mood swings with her. "It's the first week of summer for me, and y'all are up at the crack of dawn, hollering like you have no manners at all. If I can hear you from out there, then I know Savannah can hear you from down the hall."

I couldn't help but smile. Even with her fussing at me, my heart was full. All these people—my people—under one roof, the same roof that had been in my family for generations. The love swelled up like a song inside of me.

Even though Savannah hadn't been to the gala, she'd had a winning bid at an entirely different auction: the one where she bought Mother's house.

Patrick had been brought up on a number of charges, but fraud was the one that stuck. A trial would have dragged his family name down even deeper through the mud, and I was grateful for his decision to plead guilty. He was sentenced to eighteen months in a white-collar correctional facility, but because he was such a pillar of the community, his lawyer got the sentence reduced to twelve, which meant he'd be out in nine. He was also ordered to pay back the money from the imposter paintings, plus restitution, adding more for pain and suffering. Everything he owned went onto the market—the house, the gallery, and the furnishings. Money soared out the window like birds in flight.

Those same birdies must have given Mother a wealth of information before her death, because through the small-town gossip in our little city, Mother had found out that the McDade family was hanging on by a financial thread. Apparently they had made some bad business deals and used their pharmacies as collateral, even borrowing money from the gallery that they couldn't afford to pay back. It's funny how you think you know someone—even yourself—and then everyone turns around and shocks the hell out of you.

Like most Southern women, Savannah had held on to a particular guilt for twenty years: the guilt of talking me into having a party on the night that changed my life. Back then, she had promised me that someday she would find a way to right things. Honestly, I hadn't given that promise another thought, but it turned out that she couldn't stop thinking about it. When Savannah bought my family home, I knew this was so much more than any ordinary friendship. She had enough money to buy any home in Charleston, but she picked mine, and she did it for me. I would never be able to repay that amount of kindness, not with money anyway.

Jade winked at me from across the kitchen. I loved when I turned to look at him, and he was already looking at me. "What's the plan today?" he asked, apparently surrendering to the fact that it was getting crowded in there, and nothing fancy was going to be happening in the bedroom.

"I need you to drop Penny off at school and then go meet Beth at the gallery. Her appointment isn't until midmorning, but she's already there, and I know she's nervous. Help her set up with whatever she needs, please. Evie needs to get dressed, because visitation starts at noon, and it takes two hours to drive to Columbia."

I watched Evie's gaze move to the floor, while she absentmindedly bit her cuticles and continued to twirl her hair. Her words were a grumble. "I don't know why I have to go visit him anyway. He gets out in three months."

"Honey, I can't have this same conversation with you again. He's your father. He needs your support. Do you want me to go with you?"

"I'm not a baby," she said, a kick of meanness in her voice.

As I turned around to finish packing Penny's lunch, I caught Evie's reflection in the hallway mirror. She cut her eyes at me and then stuck out her tongue.

"I can see you, you know. Don't be ugly. Now, does everyone know their job today?"

"Got it," Jade said, lightening the mood while taking a huge bite of dry toast.

"I'll get Savannah ready, and then we'll meet you at the gallery for last-minute stuff before the client gets there. Oh!" I exclaimed, palming my forehead. "Lexi is bringing over the new baby tonight. It's her first time out as a new mom, so we're going to have to tone down the noise. Let's all just pretend to be normal."

In the wake of Penny jumping up and down and freaking out with excitement for a brand-new baby to be at her house, I saw the pleased look on Evie's face. After grabbing a cup of coffee, she slipped out of the kitchen and back to the carriage house. She could sulk over grades or boyfriends, and especially her father, but I knew that nothing brought her more joy than a baby, especially her half-brother.

Savannah had been right about Lexi, too. Lexi had always made men her priority, and she had just given birth to the most important man she would ever meet.

As with Mother and me, I supposed that Evie also had the best and worst of me inside her. However fleeting that look might have been, it was there; a smile had graced her lips upon mention of him.

I knew Beth would have her own kind of fit to get her hands on that baby boy. She always said that new babies were the best kind to sniff.

"Why are you so nervous about Beth's meeting today?" Jade asked, grabbing Penny's backpack off the floor. "Beth's work is amazing; everyone says so."

"I know it is, but she *has* to get this mural gig at the children's hospital. It's hardly punishment to her—you know, for *conspiring*, or whatever they're calling it. I couldn't stand to see her do jail time if the hospital doesn't want her."

Stuffing the rest of the toast in his mouth, he said, "God, I love you," while wiggling his eyebrows up and down suggestively.

I knew exactly what he was doing. "Um, no. Now go."

"What about me? What's my job?" Penny exclaimed, hopping up and down.

I bent down and kissed her cheek. "Your job is to go to school, to be kind, and to stay awesome. Can you handle that?"

Just like Jade, she yelled, "Got it!"

Amid the chaos of grabbing things and racing against the clock, I almost missed one of those little moments that are disguised as routine. I had nearly forgotten something very important.

"Wait," I called out, just as they reached the door. "I want to get a picture of you on your last day of first grade, to show your mama."

I swelled with love as Jade swooped her up in his arms, in exactly the way I had always pictured him doing. They looked at each other, and then they looked at me. Those two were cut from the same cloth. Even though I was behind the camera, my smile could not have been bigger.

After sending Penny out to the car, Jade came over and put his arms around me, this time with no ulterior motive. He hugged me tightly, and I breathed him in.

"Don't worry, it's just a phase. Evie will grow out of it."

"How'd you know she hurt me?"

He smiled and said, "Because I've known you my whole life."

"I hope you're right. It's just that I never say or do the right thing. Evie's always mad about something. I feel like I never know what's going on. Sometimes I think she hates me."

"She doesn't hate you, or maybe right now she thinks she does, but it's temporary. You're her rock. You always have been. She knows you'll always be there, and you'll never desert her. At this point, I think she also knows what you gave up for her. Aren't all girls at odds with their parents at some point in their lives? Don't you remember a time when you hated your mother?" He smiled at his own joke.

"Haha, very funny. Okay, I won't worry about it. Thanks, baby."

"Someday, when I'm ugly and you're gray, I'm going to put my arms around you in your favorite rocking chair, and we'll both know that it's only ever been us. For our whole lives, we have only ever loved each other. I have a feeling that in the end, that's the only thing that'll matter." He kissed my forehead and added, "I love you, and I'll see you soon."

———

WE WERE LATE WHEN WE FINALLY PULLED UP. FROM THE CAR, through the slats of the open plantation shutters, I could see Beth inside the gallery, shaking hands with the chairman of the board of the children's hospital. I hoped it meant she'd gotten what she wanted. When the chairman left, we hurried up to head inside.

"You all right?" I asked Savannah, wheeling her up the ramp that Jade had built, but careful to miss the one crooked board.

She smiled as the sun dappled the trees just right, creating a ray of warmth on her face. "I'm fine," she whispered, the only volume she had left.

Before going inside, we stopped to admire the newly painted logo on the outside of the whitewashed brick building. In the signature Charleston colors of vibrant pinks, warm yellows, and palmetto greens, a person-sized pineapple was the backdrop of two words: Van-Low Studios.

Savannah smiled, nodding her head.

"I like it too. Okay," I said, taking in a hopeful yet nervous breath, "cross your fingers." Throwing open the door, I yelled, "Did we get it?"

Jade's arm was wrapped around Beth's shoulder, both of them staring at me with wide eyes. Neither answered me.

"Well? Don't play with me. Are you going to work or going to jail?"

Beth threw her fists up in the air, shaking them vigorously. "We got it!"

We all howled with joy, even Savannah, dancing and cheering, hugging and congratulating each other on a huge catastrophe averted. I wrapped my arms around Savannah, kissing her face and gently swinging her arms in dance. I wanted her to feel every ounce of happiness she could, to feel alive for as long as she was. I hoped she would gather up the joy and absorb the weightlessness that came from being truly happy. She needn't have one ounce of remorse, no regret, no heaviness of the past in her body, so that when it came time to send her into the sky, there would be no earthly weight to keep her from the stars.

After we had all settled down, I wheeled Savannah's chair to the sunny corner of the studio she liked best. She stayed quiet mostly, but I liked to think that she wasn't pondering lists or checking things off. Her plan had seamlessly come together. The only part that would be missing in it was her. Maybe that's what she thought about on those sunny days.

Beth came through the front room, looking for her glasses. She was getting started on the sketches for the children's hospital.

"What are you going to paint?" I asked her. "Maybe something like the fairy-tale scene you did in the closet of my old room?"

She looked up in thought before answering. "Nah, I don't think so. Believing in fairy tales is nice, but they don't always come true, not for these kids anyway. I think it's much more practical to send your prayers up to the sky and believe in the stars." She gave me a wink. "It worked for you."

The bell on the front door rang out, and a customer walked in.

"Hello," I greeted her. "Can I help you find something today?"

The heavyset woman with beautiful blonde hair replied, "Harlow? Harlow Ausby?"

"Yes, that's me. This is very embarrassing, but I'm sorry, I can't place your name."

Hiking her purse up onto one shoulder, she slapped herself in her ample chest and exclaimed, "Caroline Coker! Remember me? God, you look amazing!"

With widened eyes, I looked at Savannah. She shrugged and mouthed, "Told ya."

"Caroline, yes, of course," I said, hugging her in one of those fake nice-to-see-you embraces, followed by an obligatory kiss on her pudgy cheek. "How are you? Things going well in your life?"

Before she could answer, Jade came out of the back room. "I fixed the board on the ramp out back. It should be fine for Savannah's wheelchair now."

Caroline pulled a look of pure shock, probably at how beautiful this man was who now stood next to her. I liked that look of hers, but it wasn't my favorite.

"Oh, sorry to interrupt. Hello there," he said, introducing himself. "I'm Jade Ryan."

"Hello," Caroline replied, all breathy and ridiculous.

"Caroline, you might know Jade from Ryan and Son's Woodworking down on Folly Beach." She was nodding as the recollection seemingly became clearer. "Jade is married to Savannah. You remember Savannah, don't you?" I turned her around to face Savannah in her sunny corner. Savannah waved, reveling in this exchange.

"I'm done here," Jade said to me. "Are you coming with me, baby?"

"I'll go anywhere with you." I leaned up and kissed him, and the look on Caroline's face was pure shock. There it was; *that* look was my favorite. "Let me just wrap this up with Caroline here. I'll meet you at the truck."

She turned to look at Savannah, and then back at me. "Yeah," I said, bringing my palm up to the corner of my mouth, as if I were telling the loudest secret. "I'm having sex with her husband."

A laugh burst out of Beth, and Caroline's face dropped in horror. She looked back at Savannah, who had an ear-hanging smile plastered across her face. Savannah slowly brought her finger up to her lips and lightly tapped her two front teeth. Caroline's face turned all shades of red; her scowl was vicious.

"It's been great seeing you, Caroline, but I have a date at the beach. Beth here is busy with her art, and Savannah, well, Savannah doesn't like you, never has. I'm sure you understand. Feel free to let yourself out."

Caroline turned in a huff, stomping toward the exit. Before she slammed the door behind her, I yelled, "Don't forget to take a pineapple on your way out!"

The three of us filled the studio with cackling laughter at Caroline Coker's expense. My face hurt by the time I managed to get ahold of myself, Beth had to get a tissue for the laughter-induced tears pouring out of her, and Savannah radiated in the sun, with a more than perfect look of satisfaction. As unconventional as our situation was—especially for women South of Broad—I wouldn't have traded it, or the road we had taken to get there. I had needed Mother to get to Beth, Beth to help me find Jade, Patrick to give me Evie, and Jade to reconnect me with Savannah. Without following this specific path of aligned stars, there was a possibility that we may have all been lost in space.

Beth had once told me that the best part of my love story was still to come. She couldn't have been more right. The best part of my story *was* love—my love for the women in it. As I took in the sight of these women, love bloomed inside of me, reaching every crevice, every fold, and leaving nothing untouched. I looked out the window, up into the clear sky, and let the warmth hit my face. It occurred to me that in that moment, I felt as though I was finally the person I was meant to be, the one I'd been searching for all this time. There were so many prayers I had lifted and thrown into the sky over the years: about Beth, about Jade, about finding my way out of that deep darkness. For so long, I thought they had gone unanswered, that they had disappeared into the clouds. As I looked up then, I understood that they had been scattered, disguised by the lightness of day and the rays of the sun. For only in the darkness can you best see the light.

THE LETTER

Dear Harlow,

Despite what you may think, I do love you. I've always loved you. I just didn't know how to show it. I know that may seem like a lazy excuse for a mother to give, but that's my unfortunate truth. I wasn't a good mother to you, or to Beth. I'm still unsure as to why God made me one. I failed both times. I take solace in knowing that my only success was bringing you two together. It took a lifetime of repeated mistakes and lost love to truly understand the value a mother holds. It seems ridiculous to me, even now as I write, that I think such absurd thoughts and make such devastating mistakes.

You can take comfort in the fact that you are nothing like me. You were born into an unfortunate lie and sucked into the engine of that machine. The reason you're here—still with me—isn't because you're weak. It's because of your strength. God knows, I didn't make your life easy. It wasn't my plan to make it so hard. I didn't start out that way. I was so consumed with the darkness of loss that I couldn't bear to seek the light. Anyone would have left me, should have left me the moment they had a chance for escape. Your mother did. But because of your strength, you stayed, and I never let you live it down.

Through all of it, through the years with me, you still know love. You know of love even though you're familiar with loss. I can't imagine staying in a loveless marriage for twenty years, or worse, holding on to the love for a man in a life with no guarantees. That is the epitome of the strength of a Southern woman. For all those years lost, you have my deepest apology.

It's a shame how we lose things in this life—love, relationships, time, and people. I'm not exactly sure how it happens. I can only speculate that pride plays a big part. Although I've assuredly lost the right to speak of such things, I can tell you that the view from a hospital bed is not the one you'd like to remember for yourself. On the path to my end, I've done what I can to make things right, but I'm familiar with the cliché of too little, too late. I pray that today I've done enough, and at the right time.

As far as funeral arrangements go, you do with me what you like. I don't need a long-winded eulogy. God doesn't need to be told who I am; He's already familiar with my work. As you know, the Ausbys have a family mausoleum in the Magnolia Cemetery, and to have a plaque there would be just fine.

Learn from my mistakes, Harlow, and don't wait until the end to start living your life. The middle is the best part.

Leaving you in love,

Vivian Ausby

Note from the Author

I started *Terms of Surrender* when I had just turned thirty-seven years old. For various reasons, I shelved the project for almost three years. I finally finished it a month before my fortieth birthday. Since the present-time sections of *Terms of Surrender* happen on Harlow's fortieth birthday, I found something full-circle to be taking place when I finished. On the time of the book's completion, I also happened to be living in the Lowcountry. I wrote the majority of this book while in and out of hospitals and doctor's offices. My husband had become very ill seemingly overnight, and specialist after specialist couldn't diagnose him. Suddenly, I became a full-time caregiver, with no specific caregiving skills, while this "thing" took over our lives.

Writing this book saved me, and I couldn't be more literal about that. It saved me from depression, from insanity, and mostly from myself—there were about a thousand rabbit holes waiting for me to fall down each day. *Terms* was a place I could go to where I knew there was a happy ending, even if I hadn't written it yet.

To all those caregivers out there, I salute you. And I wish y'all a happy ending.

You can follow me on Instagram @karynraewrites or subscribe to my website www.karyn-rae.com to find out what's happening next.

Other Novels by Karyn Rae

The Achilles Heel
The Achilles Heart
The 51ˢᵗ State
Into the Dark (coming soon)

Also coming soon:
Savannah (Terms of Surrender Series Book 2)
Beth (Terms of Surender Series Book 3)
Vivian (Terms of Surrender Series Book 4)

Turn the page to read an excerpt from Rae's debut novel,
The Achilles Heel.

ANNIE

DON'T PUT YOUR HAT ON. PLEASE DON'T PUT YOUR HAT ON.

Crossing my fingers like a grade-school child wishing for a snowstorm in August, I watched him take his time as he gathered what looked to be papers, though I wasn't quite sure. He took in a deep breath and let it out slowly, while grabbing his hat from the dashboard. For some reason, I had the notion that if he didn't put on the hat to complete his uniform, this visit would be somewhat less official. He noticed me standing through a sliver of the window framing my front door. He paused, shut his car door, and straightened his trousers a tad—a natural act when one goes from sitting to standing and is between pant sizes. Finally, he put on that goddamn hat.

As he walked toward the door, gravel from the driveway crunched under his heavy black boots. Streaks of sweat ran down his sunlit, glistened face. His heavily starched shirt sported a soaking wet "V" on the chest, connecting to the wetness under both arms. With record-high temperatures in Kansas City reaching 106 degrees during the first week of June, I was secretly glad he was hot, and it almost made me happy to think that he might be suffering a bit.

Our eyes made contact when he reached the red-brick porch steps, and I knew. He could have turned around, gotten back in his police car, and never said a word to me, but his eyes told me the whole story. Or maybe they didn't tell me the entire story, but they certainly implied the most important part: the ending. As he stood on the opposing side of the window, the glare from his name badge which read GRADY shone in my right eye, causing me to wince.

"Ma'am," he said through the double-paned glass. "Are you all right?"

I stood there, staring blankly. *Why is he here to ask me if I'm okay? Is this guy an idiot? What cop comes to someone's front door, scares the hell out of her, and opens with a question like, "Ma'am, are you all right?" I was doing just fine before he pulled into my driveway.*

"Ma'am," he started again, tapping on the window to get my attention, breaking the paralyzing trance holding me motionless. "Are you okay? You're bleeding!"

At that moment, I tasted the blood. As I'd mentally calculated his every move from the car to the door, knowing he wasn't here to give me stellar news (cops don't randomly show up at your house for no reason), I hadn't noticed that I was biting down on my lip. It must have been hard, because the blood was now running down the side of my chin.

I tried to answer, but only felt air pass between my lips; my voice was lost in translation. I only nodded my head up and down.

Officer Grady asked, "Are you Annie Whitman, the wife of a Mr. Jack Whitman?"

Again, I nodded.

"Could you please open the door? I'd like to come in and speak with you for a moment."

I reluctantly but automatically obeyed, and the creak of the screen door was synonymous with a horror movie. Apparently, I was the main character.

"Ma'am, your husband was in an accident on the highway this morning. There were no survivors. We believe he was killed upon impact and have launched an investigation into the crash. Unfortunately, we don't know many details yet. I'm so very sorry to bring you this devastating news. Is there someone you can call to be with you right now?"

"No, you're wrong," I croaked in a broken and raspy voice, like someone infected with the forty-eight-hour flu. "My husband is at work, and this is a mistake." I tried again, but only fragments of sound spit into the air. I wasn't forming recognizable words. "I'll just call him, and we can clear this up," I stammered. "You'll see it's just a terrible mistake." I pulled my cell phone off the deep-chested entry table, trying to will my hands to stop shaking long enough to dial the number.

"Oh, no, Jack. No," I whispered through gritted teeth when the call went straight to his voice mail.

I dialed again. "Shit. No. Please, no," my voiced squeaked as I paced back and forth. With my right hand barely sturdy enough to hold the phone to my ear, and my left tucked tightly under the opposing armpit, I filled my fingers with skin, pinching down as hard as possible to divert the pain of feeling my heart rip apart.

Officer Grady extended his arms and shifted his feet each time I shuffled near him. He initiated words of comfort, but quickly realized his efforts were powerless when dealing with someone rapidly sinking in the quicksand of denial.

Finally, he stepped into my path, and with a tight grip on both slumping shoulders, he softly turned me around to face him.

The fact that I had bitten entirely through a small portion of my bottom lip seemed to startle him. While the blood continued to stream, he gently took control of my breakdown. "Mrs. Whitman," he whispered. "Who should I call? You need someone with you right now. Please, let me call someone for you."

This time, a small and childlike "yes" escaped through my bloody lips. I felt like it shouldn't have taken so much effort to say one little word, a word we use a hundred times a day, but it *was* hard—and completely exhausting. It was as if the sound from that three-letter word held my lips apart just long enough for my soul to escape.

He pulled out a bandana, applying pressure to my mouth, and in exchange, I handed him my cell phone with the name Jamie lit up in blue letters on the screen. Someone would need to tell my brother-in-law that his older brother was dead.

As Officer Grady took the phone from my hand, a tiny, purple orb slowly drifted past my line of vision and across his chest. Confused, I followed the speck with my eyes, only to see it suddenly multiply a thousand times. Each orb began to swell. The purple color faded to the outside of the circle, and a bead of light replaced the center, like the dimmer switch on an LED bulb. Trying to blink the beacons away only seemed to make them brighter, and within moments, the fluorescent illumination had blinded me. My body became too burdensome for my legs; even my hair felt heavy. As if I were riding on a roller coaster and cresting the highest peak, I closed my eyes, just as I felt myself plummeting to the ground.

My name is Andrea Whitman, and those were the last moments of *this* life as I knew it.

Made in the USA
Coppell, TX
26 June 2024

33968874R00157